Hiding In Plain Sight

Sue Nelson Buckley

Hiding In Plain Sight
Published by Sue Nelson Buckley

Copyright © 2024 Sue Nelson Buckley

All rights reserved

This is a work of fiction. Names, characters, places, and incidents either are the products of the author's imagination or used fictitiously. Any resemblance to actual persons, living or dead, businesses, companies, events, or locales is entirely coincidental.

For permissions contact: sue@suenelsonbuckley.ca
Cover by Sue Nelson Buckley

ISBN: 9798227061249

ACKNOWLEDGEMENTS

I'd like to thank Peter Larsen, a fellow Saint John High School Alum who taught at SJHS, for bringing me up to date with things that have changed (or not) since our high school days.

Happily, we didn't have a Janie in our class. Unfortunately, we didn't have anyone like Ben or Alex, either. That would have been way too cool.

Special thanks to Nirmal, Mike, Perry, Marc, and Tanya for their mad story editing skills.

Also, special thanks to Robin for tirelessly proof reading this novel's second edition.

CHAPTER ONE

"Hilary, are you watching?" Shannon's voice screeched through the phone and into my ear. Her voice was so loud I could almost hear it coming from her house across the street. It was like hearing her in stereo.

Shan was rarely subtle.

Mom looked up from her laptop. She had her work stuff spread all over the kitchen table. "Shannon?"

I nodded.

She went back to her notes and even though Shannon was still talking, my attention was already back to the action on the other side of our driveway where our new neighbours were unloading their stuff from a cube van with the name of a rental company splashed over its side. "Of course, I'm watching."

"Why didn't you call me? Look at him."

I smiled. That was precisely why I didn't call her. I love Shannon. We've been best friends since Junior K, but when she's excited, the girl just won't shut up. Me? I like to observe. Not like a stalker or anything, but sometimes you just learn a lot more by keeping your mouth shut, and I was learning a lot.

"I'm coming over." The phone clicked.

I had exactly forty seconds before Shannon appeared on my doorstep. Forty-five if she had to wait for a car to pass before crossing the road. That rarely happened. Shannon rarely waited for anything.

I glanced back at my new neighbours. The mom was pretty. She had dark hair pulled back into a ponytail and appeared to be the one in charge of getting everything into the house. The dad was a bit older. His hair was greying at the sides, and he seemed stressed. The daughter appeared around twelve, but her childish attire suggested she could be younger. But the son… wow, just WOW. He's the one I'd really been watching.

If someone read my journal and made me a guy to order, he'd be perfect. Just under six feet, dark hair, darkish eyes, and a great laugh that made my toes tingle.

I'd guess he was around seventeen. Ok, that was me hoping he was only seventeen. If he was older, he wouldn't be attending school with Shannon and me, which would mean he probably wouldn't be interested in getting to know a high-schooler like me - even if I was a senior.

He reached up and pulled two of the bigger cartons off the back end of the truck. His muscles flexed under his dark blue T-shirt when the boxes threatened to tip over. For a minute, I forgot all about Shannon, the book I had been pretending to read, my mom in the kitchen and, well… everything. I just held my breath and watched him jostle the boxes to keep them upright.

Then Shannon's bright blonde head bounced past my window.

I groaned. My peaceful morning of ogling the cute new neighbour was finished—kaput.

"Hi, Mrs. F.," Shannon said as she walked in without knocking.

Sure, our door was open to catch the breeze. Even if closed, she would have entered. Her sense of entitlement always amazed me. We were both only children from middle-class families. We had many friends and were pretty good-looking, if I say so myself. Compared to her,

I was a wallflower. Shannon just had that extra 'here-I-am' attitude that could be just as annoying as it was endearing. Like right now, for example.

"So why are you just sitting there?" she demanded. Hands on her hips, she glared at the open book on my lap.

I shrugged. She already knew the answer.

"Hilary, this is no time to be shy. If Janie gets to him first, he'll be ruined."

She had a point. Janie was the golden girl. Her dad owned a bunch of businesses around town and with her posse of local celebrity wannabes, she made Shannon look like a cowering wreck. Janie and her buddies had been extras on a movie set back in middle school. Four years later, they were still milking the glory, brandishing their Apprentice Member ACTRA Cards in case we forgot.

I put my book down and stood up. Shannon gave me the once over with a critical eye. My long auburn hair hung straight down past my shoulders. I was wearing one of the tank tops she gave me for my birthday last week and my favourite shorts that, in my mind at least, made me look taller than my five foot two.

Her eyes narrowed when she saw I wasn't wearing make-up, a major faux pas in her book.

I shrugged. It was still two weeks before school started, and I didn't have to work at Coles Electronics until later this afternoon.

Shannon ignored my lack of make-up and nodded her approval of my wardrobe. She was wearing a similar outfit, khaki shorts, T-shirt, and her favourite platform sandals that did great things for her legs and unfortunately made her tower over me.

"Let's go," she ordered.

I paused at the door long enough to slip my flip-flops on to my feet. I could hear mom laughing behind me. I swear, she enjoyed watching Shannon boss me around, especially when she agreed with her. Mom had already suggested I go over to say hello. I shot her a look over my shoulder, which only made mom laugh harder. I took a deep breath and followed Shannon out the door with no choice but to walk slightly behind. Even in heels, she out-paced me as she strode across the thin stretch of lawn separating the two driveways.

The father was just reaching into the truck when he saw us coming. He stopped what he was doing and smiled.

Shannon stuck her hand out to shake his. "Welcome to the neighbourhood. I'm Shannon, I live across the street."

The man hesitated before reaching out, as if her gesture was unexpected. "Hi Shannon, I'm Norman McAllister."

The daughter appeared around the truck to get another load. She stopped short when she saw us. "Alex, come here. This is Shannon and…"

"Hilary," I stepped forward. "I live next door."

Mr. McAllister shook my hand too while Alex looked on. She looked downright unfriendly.

"Ben, Angela, we have visitors." Mr. McAllister hollered into the house. I turned my attention back to Alex. I didn't want to look like I was desperately waiting to meet the hot guy next door. "What grade are you in, Alex?"

She shrugged. "I'm starting grade nine this year."

This surprised me because she didn't look old enough to start secondary school.

"Our Alex is a genius. She skipped ahead of the rest of her class and is starting secondary school two years early."

"Daaaaad, do you have to tell everybody?" If possible, Alex looked even more annoyed.

I looked at Alex with a whole new level of sympathy. Starting secondary school at twelve was going to be rough. Especially if she got on Janie's radar, which I really hoped she didn't.

"Ahh, here they are. Ben, Angela, meet Shannon. She lives across the street."

The mom, Angela, stepped forward to shake Shannon's outstretched hand. Ben glanced at Shannon, then looked directly at me. "I've seen you around."

"I… I'm Hilary." Up close, he was incredible. His eyes were so dark they were almost black, even in the sunlight. Seriously wow.

"I know."

Shannon didn't even notice she'd been ignored. "Really? Where'd you see us?"

Ben broke my gaze to answer. "I've seen Hilary a few times when I drove by to check out the neighbourhood."

"You drive?" Shannon practically danced with delight. At our school, having a friend who drove was almost as important as driving yourself. And if you had your own car? Well, it puts you into a completely different stratosphere.

I knew Shannon's next question would be whether he had his own car. Before she got too excited about how he could increase our already solid social standing, I figured we'd better find out if he was still in school. Where Alex looked younger up close, Ben looked much older. There was a wisp of hair peeking over the V-neck of his T-shirt and the five o'clock shadow he had would take most guys in senior year a week to grow. "Are you still in school?"

"Yeah, I graduate in the spring." He cocked his head. "Saint John High?"

Saint John city center had three secondary schools. Harbourview High was the trade school. St. Mac's and Saint John High were both academic.

"Yes," Shannon butted in again. "Hilary and I are seniors too." She looked around. "So, do you have a car?"

So much for distraction. I sighed and let her run with the conversation.

Ben smiled. "Come on, I'll show you." He led us around the truck to their backyard, which had been blocked from my view when I was on the couch.

Shannon and I gasped.

It wasn't just a car. It was a mint condition classic Barracuda. Its metallic blue paint sparkled in the sun. I felt my knees go weak and thought Shannon was going to collapse from excitement. Our 'it' factor would skyrocket just by standing close to a car like that, never-mind being on speaking terms with its owner.

Ben's shoulders shot back, and his chest stuck out at our reaction. "Dad and I spent all last year restoring it."

Shannon jabbered on about how cool the car was and how smart Ben and his dad were for fixing it. She opened the driver's door and plunked herself in the driver's seat, running her hand over the crimson leather.

I walked slowly around the car, afraid to touch it in case I left a fingerprint.

Shannon called for me to look at something inside.

I raised my gaze and saw Ben staring at me, as if watching my reaction. "My dad was always working on his car. I'd go out and help him, but we'd just end up talking." I blinked back the sudden tears in my eyes. "He would've loved this car."

Ben looked as if he was about to say something when Alex came around the corner of the house. "Dad said to stop showing off your car and come back to help him."

"Did Dad really say for me to stop showing off the car?"

"No but, he told mom he hoped you didn't get distracted for long because he had to get the truck back before two."

I laughed. "Hey, Shannon, we qualify as distractions. We're moving up in the world."

Shannon looked at me in surprise. She is usually the flirt, not me. I'm the one who makes sure everything goes smoothly. When it came to talking to guys, especially ones as good looking as Ben, I usually got tongue-tied.

I glanced away, feeling the heat crawl over my face. I knew looking away wouldn't stop the blush from happening, but at least it prevented me from seeing Shannon smirk about it, or Ben, which would make me blush even harder.

Unfortunately, I looked right into Alex's combative gaze.

Her feet were planted shoulder-width apart, her arms folded stiffly across her chest. Her scowl made it clear that her brother was off limits.

Ben must have seen something change besides the colour of my face. One look at his little sister's expression and he motioned Shannon out of his car.

Alex's expression turned triumphant as she whirled around and preceded us toward the front of the house.

Ben shook his head. "Do either of you want a little sister? I'm willing to sell her. Cheap."

Shannon and I both held up our hands as if to push such a horrible thought away. Shan added a dramatic shudder, "No thanks, I like being an only child."

While we were out back, Ben's dad had moved the couch and mattresses to the edge of the truck. Ben jumped up beside him to lend a hand.

"Can we help?" I asked.

Mrs. McAllister said yes at the same moment Mr. McAllister said no. They looked at each other for a few seconds, having a silent conversation of couple-speak before Mr. McAllister changed his mind. "Thank you, that would be nice." He pointed to half a dozen smallish boxes waiting to be taken inside.

I could feel the visual daggers Shannon was shooting at my back when I reached up to grab the first box marked "living room books."

She dressed to impress. Her sandals weren't designed to lug boxes, no matter how cute the new neighbour was. I tried to feel guilty for making Shannon do hard labour in heels, but I couldn't. This was a relatively mild payback, considering all the situations she had involved me in over the years. I smiled as I walked into the split entryway and up the stairs, Shannon trailing behind me. I was feeling proud of myself until I reached the top.

Alex stood there, blocking the door to the kitchen, one hand on her hip, the other pointing to my right. "In there."

I decided this wasn't a good time to tell her I knew her new home better than she did. The previous owners used to babysit me after school when mom had to work late. After dad died, she worked late a lot. Since I was carrying books, I walked directly over to one of the built-in bookcases flanking the stone fireplace and set them on the floor.

Alex looked at me suspiciously, her glare intensifying until even Shannon noticed.

Shan was about to make a smart-assed comment but stopped when she saw me shake my head in warning.

Being seventeen is hard enough. You're not quite an adult, but at least you're on the downswing of puberty. Shannon and I had each other to get through the worst parts. Alex was a prodigy at twelve, in a new city with no friends yet. I felt sorry for her, even though for some weird reason, she was trying to pick a fight with me. The fact I wasn't taking the bait seemed to make her even more furious.

The clumping of Ben and his father coming up the stairs broke our silent standoff. Whatever they were carrying sounded heavy. They hesitated at each step to adjust their load.

"Alex, stop glaring at the girls and move." Impatiently, Ben nudged his sister out of the way as he guided his end of the sofa into the living room.

Shannon and I stepped closer to the fireplace to give them room to bring it in.

Alex stomped back down the stairs as soon as the way was clear.

Mr. McAllister looked puzzled. "Why would Alexandra glare at the girls? They are helping."

Mrs. McAllister came up the stairs behind them. "What is wrong with Alex?"

It was clear Alex wanted us to leave, and I'd thwarted her by offering to help and invaded her turf even further. I started to apologize.

Ben spoke before I could. "She's being a brat. Probably ticked that I didn't include her when I took the girls out back to see my car."

"I am not being a brat," Alex shouted from outside. "And I don't care about your stupid car."

Mr. McAllister frowned. "Well, she cannot be with you all the time. She will have to find her own friends."

Shannon and I looked at each other. There was no one Alex's age in our neighbourhood. Shannon and I were the only teens nearby. I'd just turned seventeen and Shannon's birthday was next month.

"I'm afraid she's stuck with us," Shannon said.

"I am glad you girls came over. Our frequent moves in the past two years deprived the children of the opportunity to make friends. It's been especially hard on Alex."

Shannon didn't look exactly pleased to play saviour to a twelve-year-old, but I kind of liked the idea. I'd always wanted to have a younger sibling. This was as close as I'd probably ever get.

CHAPTER TWO

I worked until six and then, after supper, went out to my treehouse. Mom thought I was too old to hang out in a playhouse, but my dad built it for me when I was eight, just before he got sick.

He built the floor over two of the lowest branches. The ceiling was just over a metre high where it attached to the tree trunk. It sloped down to the outer walls, which were barely half a metre tall. Dad had built little cabinets for me to store my dolls and tea sets and then shingled the roof and put glass in the windows just like a proper house. I was so excited when he let me help him paint the inside, bright pink, just the way I'd wanted it back then.

The tree had grown, so now the floor was almost two metres above the ground, and it didn't seem nearly as big as it did back then. The floorboards creaked now when I moved around, but coming out here had become a nightly ritual. I kept a journal hidden in the secret hiding spot dad created for me. It had become one long letter to him. Even though I knew dad couldn't answer back, I felt closer to him here in my treehouse than anywhere else.

I picked up my journal. There was so much to tell him. Not only about Ben, but the whole McAllister family.

After we finished helping the McAllisters unload the truck, Shannon went back to her place. I went back to reading my book on the couch until it was time to leave for my shift. I could hear them talking out in the yard. There was something odd about them, especially the parents. They seemed extremely formal, even with their kids. Occasionally, I thought I heard words in a different language. I tried to remember where they moved from, but I don't think they said. There was something surreal about them. They reminded me of a TV show from the old days, like when my mom was a kid.

From my treehouse, I could see into the McAllister's back yard. While I was writing, Ben and his dad came out of their back door, deep in conversation. This time, I was certain they weren't speaking English. Or any language I'd ever heard before. They walked in front of Ben's car and across their back lawn, right toward me. For a minute, I wondered if they were coming to visit me in my treehouse. Then they stopped, looked around for a minute, and then poof. They disappeared.

"What the…?"

One second, they were there and the next, they disappeared into thin air.

I blinked and leaned closer to my window, fighting the urge to freak out. I could still clearly hear them talking. Their voices had changed. It sounded like they were speaking from the inside of a big tin can. I rubbed my eyes like a little kid. Surely, I hadn't just seen what I thought I did.

Ben and his dad couldn't just disappear.

Not looking away, I shrank against the far side of my treehouse. I willed the floorboards not to creak and give away my presence while I figured out what to do. Even though I couldn't see them, I could still hear them. That meant they were still there. If I tried to leave the treehouse, I was sure they would see me.

I was trapped!

Then Ben reappeared just as suddenly as he'd vanished. He was carrying a big bluish-metal box with wires hanging down from one side. Behind him, Mr. McAllister popped back into view with another bluish box and more wires.

My heart was pounding. My back pressed so hard against the wall I was afraid I'd fall through. I had to relax and try to think this through logically. So far, they didn't seem to know I was there. Good! Until I figured this out, I wanted to keep it that way.

I watched them go back and forth, disappearing, then reappearing again with more big boxes. It looked like electronic equipment but nothing like I had ever seen before… and I work in an electronics store. After a while, I realized I had switched from being scared to being curious. Whatever they were carrying into the house looked like super-secret spy gear, or components to make a terrorist tracking system.

Okay, now I was back to scared.

If you drew a triangle on the bottom half of a map of New Brunswick, with one point on the oil refinery, one on the nuclear power plant and the other on the military base in Gagetown, my neighbourhood fell in the middle. Sure, the McAllister family seemed friendly, but wasn't that what people always said about the serial killer who used to live beside them? No one ever suspected a thing.

Holy crap. It had been almost an hour. How much stuff did they have in whatever it was? And how did they just disappear into thin air like that?

My journal lay forgotten on the floor of my treehouse as I peered through the window, waiting until it was dark enough for me to escape my hiding spot. It was only fifteen metres to the back door of my house, but it might as well have been a million. The sun had finally set, but it was still too light for me to leave undetected. I had at least another half an hour to wait. Hopefully, that'd give me enough time to stop shaking.

I wasn't sure if it was fear or excitement that made my hands tremble. Maybe Shannon was right when she complained I read too much science fiction. Or maybe I was just losing my mind.

I hoped mom was watching TV when I finally made it inside. The last thing I needed was to have her ask why I looked freaked out. I'm not a good liar. She wouldn't believe me if I told her everything was fine. Especially since right now, I wasn't sure it was.

CHAPTER THREE

After watching Ben and his dad do their disappearing act, I tried to avoid close encounters with any of the McAllister family. I had so many questions, but couldn't exactly say, "So I saw you guys disappear in your backyard the other day. Are you magicians or terrorists?" I wanted to explore their backyard and figure out what was happening, but they were always outside.

So, I took the coward's way out. Whenever I had to leave for work and one of them was in their driveway, I ran to my car, pretending to be late. I'd wave and call out a hello then drive away.

Ok, so it wasn't really my car, it had been Dad's. It was mine to use as long as I paid for gas and maintenance. It didn't quite qualify for the same realm of social status as Ben's Barracuda, but it let me be cooler than Shannon, car-wise at least.

Shan's parents were over-the-top-protective. They wouldn't even let her get her learner's permit. Shannon was understandably upset. They also wouldn't let her get a job.

At first, I was resentful about mom making me get part-time work since Shannon didn't have to, but now I appreciate having my independence. I didn't have to ask for permission to buy things like Shannon did.

A week later, I looked out the window before leaving for work. The coast was clear. I grabbed my purse and made a dash for my car. I'd just opened the driver's door when Ben appeared beside me.

"Ack." My hand flew to my chest. "You scared the crap out of me."

My heart was pounding in my throat and my hand shook against my uniform shirt. I wasn't usually jumpy, but after the other night, who could blame me for overreacting when Ben seemed to come out of nowhere?

"Sorry, I didn't mean to surprise you. You come and go so fast it's hard to catch you."

I felt a little guilty. After all, he was new to the neighbourhood, and I was shunning him. It was ridiculous when, aside from the potential link to terrorism, he was the hottest guy I'd ever met.

"I'm doing double shifts this week at work to help with the back-to-school rush and to increase my back-to-school wardrobe fund."

"Ugh. I don't even want to think about clothes. That's all mom and Alex have been arguing about this week."

I laughed before I could catch myself. He seemed so normal. Face-to-face with Ben made it hard to remember why I panicked. There was just something so strong and comforting about him. I shrugged. "It's a girl thing."

"Makes me glad I'm a guy."

"Me too," I said to myself. Even though I knew he couldn't read my mind, I could feel another blush starting. I looked down to hide my face and caught sight of Ben's jean-clad legs. They were thick with muscle. I bet he played rugby. Oh God, this wasn't helping. I looked up farther. Today he was wearing another dark blue T-shirt. It wasn't tight, but it showed off his biceps and made me sad beach season was over. He would look great up at Crystal Beach, diving off one of the wharf towers in just his shorts.

"So, where do you work?" He interrupted my mental inventory, which I'm ashamed to say got stalled around his shoulders. I felt my face get red again.

"Cole's Electronics. Their new store over by East Point Mall." Something about the way he nodded made me wonder if he already knew where I worked. Gawd, I had to get a grip. Now, I was just being paranoid.

"Really?" At least he sounded surprised. "That's great. I need a new laptop for school. My old one is too slow to get me through senior year. Oh, and I need a TV. Dad set up a box in my basement suite. Maybe I'll stop by later and see what you've got."

"Basement suite?"

"Yeah, I turn seventeen in January, so we converted the basement into a mini-apartment for me so I can have some privacy."

"Wow, nice." This new piece of information intrigued me, although part of me wondered if it was to help hide whatever he was doing with all that strange equipment. I'm a techie, but I'd never seen anything like that stuff before.

"Yeah, it's a combination Christmas, birthday and graduation gift from my parents."

"Lucky." I meant it too. I glanced at my watch, even though I knew exactly what time it was. "Crap, I've gotta run, or I'm going to be late."

"Ok, I'll talk to you later."

I climbed into my car, turned the key, but released the clutch too fast. My car jack-rabbited ahead a few feet. Oh, for Pete's sake, I've been driving Dad's stick shift for over a year and now I stall my car as if I'd never used a clutch before? I glanced behind me in my side mirror to where Ben was still standing. I had to give him credit. He looked like he was trying hard not to laugh.

I started my car again, and this time made it out of my driveway without embarrassing myself any further. As I turned on to the road, I caught sight of Alex, standing on the front steps of their house, arms crossed over her scrawny chest, glaring daggers at me. I didn't understand what her problem was. Then I looked at what she was wearing. Pigtails and a pink and blue gingham dress that I truly hoped was her mom's idea. Where they found a dress like that outside of the toddler's section was a mystery. Alex was dressed more like a character from Anne of Green Gables than a secondary school student.

Barely an hour into my shift, I was a basket case. I kept finding excuses to walk near the windows at the front of the store to check the parking lot for Ben's car. I wanted to avoid another pop-up encounter like he'd done beside my car. Squealing in surprise during your shift was never a good idea, no matter how gorgeous the reason.

It was a mixed blessing when Jocelyn asked me to cover breaks on cash. I could see out the window, but wouldn't be available to help Ben when he came in.

Unfortunately, I saw Janie's car arrive instead. She and three of her closest BFFs climbed out.

"Please let them go anywhere but here," I whispered fervently under my breath. The last thing I needed was Ben to walk in when Janie was taking cheap shots at me, and the other staff members.

Her dad owned this store, making us powerless against her. She'd already had three clerks fired because they stood up to her. Although that's not the story she told her father to get rid of them.

"Damn." She was coming this way. I motioned to Jocelyn, the shift supervisor.

She looked outside, and her shoulders slumped. Our smooth evening shift had just tanked.

The unmistakable giggle of Janie and her entourage echoed through the large electronics store. Seriously, the girl was every stereotype of a wannabe celebrity. She was beyond-belief annoying when she put on a show for her friends.

Suddenly I felt lucky to be working cash. That meant Janie would have to get someone else to help her. I felt my stomach unclench.

"There she is." Janie drawled in her fake look- at-me-aren't-I-something-else voice. "Hilary, I need you to help me pick out a new cell phone. The one you made me get for the summer is already out of date."

Jocelyn, the traitor, was at my elbow in an instant. "I'll look after the cash while you help Janie."

I suppose I could take it as a compliment that she trusted me with the boss's daughter, but we both knew I was just the unlucky winner of tonight's front-row seat to Janie's mystery performance. Mystery because we still didn't know what part she'd be playing tonight. Past performances included the spoiled rich kid, super cool teenager, who I was kind of hoping for, or wronged heiress to the company. It sounded like it was going to be the latter.

"Hilary, I thought you said this was the latest phone." She held the electronic out from her body between her thumb and index finger, as if it offended her.

I looked at the bright pink case and groaned at the memory. That phone arrived in stock the day she bought it. We hadn't even put them out on the display shelves when she demanded I find her one… in pink. It took forever for me to find a pink one out back, and it had to be the pink one. Even though she immediately bought a case in an even brighter shade of pink to cover it up. I'm talking Pepto Bismol pink.

"We got a shipment yesterday, but there will be newer ones coming in next week."

"But I don't want to wait until next week. I want a new phone tonight."

I held in a sigh. Of course she does.

I motioned her to follow me to the bank of phones on display. "These are the models that came in yesterday.

One of the girls in the group made the mistake of saying, "Oh, look at this one."

Janie just arched her perfectly shaped brow. The girl immediately slunk back a pace and hung her head.

Half a torturous hour later, Janie and her posse left the store. Jocelyn called over to me from the service desk, "Hilary, take a break. You deserve it."

"Just a sec." I skulked behind a display of activity trackers, watching to make sure Janie was really leaving and not just teasing us with her departure. With my luck, she'd come back in to return the phone because she'd forgotten she didn't want to buy it today after all. The girls were safely across the parking lot when Ben's car pulled in. "I'll take my break in a minute if that's ok. My neighbour just arrived. He needs a new computer, and I told him I'd help him chose one."

Jocelyn nodded. "Sure, just let me know when you're done."

Damn. Janie had turned around and was also watching the Barracuda pull into the parking lot. She didn't take her eyes off Ben as he crossed the parking lot and entered the store. "Please don't let her follow him back in," I whispered.

My prayer was answered. She turned back around and kept walking to the row of clothing stores, leaving Ben to walk through the automatic doors alone and make a B-Line to where I was standing. He couldn't see me from the parking lot, yet he seemed to know exactly where I was. I should have found it really creepy and probably would have, if I wasn't still recovering from Janie's toxic presence… and if he'd been less of a hunk.

I know, I know, I'm being superficial, but I'm seventeen, superficial happens.

"How goes the sales thing?" He smiled as he looked me up and down as if checking me out.

I could feel myself blushing. "Better now that you're here… I can smell a huge commission from all the stuff I'm about to talk you into buying."

Jocelyn looked up. She looked startled to hear me be so flip with a customer. Plus, we weren't supposed to advertise that we earned commission. When she saw Ben smiling, she looked back down at her paperwork and smiled to herself. It was pretty obvious that a commission wasn't the only reason I was so willing to delay my break.

Ben and I got down to business quickly. I'd just helped him decide which laptop to buy and we were moving over to the televisions when Jocelyn came over. I glanced at my watch. We'd been at it for over thirty minutes. "Hilary, are you almost finished with your 'customer'? We have other people waiting."

I hated the way Jocelyn emphasized the word 'customer'. I'd heard her use the same tone of voice with my co-workers when their boyfriends came in to hang out. I was a bit offended.

Ben spoke before I had a chance. "Hilary's been very helpful. If it is all right, I would like to keep working with her for a little while longer. She's helped me pick out a laptop, but I still need a TV and speaker system. If you need her, I can wait until she's finished with the other customers."

Jocelyn paused for a minute, as if she had been expecting an excuse. "No. That's ok, you keep going."

By the time Ben left, he had a new laptop, a new cell phone with an extra battery, and a fifty-inch TV for his basement suite. I tried to tame the smile that threatened when Jocelyn heard the total.

She came over and put her hand on my shoulder. "Sorry."

"It's all right."

I helped Ben take his purchases out to his car. "So, do you want to come over tomorrow and help me decide where to install the TV?" he asked as he angled the box into the trunk.

"Sure, but it'll have to be in the morning. I have to be back here for work at two."

"No worries, I can't imagine it will take too long. Dad has already hooked up the extra box for me."

"Must be nice. Mom and I just have the basic package. She won't let me get anything like Netflix because she doesn't want me to spend my life on the couch watching movies."

"She may have a point. They tend to suck you in two hours at a time," he agreed. "Mom and dad rarely let us watch movies. It was a long hard fight for me to convince them to get digital when we moved here."

Out of the corner of my eye, I saw movement. Crap, Janie was coming toward us. Thankfully, at least this time, she was alone. She must have ditched her friends.

I still groaned. Hadn't I already endured enough Janie for one night?

Ben turned to see what had caught my attention. He looked confused at first and then his eyes narrowed.

Janie didn't hesitate. She walked right through the empty parking space beside Ben's car and stood between us, forcing me to move back to avoid having her step on my toes in her strappy high heels.

I managed not to roll my eyes. But looking over Janie's shoulder, I saw Ben didn't have the same resistance. I pinched the soft skin under my arm to keep from laughing aloud at his expression. There would be a bruise there tomorrow, for sure.

I didn't need to see Janie's face to know what was coming next. I'd seen her in action before. As if cued by an imaginary director, Janie started preening. She twisted the ends of her blonde hair between her fingers, angled her shoulders and face into a come-hither look, then lowered her chin and looked up at Ben. A move she learned from Cosmo Girl, guaranteed to make her eyes look bigger and more appealing.

I'd read the same article, but there is no way I'd ever be able to pull it off without giggling.

"Hello," Her voice was huskier than usual. "I haven't seen you around before."

Ben gave Janie a dismissive once over and stepped around her. "No, you haven't."

I had to take another step back or he would have ended up flush against me, which would be fun any other time than when we had an indignant Janie about to explode less than a foot away.

He put his arm up to brace it against the roof of his car, blocking Janie from getting in between us again.

She barely looked in my direction. Her eyes glued to this poor, misguided male who obviously didn't know what he was missing. She wasn't quite sputtering, but she was close.

Ben continued our conversation as if there had been no interruption. "Come on over when you're ready. I'm usually up early and will be out back working on my car. There are a few things I want to adjust on it before school starts."

"You're not taking the bus?"

"Nah, mom wants Alex to get involved in a bunch of after school stuff. She thinks it'll help her fit in. It's easier for my parents if I just hang around to drive her home instead of them having to go all the way downtown to pick her up.

"Sounds familiar. Mom was working crazy hours and wanted me to do stuff after school instead of having to come home and be stuck at the house. So, she didn't sell Dad's old car and let me use it instead."

I watched Janie out of the corner of my eye. She had gone from confused to furious. I don't think anyone had ever ignored her in her life. She spun on her heel and stalked away, her sandals making an angry clicking noise on the pavement.

"You shouldn't have done that." I murmured low enough so only he could hear.

"What's she going to do?" He shrugged off my concern. "Does she have a big, bad boyfriend who'll punch my lights out?"

I giggled at the image that popped into my mind. Janie was between boyfriends, but last year Jimmy Rogers was so infatuated with her he'd do anything she asked. While he was better equipped for doing Janie's calculus homework, there was no doubt he would challenge Ben if Janie asked him to.

"No, I think you're safe. But..." Then I thought about Alex and the way she'd looked when I left for work. Janie was a sore loser. She wasn't used to being bested, and she wasn't above using Ben's little sister to retaliate. If Alex showed up at school dressed like she was today, she'd be toast. It took me only a split second to decide there really was not any point in warning Ben. He would just laugh anyway. Guys didn't understand how devastating teenage-girl warfare could be? He'd probably never had a moment of self-doubt in his life.

He jerked his thumb over his shoulder in the direction Janie departed. "Is she really as popular as she thinks she is?"

"Only with the other wannabes." I shrugged. "Most of my friends stay out of her way. She can be a first class..." I lowered my voice, "bitch when she wants to be. No one is safe from her claws. I don't know whether she just does it for fun or because she thinks it makes her more popular."

"Either way, that's pretty pathetic."

"That's our Janie."

We stared at each other for a minute.

"I have to get back to work." I handed Ben the bag. "I'll see you tomorrow."

"Great." His smile was wide enough to make me a little weak in the knees. He climbed into his car and pulled up alongside me as I walked back into the store. "Hilary don't worry about Janie. I've seen her type before. They're all the same and they usually end up causing more trouble for themselves than anyone else."

"I know, but sometimes she just gets under my skin."

"Just like a pimple, eh?"

I burst out laughing. I don't know which was funnier, his joke or imagining the look on Janie's face if she ever found out she had just been called a zit.

CHAPTER FOUR

I carefully dressed the next morning, choosing my favourite khaki shorts that showed off the tan on my legs and a sleeveless periwinkle-blue blouse. From the way Ben smiled at me last night, I'll admit I was leaping to the assumption this was a prequel to a date, or at the very least, a chance to explore the possibility of dating.

Yes, I know… I have to be careful. Normal guys don't just disappear into thin air. The what-ifs played in my mind, giving me not only a headache, but they made me incredibly nervous as I walked across the yard to where Ben was working on his car.

He must've been watching for me because he stopped working and stood up before I was halfway across my driveway. He was wearing old, grease-stained jeans, and a faded T-shirt.

My smile faltered a bit. He seemed to be very casual about my visit to his inner sanctum. Maybe I'd read him wrong after all. Then I noticed he'd shaved. Showering was nothing but shaving on a Saturday morning when he was planning to do nothing but work on his car all day? I smiled. Judging from his stubble on the day we met, he didn't seem to be the type of guy who shaved when he didn't have to.

Alex came around behind Ben and scowled. "What's she doing here?"

"She is helping me." Ben's tone of voice was patient, barely.

"Dressed like that?" she pointed to my flip-flops with the cute fabric flowers clustered along the thong part.

"Yes, like that." He picked up a rag from the edge of his car and wiped his hands as he walked toward me.

"Any annoying customers after I left last night?"

"No, I made a few more sales and re-stocked some shelves."

"Where are you going?" Alex demanded.

"Inside." Ben didn't bother turning around. "I asked Hilary to help me with something, if that's all right with you, your highness." He didn't wait for an answer. He put his hand on the small of my back and nudged me forward.

I shot an apologetic look back at Alex, just in time to see her storm away and vanish, just like Ben and his dad had that first night. Shock made me stumble.

Ben caught me, then looked back at his sister to see what she had done this time. The look on his face changed from impatient to angry. "Stupid brat."

I felt frozen to the spot until Ben grabbed my hand and tugged me around the corner of the house to the front door.

I should have run away, but my curiosity got the better of me. Distracted, I waved at Ben's parents sitting in the kitchen as Ben led me down into his basement suite.

He guided me along down the short hall, past the open door to his bedroom, to an open area that took up the entire front end of their house. He motioned for me to sit on his couch. "Hang on a minute. I have to talk to Mom and Dad about Alex." He left me alone and took the stairs two at a time from the way it sounded. I couldn't hear what he was saying to his parents, but the tone of his voice sounded far angrier than if he was simply complaining about Alex's rude behavior.

While waiting for Ben to return, I looked around his living space. The first thing I noticed was that it was incredibly neat. I wondered if he had cleaned up because I was coming or whether he was always this tidy. I was a little ashamed of the state of my bedroom in comparison.

I stood up and walked down the hallway. They had done an amazing job renovating the basement in the short time since they moved in. The entire front of the house was Ben's living area. It had a kitchenette on one side and the box with his TV still inside rested against the opposite wall. His bedroom was beside the staircase, and it looked like they had enlarged the bathroom. I peeked inside and saw my guess was right. They'd added a shower stall.

The Jennings had used the basement as a games room. They had a full-sized pool table set up near the back of the house and a bar area where Ben's kitchen was now.

Wait, a second. The room was too small, well too narrow really. The width of the house was the same, but there wasn't enough room to play pool anymore. It was like the back windows were a lot closer than they should have been.

Impossible!

Ben was still talking upstairs, so I walked back to the front of the house and then counted my footsteps as I moved toward the back wall. If each of my extra-long steps measured a metre, then it was missing at least three.

I heard Mrs. McAllister call Alex.

I looked out the back window to see if Alex would reappear as quickly as she vanished and if it would be in the same spot. She did, and it was. As she stomped up the back stairs, I walked back out to Ben's living room.

There were more angry whispers and then what I assumed was Alex racing to her bedroom and slamming the door. A few seconds later, Ben came downstairs again.

"Sorry, Alex has been a real pain since we moved in. She seems to have it in for you."

"It's kind of nice having someone's sister ticked off at me. As an only child, I missed out on all the sibling dramatics."

"You didn't miss much, trust me." He shook his head as if to dislodge his irritation. "You said your dad died?"

"Yeah, I was only eight when he was diagnosed with cancer. He hadn't been feeling well and I guess he figured he could just tough it out on his own. By the time he went to the doctor, it was too late. He died six months later."

"I'm sorry." Ben looked solemn. "That must have been really tough for you and your mom."

"It was in the beginning. It's better now."

I took a chance and mentioned how familiar I was with his house to gauge Ben's reaction. "Actually, I used to spend a lot of time here. Mr. and Mrs. Jennings looked after me. After dad died, my mom had to work. Mr. Jennings let me help him paint these walls when he was building his games room." I gestured around Ben's basement. "For a while, it seemed like I spent more time here than at home." My gaze lingered on the back wall for an extra beat, hoping to see everything was back to the way it should be. It wasn't.

Ben's forehead wrinkled as if I had just made his life more complicated. He was silent for a moment, looking at my face as if my expression could help him make an important decision. Finally, his shoulders dropped. "I guess we need to start with the obvious. You saw Alex disappear, didn't you?"

Suddenly, we were at the moment of truth. It surprised me how calm I felt. I wasn't frightened and I should have been terrified. "Not just Alex."

Ben looked perplexed for a minute before his face cleared. "The night we moved in."

I nodded. "I was out back in my treehouse when I heard you and your dad in the backyard. I looked to see what you were doing and then poof, you vanished. A few minutes later, you reappeared, just like that." I snapped my fingers.

"That's why you were avoiding me."

"It seemed the smart thing to do until I figured out what happened." I paused. "Or convinced myself I hadn't seen anything after all."

Ben sighed and leaned against the wall. He was not blocking my way out of the basement, which was a relief, but his expression made me sad. He suddenly looked older somehow. The longer he went without speaking, the more I was sure I didn't want to hear his explanation. No matter how curious I was. Without thinking, I looked down at the other end of the house again.

"You figured that out too?" Ben shook his head and smiled to himself. "Who am I kidding? Of course, you did."

"This used to be my playroom and then after he bought the pool table, Mr. Jennings taught me to play eight-ball and snooker." I looked around the room again, then back to Ben. "There isn't enough space back there to set up the pool table anymore.

"Hilary, please sit down." He pointed to the chair beside his desk where his new laptop sat. "We need to talk." He glanced to the foot of the stairs as if looking for eavesdroppers before opening a folding chair and pulling it close enough for our knees to touch.

"Does Shannon know?"

"No, she's visiting her grandparents in Ontario this week. I'm not sure I would have told her, anyway. She would have made me sneak over here at midnight to investigate."

"Yeah, she seems the type."

I raised my eyebrow in warning. "You're talking about my best friend since kindergarten."

He backed off a bit and raised his hands as if to ward off a barrage. "I didn't mean that as a bad thing. It's just that you seem to take your time and think things through. Shannon strikes me as the impulsive type." Even though he had leaned back, our knees were still touching. "I'm guessing you end up bailing her out a lot more than she has to rescue you."

He was right, but it seemed disloyal to agree. So, I shrugged my shoulders.

"If I ask you to leave it and not ask questions, could you?" His gaze was intent. He stared right into my eyes, as if trying to see the answer before I spoke.

"I guess it depends."

"On what?"

"Will not asking about what I saw hurt anyone?"

Ben looked relieved that I wasn't panicking. Even though we both knew there was nothing logical about his dad, sister and him just appearing and disappearing in their backyard. "No, keeping our secret will save my family from harm."

I'm not sure why I believed him. You'd probably think it was because I could feel the heat from his legs through the rough denim of his ragged jeans still pressed up against my knees, or because I had made a great commission from the TV in the box beside us. There was something more. He seemed frightened about what I was going to do as if there was a lot riding on my answers. More than I would have expected if he and his family were just running a scam. It seemed more likely they were in hiding.

That's it. I felt like doing a face-palm. They are hiding. That would also explain Mr. McAllister's reluctance to let Shannon and me help to unload the truck and why, when he had no choice, he'd given us the boxes marked for the living room. It all made sense. Well, except for the disappearing part, but I doubted I would ever figure that one out.

"You're in some kind of witness protection program, aren't you?"

Ben hesitated, choosing his words carefully. I could tell he was really trying not to lie, but also not betray any confidence. "Yes, I guess you could call it that."

A thought struck me that made me shiver. Ben couldn't help but notice my sudden tension since our legs were still touching and somewhere during our conversation, we were no longer kneecap-to-kneecap, but we had shifted so we were sitting even closer, my knees tucked safely between his. Interesting since neither of our chairs could move on the thickly carpeted floor.

"What?"

"Does what's going on with you and your family mean mom and I could be in danger?"

"No." Ben was quick to reply, and his voice sounded confident. "We've got things under control. There is no risk to anyone around us."

"I'm really not sure if that makes me feel better or worse." I said with a nervous half-laugh. "Better, because you have it under control, worse because you've just confirmed there is something that needs to be controlled."

Ben just looked at me. "You have got to be the smartest person I've ever met." He started listing on his fingers, "One, you figured out there was something different and two, you don't freak out. You apply logic as if it's a physics assignment. I think, you're actually starting to freak me out and I'm the one who can vanish whenever I want."

"Whenever you want?"

Ben looked down and muttered something under his breath that sounded suspiciously like he swore, even though I'm sure it was not a word I'd ever heard before.

"You didn't just seem to appear beside me yesterday. You really did."

"Shh, keep your voice down. Mom and Dad will kill me if they know I did that."

Ben did not look like a worried adult anymore. He looked more like a little kid who'd been caught with his hand in the cookie jar.

I recognized that look. It was the same one I had when I dinged the car and hoped mom wouldn't notice. "So, since you can't tell me what's going on or how you can appear and disappear at will... what can you tell me?"

"I can tell you I convinced mom and dad to choose this house. We'd been checking out different cities and potential neighbourhoods for quite a while. I put this house as number one on my list."

I cocked my head. "What's so special about this place?"

It was his turn to blush. Colour highlighted his cheeks, and his ears got all rosy. He was normally so confident, I'm sure it was the first time he's ever felt unsure of himself. The way he avoided looking me in the eye told me his answer was going to be a good one. It had to be, since it was making him squirm so much.

I was not expecting the answer he gave me.

"You."

"What do you mean me?" I was genuinely confused.

"I saw you when we were driving through this neighbourhood. Then I convinced Mom and Dad this was the best choice for our new home."

"You risked your family's security by choosing a place based on what the girl next door looked like? Are you nuts?"

He looked even more uncomfortable now, as if he'd started a conversation that he no longer had control of. "I expected you to be so flattered that you would blush and change the subject." He rolled his eyes up toward the ceiling. "Leave it to me to pick the one girl in the universe who would yell at me for compromising my family instead of taking the compliment gracefully."

"But Ben." I let my voice trail off.

He held his hand up to ward off further comment. "Look, it finally came down to here or in the middle of nowhere. Seriously, where would you choose?"

"Ok, ok, point made."

"Great, now can we hang my TV?"

I gave up and nodded. There was so much I still wanted to know, but I trusted him enough to let the conversation shift for now.

Ben was already up, and fighting with the cardboard corners cushioning his TV, which made it almost impossible to pull it free from the box. I grabbed the cardboard, and he held the TV, pulling it gently. When it was out, Ben tossed the box aside and helped me sort the wires and cables until we finally had everything ready.

We were back to being two regular teenagers.

I tried not to laugh when he made an innocent comment about mounting his TV, then turned red again when he realized what he had said.

He did a terrible job of pretending not to notice the way I looked at him while he stretched above me to hold the TV in place while I tightened the clasps on the bottom. I'm positive he did not need to flex as much as he did. He was the total package: smart, confident, built with sinewy muscle and a clean male scent combined with an eau de tinkering-with-car that made my toes curl.

At seventeen, I am not exactly a virgin, but I'm also not exactly not a virgin either - it's complicated. Ben had me thinking wicked thoughts that belonged in a spicy romance novel. When we finished, we stood back and viewed our handiwork. The TV was straight and solid. Ben put his arm around my shoulders and hugged me to him for a second. My heart pounded, but instead of leaning in for a kiss like I wanted to, I retreated. There were too many other things to think about.

"I've gotta run," I backed out of his half embrace and darted out of his basement suite and headed through my house to my treehouse. I had so much to sort out in my mind before I went to work.

CHAPTER FIVE

Safe in my treehouse, I tucked my legs up protectively to my chest and rested my chin on my knees. Sometimes I wished I didn't over-analyze stuff so much. It gave me a headache. I half-wished Shannon was home. I needed to talk to someone about what was happening. I thought about calling her, but I promised Ben I wouldn't say anything. Maybe it was a good thing she was gone after all. I was a horrible actor. She would know something was wrong, and she'd be hurt if I didn't tell her.

I don't know why I felt so drawn to Ben. After Trent, you would think I would know better than to fall for a guy just because he looked good. When Trent first asked me out, even Shannon, who was always trying to convince me to take chances, warned me away from him. She'd heard some bad things about him. I'd ignored her. Trent had told me all about the other girls. He'd convinced me they kept telling stories because they still wanted to be with him. I admit, he hadn't been one of my smarter choices.

This thing with Ben was different. It was not just a simple crush. One thing I learned from my experience with Trent, good looks didn't mean they were a good guy. Personality was more important.

Ben's little sister was a pain, but he treated her gently. He realized how much more difficult their move and everything else was on her than him.

She seemed to have it in for me, and I didn't know why. Was she upset about not having her big brother all to herself anymore, or did it have to do with the other stuff?

I knew I should run screaming to the police, or at least tell my mom, but something held me back. I decided to wait to see what would happen next.

CHAPTER SIX

The first day of senior year.

What was going to be different? Who is going to be different? Since kids bussed in from all over the city, I hadn't seen most of my classmates since last June.

My bus was one of the first to arrive at the school. Instead of going directly in, I leaned against one of the cement pillars in the large open plaza area and watched the other students arrive. The place was crazy busy. People gathered in groups, shouting out to their friends. It was easy to pick out the new grade nines. It hurt just to watch some of them. Zits, baby fat, klutzy… all with the same excited yet terrified looks on their faces.

I remembered how awkward I felt on my first day. It was exhilarating, but not what I would call fun. It was a harsh transition.

They'd lost their place as the ruling class of middle school and were reduced to be the butt of everyone's joke in secondary. I was so glad I was not fourteen anymore.

Shannon normally would have taken the bus with me and been standing here beside me. But this morning, her mother unexpectedly insisted on driving her instead, probably to give her a lecture about how important this year was going to be. This was the first time Shannon, and I did not sit together to catch up with everyone. It was so much fun, being surrounded by so many conversations going on at once. You learned about everyone. Shan had been royally ticked about having to miss it. She made me promise to update her on everything when we met up in the auditorium for the Welcome Assembly.

It didn't take long before I was surrounded by my friends and then friends of friends. I waved to other students I knew as they walked by. The first bell rang as the last of the buses cleared away. People began drifting away and heading inside. The assembly would start in fifteen minutes. I bent down to retrieve my laptop bag. Working for an electronics company had its advantages. I had a sweet laptop, at just above cost, which would really come in handy for school.

I was just about to head into the building when a flash of metallic blue caught my eye. Ben had just parked his Barracuda and was walking toward me. Alex trailed behind him. When he shifted direction toward me, Alex glared, crossed her arms over her long jacket and stalked away into the building as if she knew exactly where she was going. Ben shook his head, shrugged, and kept walking in my direction.

I started to warn him he'd parked in a residential zone. Vehicles were towed unless they had a residential parking permit, which was almost impossible to get without a valid uptown address. I had barely opened my mouth to speak when I noticed the tag hanging from his rear-view mirror. Seriously, how did he get that? I didn't notice the last of my friends elbowing each other and walking away, leaving me alone with Ben.

Ben was getting way too good at reading my thoughts. "Connections" was all he said before taking my bag and looping the strap over his shoulder, leaving me to trail behind as he turned toward the school. He stopped just before the door. The mass of kids rushing toward the auditorium was daunting. There didn't seem to be space for us to merge into the throng.

"Shall we?" He reached out for my hand.

I hesitated. If we walked in holding hands, my friends would accept him faster than if I introduced him as the guy next door, and he wouldn't be the only one benefitting. I would start my senior year with the hottest guy in the school on my arm. I smiled and, in the boldest move I'd ever made, I dodged his hand and put my arm around his waist until we were hip to hip. "We shall."

I'm not sure who was more surprised. Ben, me… or Shannon.

The look on her face when we entered the auditorium made me wish I had my camera. She was saving a seat for me beside the aisle in the centre section. As seniors, we had the best seats in the house, the rows directly in front of the orchestra pit. The grade elevens sat behind us leaving the grade tens squished in the back and the grade nines up in the balcony.

"There's Shannon." I nudged Ben with my hip to direct him to where she was standing. By the time we got there, she had snagged another seat so the three of us could sit together. I glanced around, waving at people I knew. Janie and her entourage were standing close to the stage. She watched us with narrowed eyes as I introduced Ben to my other friends. It was obvious she recognized Ben from the incident at the store. I smiled. Ben walking in with me trumped her last-minute catch of Jason Wheatley, star of last year's drama production and MVP of the track and field team. Jason was gorgeous, with blonde hair, blue eyes, and dimples to die for, but next to Ben, he looked like a pretty little boy.

The principal stepped up to the microphone and asked everyone to take their seats. Ben and I sat down beside Shannon. She looked at his arm draped across my shoulder and demanded, "When did this happen?"

Ben answered her truthfully. "About five minutes ago" then he looked at me even though he was still answering Shannon, "It would have been sooner, but Hilary was playing hard to get."

I elbowed him in the ribs. "I wasn't playing hard to get and you know it."

He gave in, "No, she wasn't playing, she was hard to get. I've been trying to attract her attention since we moved in."

Shannon laughed. "Yeah, Hilary can be dense like that sometimes."

"Et Tu Brute?" I tried to look offended.

"Hilary, you have guys drooling over you all the time and never seem to notice."

I was about to say something smart-assed when the drone of the loudspeakers drowned me out.

"Welcome to the start of the best year ever at Saint John High School."

I looked up to the stage to see the curtains swishing from movement behind them. The first assembly of the year was a bunch of skits by the different teams and membership pitches by the academic clubs to encourage students to get involved. I thought it was strange that Janie was sitting in the audience, especially this year, since she was president of the Drama Club. Usually, she was backstage, telling people what to do. I glanced over to where she sat and rolled my eyes. She was speaking irately into a lapel mic, bossing people around remotely. I had to resist the urge to take a box of Kleenex backstage to the poor person who had to listen to her. Instead, I relaxed back into my chair and rested my head against Ben's shoulder.

I had to pinch myself.

As soon as Principal Murdoch finished her welcome speech, the curtains opened to reveal the football team dressed as cheerleaders and the cheerleaders dressed in football gear. They weren't the most creative bunch. They had the same skit every year.

In between performances, representatives from the other clubs like math and chess stumbled up to the podium to make their bid for new members. I always felt bad for them. Most didn't want to be on stage, and it showed. Traditionally, the drama club closed the show. This year was no different. Janie was shifting in her seat preparing for her grand entrance, which apparently was going to be from the audience this time.

The opening chords of Mamma Mia blasted through the speakers. The auditorium exploded with applause. We'd tried to do Mamma Mia last year for our big school production, but something happened with the copyright, and we ended up doing one of Shakespeare's plays instead. If they were playing ABBA now, it meant we got the musical this year.

The spotlights swung down to Janie, who jumped up from her spot in the audience and started belting out the title track. Instead of singing to Jason, which he seemed to be expecting, she danced her way up the aisle to where Ben, Shannon, and I sat. She pulled Ben to his feet and started serenading him.

Mamma mia, here I go again
My, my, how can I resist you?

Mamma mia, does it show again?
My, my, just how much I've missed you?
Yes, I've been broken-hearted
Blue since the day we parted
Why, why did I ever let you go?
Mamma mia, now I really know
My, my, I should not have let you go

The music changed to the next song in the montage. The lights swung up to the stage where Amanda was waiting with a group of guys to re-enact the beach scene from the movie.

But Ben unclipped the lapel mic from Janie and started to sing. He had a spectacular baritone that easily drowned out Amanda. The lighting crew must have realized something was up and swung the lights back to him.

You're so hot
Teasing me
So, you're blue but I can't
Take a chance on a kid like you
It's something I couldn't do

There's that look
In your eyes
I can read in your face
That your feelings are driving you wild
But girl, you're only a child

Ben handed Janie back her microphone with a smirk and then spun her around to face Jason, who had moved up the aisle behind her. Then, Ben turned his back on her and sat down and put his arm back around me.

Another change in the music partially disguised his snub. This time it was Dancing Queen.

From the look on his face, Jason was furious with Janie's little improvisation.

The other drama club members came running down the aisle, apparently adjusting their dance to Janie and Jason's new position. They swirled around them, sweeping them up the side-stairs to the stage for the finale. Janie kept in step with everyone else, but she looked a little shell-shocked at the outcome of her prank. It obviously didn't turn out the way she'd expected.

Shannon and I could not stop laughing. People sitting closest to us were congratulating Ben. It wasn't often someone got the better of Janie. Ben's position in the SJHS social network was rock-solid, less than an hour into his first day.

No one paid attention to Janie, who was now at the podium making her plea for new drama club members.

I looked around at the rest of the grade twelves. They were still howling with laughter. I tried to feel a twinge of regret at her public humiliation and couldn't. Janie was a bully. Many of the students were straining to get a better look at the new guy. I glanced farther up the auditorium to the grade ten and eleven kids. They were laughing, too. Up in the balcony, the grade nines looked confused. They didn't know what just happened, but they knew it was big.

Then I saw her. Alex was sitting in the front row of the balcony. She was glaring down at Ben and me. Well, okay. The glare was just for me. Meh, I was getting used to it. What disturbed me was what she was wearing.

Apparently, she had lost another argument with her mom about her wardrobe. At least I hoped the outfit wasn't her choice. Her hair was in pigtails and, from what I could see, she was wearing a dress that might have been cute if she were a normal twelve-year-old going to middle school, but she wasn't. She might as well have been wearing a target on her back.

I nudged Shannon. "We have a mission, balcony, first row centre."

Shannon looked up. "Oh, dear God, they'll slaughter her."

"Exactly."

Ben looked at us confused, "Who will slaughter who?"

Shannon smiled indulgently. "Now don't you go worrying your pretty little head about it. We've got it under control."

The Assembly finished a few minutes later. The grade nines would stay for orientation and then be escorted to their homerooms by their new teachers. The rest of us had an extra long break to get to our classes. Our room assignments had been emailed out the week before, so we already knew where to go.

As we walked up the stairs, I asked. "Ben, who does Alex have for homeroom?"

"I think Nason, room 205. Why?"

"I don't have time to explain it right now. We've got to get to class."

Ben appeared confused but seemed to accept my non-explanation. "Ok, you can tell me about whatever it is over lunch. Where should we meet?"

"By your car," I said, "We have something to do first, so we'll be late." Before he could say or ask anything else, I turned away and grabbed Shannon. We rushed away to our homerooms, which were just down the hall. Ben's was upstairs on the fourth floor.

"Any suggestions?"

"You mean aside from a total makeover?"

"Yeah, depending on who else is in her homeroom, they could completely crush her before noon."

Shannon and stood in the middle of the hall between our homerooms trying to decide on a plan. "I'll meet you in front of 205. If you get to her first, take her to the girl's locker room. It should be quiet there. We'll have some privacy."

"Ladies?" Mr. Larsen was standing in the doorway, ready to close the door.

"Sorry, sir." I slunk in past him, did a quick scan of the room, and groaned. Alex had better appreciate this, I muttered to myself as I slid into the last seat, which was right in front of Mr. Larsen's desk.

Homeroom was usually ten minutes in the morning and again first thing in the afternoon to take attendance and go over announcements. However, today, it took the rest of the morning while we got our locker assignments and a not-so-brief lecture about how we were seniors this year and, as such, should set a good example for the younger grades.

I wondered if saving stubborn grade-niners from social suicide would get me any extra credits.

My attention kept wandering. I was worried about Alex. I didn't get a good look at her dress, so it was hard to plan what we could do to improve her appearance. I did a mental inventory of what was in my bag. It relieved me to remember I had packed my emergency sewing kit to store in my locker.

After an eternity, the bell sounded. I was the first one out the door. I met Shannon as she ran out of her classroom. Together, we pushed past the crowd of kids standing around in the hallway and ran down the stairs closest to Alex's homeroom.

When we arrived, Alex was crouching beside a desk, picking up papers scattered all over the floor. Her shoulders were slumped. Even with her head lowered, I could see her chin trembling.

In the back of the classroom, Jenny, Janie's sister, and her friends were snickering.

"Crap."

Shannon and I walked into the room. "Hi Mr. Nason." Shannon smiled at her old grade nine teacher who'd been writing on the wall and missed all the action behind him.

"Come on, Alex." I grabbed the rest of her papers and shoved them into her hands. It didn't surprise me they were shaking.

In less than a minute, we were out of the classroom, past the principal's office and halfway across the breezeway.

Once we were in the girl's locker room, Alex broke away from us and stood with her feet planted firmly and her arms crossed. "What do you want?"

She tried to look ferocious, and she almost succeeded except for the tears clinging to her eyelashes. The poor kid hadn't stood a chance. Jenny had learned from the best. Find someone weaker than you and then bully the hell out of them.

"We're here to fix you," Shannon said.

"I'm fine," Alex shot back.

"So, you're ready to go back to face Jenny and her group of bitches-in-training?"

Alex crumpled to the bench. "No."

I crouched down beside her. "Alex, let us help. We have both gone up against Janie, Jenny's big sister and her friends. We know what we're doing."

"You just want to help me in order to get closer to my brother."

Shannon laughed in her face. "Umm, Alex, in case you haven't noticed, she doesn't need any help and just so you know, your brother is the one who's been chasing Hilary, not the other way around."

Alex looked surprised, as if she hadn't considered that perspective before. "But why are you being nice to me?"

I smiled at her. "I like you. You have attitude and you look out for your brother. That makes you worth ten Janies and Jennys combined."

Alex's eyes were still watering, but she started to smile.

"Ok," Shannon interrupted, pulling Alex to her feet. "Let's get you secondary school appropriate."

Up close, I had to revise my opinion. The dress Alex was wearing would have been adorable... if she were eight. Tiny, bright pink, taupe, and white swirls covered the bodice with lace along the collar and on the cuff of each puffy capped sleeve. Luckily, the skirt wasn't quite as bad. It was mostly taupe with larger pink and white swirls. Thanks to mom and me making so many Barbie clothes when Dad was in the hospital, it didn't take me long to figure out how I could fix Alex's dress.

I took out my sewing kit and made tacks along the seams of the skirt. It took me about ten minutes to get rid of all that Cinderella-like puffiness. I took my sweater out of my bag and made her put it on to cover the top of the dress. Luckily, it matched. The sleeves were way too long for Alex's short arms. I thought for a minute about my options before I folded the sleeves under, and safety pinned them in place so they wouldn't fall. By the time I finished, Alex looked like she belonged in grade nine, at least as far as her clothes went.

Shannon was waiting by the mirror, hairbrush in hand. "My turn."

Alex walked over to Shannon. She looked a little shocked at the way we had just taken over.

Five minutes later, Alex's ponytails were gone. Her hair hung down her back in one long, elegant braid. Shannon applied the lightest touch of make-up before stepping away from between Alex and the mirror.

Alex was in awe, and I have to admit, even I was impressed. She wasn't a bad-looking kid to begin with, and thanks to Shannon's magic, she was a knockout.

Her eyes started to well up again, and Shannon spoke sharply. "Don't you dare cry. It'll ruin your mascara!"

Alex hiccupped and laughed. The danger of a meltdown passed. She looked helplessly at us. "I look…"

"Fabulous?" Shannon offered.

"Gorgeous?" I looked at my watch. "Come on, we're late to meet your brother."

Shannon gathered her stuff back into her bag and the three of us walked out of the locker room. Shannon and I flanked the 'new' Alex.

Ben was leaning over under the hood of his car with a crowd of guys when we crossed the plaza. Dave's voice echoed over to us as he elbowed John, who was standing beside him.

"Whoa, who's the fox with Hilary and Shannon?"

Ben straightened and turned toward us. He stiffened the instant he realized the 'fox' was his baby sister.

I walked up, wrapped one arm around his waist, and leaned in close enough to whisper in his ear. "She's had one hell of a morning. Be supportive."

I felt him nod against my cheek. His arm had tightened against me for seconds before relaxing. I kind of liked this whole couple thing.

"So big brother, whaddya think?" Shannon asked. At the word brother, most of the guys stepped back. Little sisters were out-of-bounds, especially when the brothers looked as protective as Ben did.

"Well," he paused, "you don't look like my baby sister anymore." He glanced back at me. "You'll have to fill me in later."

I nodded. I had to stand on my toes and lean back a bit to look at Ben from so close beside him. "I'm not working tonight. Do you think your mom would mind if Shannon and I took Alex shopping?"

He nodded. "She'll probably want to go too."

"I can deal with that."

Alex still looked a little dumbstruck. Even though the boys had backed off, one or two were still eyeing her appreciatively. "Down boys." I looked pointedly at Dave. "She's in grade nine. "

"Aw." he replied, then looked back at Alex and winked. "Call me when you hit grade eleven."

Ben put his hand up. He looked over at Dave. "Baby sister, she can call you when she's thirty!"

CHAPTER SEVEN

It was after nine by the time we got home from shopping. Even with Shannon and me loaded down with bags, Alex hadn't wanted to leave the mall.

"But we haven't been to that store yet," Alex pointed. "Or to that one."

The last one she pointed at was a lingerie shop. Mrs. McAllister paled. She was reluctantly taking our advice about Alex's wardrobe. The notion of her baby girl in sexy silk was more than she could handle right now.

"Alex, the stores will still be here on the weekend," I intervened. "Besides, I have a homework assignment for English."

"You do?" Shannon asked, surprised.

I shot her a look. She is usually quicker than that.

"Oh crap, I forgot. Me too."

Alex didn't look like she believed us, but I could tell Mrs. McAllister appreciated the escape we'd offered. When we first arrived at the shopping centre, she headed right for the girl's section of the big box store. We steered her out of the department store and toward the trendier shops in the mall.

Ben mentioned they had attended private school before coming to Saint John. They had to wear uniforms, which explained even Alex and her mother's lack of understanding of teen couture. We were gentle and chose the more conservative outfits, but poor Mrs. McAllister still seemed to be in shock.

I was exhausted, even though it wasn't even close to my regular bedtime. My body wanted to collapse onto my bed, but my brain just wouldn't stop. I took my book-light and slipped out the back door to my treehouse. I hoped if I wrote everything down, it would stop spinning around in my mind. If it didn't, I would never fall asleep.

Once I was up in my hideaway, I realized my thoughts were still too jumbled to put down on paper. I leaned back against the trunk and stared out of the back window, willing my mind to calm down. From here, I could see over the huge bog behind our house. It extended all the way to the woods that stretched up over the big hill a kilometre away. I watched the curve of the small mountain fade away into the last bit of twilight.

Finally, my mind settled. I pulled my journal out from its hiding spot and took one last look out my window.

"What the hell?"

There were weird lights out in the bog. At first, they looked like fireflies playing tag over the low shrubbery, but then I realized they weren't yellow. They looked… purple? I leaned forward, pressing my nose up to the glass.

The lights moved randomly across the bog.

No wait.

There was a definite pattern. They were criss-crossing over themselves every few metres and they were further away than I had thought too. They were at the back of the bog, weaving in and out between the trees before shooting closer, then retreating again. That made them a lot bigger than fireflies. The lights dipped and weaved as if attached to long sticks, but they moved so quickly in and out of the tree line, I didn't know of anyone who could run fast enough to carry them.

"I thought I'd find you here."

I cracked my head against the glass. Ben's voice scared me. "Ben, come look at this."

I felt the treehouse shudder as he climbed up onto the tiny platform beside me. He was so big he filled the small space. To see out the window, he had to rest his chin on my shoulder.

"Look."

He tensed immediately. "How long have they been there?"

"Just a few minutes." I tried to see his expression, but it was too dark. "What are they?"

"Sensors."

Surely, I misheard him. "Centaurs? Aren't they those mythical half-man half-horse creatures?"

"Not centaurs," he corrected, "Sensors. Rat sized, flying robots designed to find and track residue from… certain types of exhaust fumes."

I shifted my position vainly, trying to get a better look at his face. His body was rigid, and I was sure he was skipping important details. "How do you know what they are? And why are they over the bog?"

"They shouldn't be here. We covered…" He backed up and dropped to the ground through the trapdoor.

"Ben, what's going on?"

"Come on. I've got to tell Dad." He looked up at me through the hole in my treehouse floor. "And I think we need to tell you what's going on."

I shifted around to get my feet out first and started to climb down from my treehouse. Ben's hands grasped me around my waist and lowered me down the rest of the way, holding me for an extra second, just enough to set my pulse racing in a different way than it already was. We ran across the back lawn to his house.

"Downstairs now!" Ben hollered when he opened the door.

I saw a glimpse of Mr. McAllister's face as I raced down the stairs after Ben. He reacted instantly to the worried tone in Ben's voice and looked very confused to see me running downstairs behind his son.

Ben led me to the back of his basement suite. To the wall that was in the wrong place. Without slowing down, he disappeared in front of me.

I skidded to a stop and tried to yank my hand out of his grasp.

My sudden halt jerked him back toward me. His face reappeared. Only his face stuck out from the wall like an animal head on display. He still held my hand, but just above his elbow, the rest of his body disappeared into the wall. He tried hard not to look impatient. "Come on Hilary. Trust me. It will be all right. I promise."

I felt him tug my hand again. I closed my eyes; not sure I could handle seeing myself disappear into the wall. I took two steps when he said, "Open your eyes, Hilary."

I hesitated another second before I peeked out through my lashes and gasped. I felt like Alice after she had fallen down the rabbit hole into Wonderland, except this was no Mad Hatter tea party. Instead, I was standing in a room that could have doubled for the set of any sci-fi flick. Blinking lights, floating holograms and more clicking and beeping sounds than I had ever heard in one place before. Apparently, I had found the missing space from Mr. Jennings' game room. I looked back the way we came, and the entrance looked like a normal doorway.

From this side, I could see down the hall into Ben's living area. This was way too weird.

"Are you ok?" Ben looked concerned. "I'm sorry Hilary, I should have warned you." he wrapped his arms around me for a second. "I meant to ease you into all this, but the Sensors made me forget to tell you about the hidden doorway."

"I didn't just walk through a wall?"

"Nope, just a hologram of one."

Before I could say anything else, Ben's dad came into the room. Ben let go of my hand and then walked through a couple of hologram maps to the other end of the room. He slipped into a high-backed chair and immediately started flipping switches and typing on what I assumed was a keyboard, even though all I could see were wispy lines of light suspended in midair. Mr. McAllister patted me on the shoulder before he walked past me to join his son.

Alex and her mother ran down the stairs and into the room. "What happened?" "Why is Hilary here?" Their voices blended so that I could barely make out the two separate questions. Forget about who asked what.

"We saw Sensors." Ben said without turning his head.

I noticed his voice had changed. It seemed deeper and more authoritative.

"How did they find us?" Mr. McAllister asked as he sat down in one of the smaller chairs along the back wall of the house, the real back wall. "There should not be any residual exhaust to track. We drove all the way here in a rented truck to make sure of it."

Alex was already in her chair, hands flying over the controls. "I think we're okay. They are all over the planet." In front of her appeared another hologram. This one was a three-dimensional picture of the Earth. Purple specs seemed to swarm in groups over the major centres of the globe.

I moved over to stand behind Alex. She was flicking more buttons. Seconds later, a vast display appeared in from her. It showed miniature images of news broadcasts from around the world with banners along the bottom identifying each city: London, New York, Tel Aviv, Moscow, Los Angeles, and Bangkok. None showed any reports of purple lights. I watched Alex flip more buttons, and the display switched to what looked like military communications. I stood back, stunned. Who were these people, anyway? There was so much I needed to ask, but everyone seemed so busy. Even Mrs. McAllister's hands were flying over the keyboard in front of her.

The tone of the chatter from the military channels was urgent. Fighter jets launched, targets acquired, then vanished.

"What happens if a jet hit one of them?" I asked. I was watching one broadcast showing the view through a nose camera as the pilot tried to zoom in on the object. The Sensor's light was so bright it fried the lens, making it look like a glowing beach ball.

Alex laughed, as if I had just told a silly joke. "You don't have anything fast enough to hit one of them."

"Will they attack us?"

Alex swivelled her chair around to face me. She put a comforting hand on my arm. This was her turf and our roles had just reversed. "No Hilary, they won't attack. They're seekers, programmed to find certain combinations of chemicals." Alex turned back to the display. She made more adjustments. "That's weird. Most of the Sensors have stayed above the twenty thousand metre mark and they run dark. They only light up when they're sniffing. That is why the news broadcasts aren't picking up the story. Only the long-range commercial flights would be high enough to see them, and even then, it would be from a distance and only if they wanted to be seen. There are only a few locations where the Sensors have come close to the ground."

"But why are they on this planet? If they know we're here, then it's only a matter of time before they find us." Mrs. McAllister left her chair and walked to the other side of the room to where Ben and his father were working.

My brain had stopped trying to merge what I was seeing with reality. I was just going with the flow until something made sense again.

"I'll check around to see if any of the other refugees we know have seen the Sensors on their planets." Alex reached up to flip another switch on her console dashboard.

"Wait!" I grabbed her hand. "If these Sensors can detect exhaust from your engines that you haven't run in a while, can they monitor a signal from here going to another planet?" I let go of Alex's hand.

Ben and his parents had been so intent on the displays in front of them they hadn't been paying attention to us. The entire McAllister family stopped what they were doing and stared at me. Suddenly, I felt uncomfortable. Who the hell did I think I was? The high-tech beeps, flashes and holographic images surrounding me should have clued me in. I knew nothing about what was happening. "Sorry, I shouldn't have said…"

"She is right." Mr. McAllister interrupted my apology. "If we stay silent, they may move on. If the Hurliingen knew for sure we were here, they would not have sent the Sensors. They would have come to find us themselves."

Ben nodded. His eyes were full of pride when they met mine for a brief second, before he looked back at the controls in front of him.

I didn't feel lame anymore. Even though I had no idea who or what the Hurlin-whatever were, or the faintest clue about what was going on, I felt like part of their team. It was the coolest feeling.

Before I could pat myself on the back too much, a horrible thought struck me. I didn't actually know if the McAllisters were the good guys. I assumed these Sensor things were evil, but what if they belonged to the police and Ben's family were fugitives? What if I just helped the bad guys dodge the law?

Mrs. McAllister walked back to her console and must have seen my expression. My poker face sucked, so I'm sure my thoughts reflected clearly on my face. "Come upstairs with me Hilary, I will explain everything."

She took my hand and led me from the hidden room. This time, I paid attention as we walked through the doorway. From the inside, it looked like a regular doorframe. As we walked through it, the room behind me faded and disappeared. As soon as we were back in Ben's part of the basement, the overwhelming noise from the electronics disappeared. It was as if that whole room no longer existed.

I followed Ben's mom up the stairs and into the kitchen. "Sit down, dear, Ben said we could trust you and he has not been wrong yet."

I fell more than sat on the chair. "You make it sound like Ben is in charge?"

"He is." Mrs. McAllister filled the kettle and put it on the stove. We both looked out the back window, facing the hill. The bog was dark, no sign of the Sensor's purple lights. "Even though you have just seen some odd things, our story is still going to sound unbelievable."

"I need to know what's going on." It amazed me at how calm I sounded. I didn't feel that way. "Ben says my mom and I aren't in danger, but that was before he saw those Sensor things."

"They change nothing regarding your safety. Our arrival has put no one else in danger." She sat down, facing me. Her hands clasped so tightly her knuckles were white. Despite her assurance that my family was safe, it was clear hers wasn't.

Exuding a confidence, I didn't know I had, I put my hand over hers. "Tell me."

Mr. McAllister raised her eyes to mine. "Ben was right to choose this place. We thought he was just being a fahrib."

"A what?"

"A fahrib. A hormone driven teenage boy." Her smile was full of pride. "We had narrowed our choices to two locations, a remote suburb in the United States and here. With all the changes happening in the United States, we decided we would be better off in Canada. Ben and the General did a physical check of both potential places. We'd made a list of houses that would suit our needs, but when Ben saw you and Shannon on your front steps, he was insistent about not only coming to Saint John, but about buying this house.”

That part I already knew. “Who is the General?”

“Mr. McAllister is really General Tsad. He is one of the top military strategists on our home… where we come from. He is here to protect us. When we arrived, we decided it would be better if he pretended to be Ben and Alex’s father to help us blend in and look like a normal family.”

I had many questions and her answer only added more. They had alluded to so much over the past hour that I didn’t know where to start. “Who is Ben? And why can he override a General?”

Instead of answering, Mrs. McAllister stood up and started puttering around the stove. Her hands shook as she reached into the cupboard for mugs. She wasn’t ignoring my question, so I stayed quiet. She put instant coffee grounds in three and hot chocolate powder in another then paused over the fifth one. “Would you prefer coffee or hot chocolate?”

I didn’t drink coffee this late, but tonight I felt like I needed it. “Coffee please.”

“Sorry for the instant. We’ve travelled so much, instant food seems so much easier and your planet has a much better variety than ours.”

I could tell she was stalling, and I needed answers. She kept referring to ‘this planet’, but it seemed too surreal to ask what other planets she was comparing us to.

“Mrs. McAllister, who is Ben?”

Her back was still toward me. She sighed and braced her hands against the counter as if to support herself during the explanation. “Forgive me, dear. This is harder than I thought it would be. Telling someone outside the four of us makes us very vulnerable."

"It's okay Mom, I'll take it from here."

Ben stood in the doorway, looking older than his almost seventeen years. He hadn't shaved since this morning and the dark stubble on his chin gave him a dangerous look. His eyes softened when he looked at me, but the grim determination in them frightened me a little. Suddenly, I was not sure I wanted to hear their story after all. But I was in too deep to stop now.

Mr. McAllister, or rather, the General and Alex, followed Ben into the room. The three of them sat around the kitchen table while Mrs. McAllister poured the boiling water from the kettle into the five mugs. Ben got a bottle of coffee flavouring from the fridge and set it down on the table. "We can't quite get used to the taste of fresh milk. I hope this is ok."

"Southern Butter Pecan is one of my favourite flavours."

It took a few minutes for everyone to settle around the table. I glanced up at the clock on the wall. It surprised me to see it was only ten thirty. Shopping at the mall seemed like an eternity ago.

Ben put his spoon down and all eyes went to him. It seemed so odd to me that his parents, or whoever they were, looked to him for guidance. My fear was gone, at least temporarily. Now I was curious.

"We arrived on Earth just over two years ago." He did not look at me as he spoke. Instead, Ben seemed to be fascinated by the coffee swirling in his cup. "We escaped from Myonus, our home planet, after a military coup destroyed our government and killed our father."

Ben's mother interrupted him. "We don't know he's dead. He might have survived." Even though her words were hopeful, I could tell she didn't believe them anymore.

Ben did not respond, but his expression when he looked at his mom told me he did not believe them either.

The General took over the explanation. "Our system of government differs from yours. It is global. It is also based on the level of a substance called Tixlar in our blood. Tixlar amplifies the production of energy from Ancfu, an element on Myonus similar to gold here on earth. On its own Ancfu has no special property. But when physically handled by the Tixlardine it becomes an almost endless source of fuel."

"According to our history, everyone was once Tixlardine. As time passed, the Tixlar levels in our blood dropped. The Tixlardine became the ruling class and the non-Tixlardine lost their status. Each generation had a new leader. Those individuals with the highest level of Tixlar would succeed the previous ruler. I guess you could call these individuals the elite of the elite. Two centuries ago, barely a third of Myonusians were Tixlardine. The balance in the population had shifted, but the rules of society had not. Those without Tixlar still could not hold office or take part in our government.

"By the time Ben's great grandfather was born, the Tixlardine composed less than ten percent of the population, and the levels of Tixlar in many of those remaining, was a fraction of what it had once been within their family lines. Because of the dwindling population, it had been necessary for Tixlardine to marry non-Tixlardine to prevent in-breeding. Which of course, diluted the Tixlar concentration even further. It was a nowin situation." The General paused for a minute to take a sip of his coffee.

"Some families began to secretly experiment with genetic modification. They tried to create children with higher amounts of Tixlar in their bodies. It was a disaster. Some of these children became Anti-Tixlar. Their systems did not amplify the energy in Ancfu but depleted it. They were like miniature black holes. To hide the failure of these illegal experiments, these children were hidden away in exile and forgotten."

"Ben's great grandfather had heard of these children and devoted himself to finding them. Because of their condition, they could not be part of mainstream society. He built them clean villages to live in and treated them with respect. In the eyes of the planet, he was a hero."

My mind was whirling. Ben was not only from another planet but also part of the ruling class. Part of me wanted to laugh and congratulate them for this impressive prank, but their fear was so real you could almost touch it. This was no joke.

"His son, Ben's grandfather, came into power. Having a single family in control for three generations was rare. Now, with even fewer families with significant levels of Tixlar in their bodies, something had to change. It was up to Ben's grandfather to make it work or there would be a war. Our supply of Ancfu was not running low, but our ability to pull energy from it was fading exponentially with each new generation. Our entire economic system and way of life were in danger of collapse.

"Myonus was a member of the Alliance of Eight, eight planets spanning three solar systems. Thanks to interplanetary trading, other technologies were adapted to

Myonus. They helped to lessen the planet's dependence on the Tixlardine. Even so, the Tixlardine were practically enslaved because there were so few left to produce the quantities of energy needed. The situation was perilous.

"Ben's grandfather proactively introduced a new system of government. He created an Integrated Council. Everyone, Tixlardine or not, were encouraged to work together for the good of the planet. Even though he remained at the head of the council, he was hailed as a revolutionary, a hero, just like his father."

The General paused for a minute to take a sip from his mug.

Mine had sat ignored on the table so long it was cold. I took a drink anyway. I needed to do something with my hands. Part of my brain was amused about how calmly I was accepting what the General was telling me. I should be freaking out. My boyfriend was… an alien prince.

"So, you're royalty?"

"Not so much anymore." Ben set his mug back on the table. "With the separation between Tixlardine and the leadership of our planet's government, we became just regular people with a rather unique skill set."

"When we started exploring planets beyond our solar systems, we drew the attention of another alien race, the Hurliingen. They are a race that thrives on competition, moving from planet to planet, stealing technology and resources like pirates. They started to monitor Myonus and the Alliance of Eight and eventually decided our resources would be useful to them. Instead of coming to the council and establishing a trade process, they found some of the old-school elites who resented their loss of status within the new mixed council."

"The Hurliingen promised to reinstate the old ways and put them in charge as a reward for their help. Our father, the fourth-generation leader, knew there was a growing movement against the Integrated Council." Ben nodded to the General. "General Tsad, had been investigating, but the Hurliingen were wise. None of the old-school elites knew their real plan. Each thought they would be richly rewarded for their participation. Their greed kept them quiet. By the time they realized they had been used, it was too late."

"My father had already prepared a ship. He knew something was happening and feared Alex and I would become collateral. He planned to send us to Earth until he could regain control of our planet. Since he couldn't leave Myonus to come with us, he sent General Tsad along for protection and to be my mentor. We barely escaped in time."

I listened in fascination. "What happened to your father?"

The General started to answer. Ben held up his hand. "From what we know, my father is dead."

Mrs. McAllister reached over and put her hand on her son's arm. He might be in charge, but he was still her child.

"We were one of the few families able to escape from Myonus. Since we have been here on Earth, we have heard bits and pieces of news. We have a network, much like your internet, only it spans between planets several solar systems away. Unfortunately, because it is so big, it is hard to validate any of the information we receive. All we know for sure is that the Hurliingen are still looking for us."

"But why? They've taken over your planet and have captured the Tixlardine who helped them. They have what they want. Don't they?"

"Almost. They want what we once had. Their plan was to capture the Tixlardine and force them to reproduce. Their strategy was to inbreed them, hoping to purify the bloodlines again and regain the lost levels of Tixlar."

"I'm still confused. Why do they need Ben and Alex if they have other families? What makes them so important?"

"Because we are elite, even among the Tixlardine." Alex said. Her voice had a quiet confidence in it. "Grandfather couldn't have restructured the government of our entire planet if he didn't have significantly more Tixlar than anyone else. It makes us genetic deities, at least on our planet." She added with a wry smile. "It doesn't seem to count for much here."

"Yeah, here it's all about clothes and hair." Ben laughed, lightening the mood. I was reluctant to bring it down again, but there was still the issue of those lights in the bog to discuss. "What about the Sensors?"

The General took over the explanation. "Sensors are an old Myonusian technology. I guess you could call them robotic bloodhounds. They were developed to track criminals. Now the Sensors are being deployed for what I can only assume is a search party for us."

"What happens if they find you?"

"They need Ben and Alex alive." Mrs. McAllister looked worried again. "If they find us, Ben will be kept prisoner to produce heirs and pull energy from Ancfu until he dies from exhaustion and Alex will…" she stopped as if she could not voice the words.

"I'll be used to procreate." Alex said it matter-of-factly, but I heard the underlying fear and tension in her voice.

Mrs. McAllister seemed to age before my eyes. Ben and the General looked grimly into their coffee cups.

It was too much to absorb. I looked out the window toward the bog. Thankfully, there was no sign of the Sensor's lights. When I was little, I was scared of the dark. Right now, I was more afraid of the lights. I took a deep breath and looked at Ben, who had been watching me as if waiting for my reaction.

"So, how can I help?"

CHAPTER EIGHT

Ben stopped me just before I left his house. "Why don't you drive to school with Alex and me instead of taking the bus?" He paused. "It would look odd if we didn't."

The smile spreading over my face at his invitation faltered. I was disappointed how he needed to rationalize the invitation by saying it would look odd. Maybe being my boyfriend was just a cover after all. "You realize Shannon will talk herself into your car, too."

"That's not a bad idea." He replied. "If the Hurliingen are nearby, they'll most likely be looking for a family hiding away or trying to be invisible. Not people surrounded by friends. It's part of the reason the General and I restored the Barracuda. We looked for a car that would stand out. The Hurliingen wouldn't look twice at anyone driving a car that attracts attention. I could drive by them, and they'd ignore me."

The rest of my smile vanished, and I could feel my shoulders slump. What he said made sense, but it made me feel even less secure about our relationship as I left.

It was almost midnight when I paused outside the front door of my house. Even though mom and I had a deal that I could stay up late, as long as I promised never to complain about being tired or let my grades slip, she wouldn't be thrilled about me staying out this late on the first day of school.

"Oh good, you're in." Mom was sitting on the sofa drinking her tea and watching the news.

I felt a little guilty. She was usually in bed before now. I may be grown up enough not to have a curfew, but I was still my mom's little girl. "Sorry, I lost track of time. Alex and I were having fun reorganizing her wardrobe. She won't look like a twelve-year-old tomorrow." I'd already filled mom in about the fiasco at school.

"I'm surprised Mrs. McAllister let Alex stay up so late." She said with a smile, knowing full well Mrs. McAllister didn't really have a choice. Alex would have continued by flashlight if she had to.

"She tried to make Alex go to bed two hours ago. It didn't work. Honestly, I think she was so relieved that she didn't have the heart to force Alex put her clothes away. Alex was so excited."

"Poor Alex. She'll be exhausted in the morning."

Apparently, I'm a better liar than I thought, but then mom had no reason to be suspicious. She knew where I'd been, and I wasn't really telling lies. I was just leaving out some important details. "Probably, but at least she's not dreading going to school tomorrow. Today was so horrible." I shuddered, remembering how Alex looked when I saw her on the balcony during assembly. "Oh, mom you should have seen her. She might as well have been wearing a huge pick-on-me sign, especially with girls like Jenny Bloche around."

Mom nodded. She remembered the situations I had endured because of Jenny's big sister Janie. "Poor Alex."

"Alex might be up all night, excited about her new clothes, but I'm bushed." I walked across the living room to where mom sat and kissed her cheek. "Night Mom, love you."

"Love you too, Hilly-bean. I'm very proud of you for what you did for that little girl today. I know she hasn't been very nice to you."

"Meh." I shrugged my shoulders. "She's not so bad."

I climbed into bed and shut my eyes, but my mind refused to slow down. I considered running out to the treehouse to retrieve my journal, but thought better of it. After all, most of the information running through my head was too risky to write, just in case someone found it.

Who would have thought the fifth-generation leader of the planet Myonus was my new boyfriend?

After a restless night's sleep, I met Ben and Alex in front of their place. Unlike me, Alex didn't look tired at all. She was practically bouncing and not a pigtail in sight. She looked great and, best of all, confident. Jenny wouldn't be able to make fun of her today.

My cell phone rang as we were about to get into the car. It was Shannon.

"Is Ben driving us?"

"He is if you get your butt over here before he leaves."

"Two minutes." The phone clicked in my ears.

This made Alex laugh. At the mall with Shannon and me last night, she got a crash course on how teenage girls relate to each other. At their old school, she and Ben had done their best to blend in. They had been mostly successful, at least they didn't stick out. However, they missed some intricacies of teen communication. There was a lot of body language and innuendo that was difficult to recognize and decode without a translator.

Shannon and I did a lot of translating during our four-hour stint at the mall.

Ben was not as lucky as he had been yesterday. There were no empty parking spaces beside the bus drop off area. He dropped Alex, Shannon, and me off near the concrete plaza behind the school and then drove off in search of a place to park.

"Ok Alex, let's see." Shannon demanded.

We had been in the car by the time Shannon arrived. She hadn't seen Alex's outfit. Alex obediently did a three-sixty. Her jeans made her look taller and the detailing on her top made her look slender instead of scrawny.

"You look great. Jenny won't be able to pick on you today."

"At least about your clothes," I warned. "She'll find something else if she thinks she can upset you."

"I know. You told me already." She rolled her eyes. "You keep forgetting I'm a quick learner. Child genius, remember?"

"Yeah, but only in subjects that make logical sense. Teenage interaction has a logic all its own."

"You can say that again." Ben came up behind me and wrapped his arm around my waist. "Teenage girl interaction defies all reasonable logic."

I elbowed him in the ribs. "Watch it or I'll take me and my teenage girl logic somewhere else to play."

He pulled me back against him, holding me securely with both arms. "Nah, I kind of like where you are right now."

This time Shannon and Alex both rolled their eyes before leading the way into the school.

Over the next few weeks, we settled into a routine. By day, Ben and Alex played the part of regular secondary school students. At night, the three of us sat in the tactical room in their basement where they could show me images from their life before they came to Earth. We had so much fun comparing the differences and similarities about growing up on different planets. Parents, we decided, were the same everywhere.

Friday night, I had to work and then planned to go out with the girls. The six of us had been friends since primary school. We didn't get together very often because most of us worked and the homework so far this year was brutal.

Alex was a little upset because we didn't invite her along. Mrs. McAllister intervened. "Shannon and Hilary do not need to take you everywhere with them. I think they have done quite enough for you already."

I sighed. Sometimes moms can be too harsh no matter what planet they are from. She made it sound like Alex was a charity case we had taken on.

"It's not that you don't deserve to hang out with us. You'll just enjoy secondary school more if you have your own friends. After Shannon and I graduate in the spring, you'll be alone. You should make friends with some girls in your class."

Alex looked unconvinced.

"Shannon and I can remember what it was like when we were asked to dance for the first time, but it's more fun telling your friend who just had the same thing just happen to them."

Shannon added, "It's almost better than having the guy ask you to dance in the first place."

Alex nodded slowly, as if pondering our rationale, before she smiled. She liked our explanation a lot better than her mom's. Then her smile got bigger. I could tell her mind was already racing ahead to decide who would make the best new best friend. She didn't have much time. The first school dance was in two weeks.

Mrs. McAllister didn't look as pleased. I am sure the thought of her baby girl dancing with a boy made her want to reach for the ponytail holders again. However, she had agreed to let her daughter blend into school life. Now she had to trust Alex to be smart enough to remember she was still only twelve.

Out with my friends after my shift, the conversation quickly turned to my new boyfriend. Shannon wasted no time telling everyone how Ben made sure his family moved in next door because he had seen me in my front yard. Everyone in the group ahh'd. I could feel my face turn red. I didn't mind so much this time.

Kathy and Serena went to our school and had already met Ben. They thought he was gorgeous and nice. They helped Shannon tell Janet and Kate all about him. I think my friends felt relieved. They'd all worried when I started dating Trent last spring and were there for me when, thanks to him, I wasn't exactly a virgin anymore and how, thanks to a well-placed knee in his groin; I wasn't exactly not a virgin, either.

Sandra whispered across the table, "So tell us, does he kiss as great as he looks?"

The heat on my face upped itself to a completely new level. I tried to stutter out a smart-assed comment but couldn't think of a thing.

They thought it was cute and started giggling.

It filled me with self-doubt. Why hadn't we kissed yet?

CHAPTER NINE

After my Starbucks date with the girls, I dropped Shannon off, let my mom know I was home, and headed out to my treehouse to think. I was upset at myself for being upset. Why was I letting it bother me that Ben hadn't kissed me yet? Maybe he was just being a gentleman. Maybe they didn't kiss where he came from. Maybe their culture frowned on physical contact between teenage couples. But he always had his arm around me and held my hand when we walked together. I sighed and stared out over the bog, wondering about our relationship.

"Can I come up?" As if I had summoned him, Ben's head appeared at the open trapdoor.

I scooted my butt over to give him room to manoeuvre, glad the shadow he cast as he got settled hid my expression. As much as I wondered why he hadn't kissed me, I wasn't sure I wanted to know the answer. If he saw I was sad, he would want to know why and I'd have to ask.

He seemed to fill the interior of my treehouse. The last time he had been here, I'd been too shocked by the Sensors to notice how close he needed to press against me just to fit. He put his arm around me and pulled me even closer until my head rested on his chest. I could feel his heart beating. It wasn't exactly steady or slow, which made me smile. He may not have kissed me yet, but that didn't mean he was completely unaffected by me.

"I thought you'd still be out with the girls."

"We don't stay out late. Except for Shannon, we all have to work tomorrow."

"Gee, and I thought the kids on this planet had it easy."

"Nah, that's three galaxies over to the left."

"Darn, I'll have to get the family to move there next."

"Somehow, I think you'll have a rough time convincing Alex. I hear they don't have school dances there and she's really looking forward to ours."

"This is true." He paused for a moment. He took a deep breath. "Do you want to be my date for the dance?"

"I'll check my dance card." I looked at my hand and pretended to read my imaginary itinerary. "Hmm, I think I might have a couple of free dances I can save for you."

"Aw? I'm an excellent dancer. I promise I won't step on your toes. Does that help?"

"Maybe."

He seemed to be sure I was joking, but not entirely.

I decided to tease him a little. "Hmm, let's see. What are my options?" I pretended to ponder. "Go to the dance on the arm of the hottest guy in school who drives one of the coolest vehicles in the city or not?" Playfully, I pointed to two spots on the wall. "Eenie meenie miney mo…"

"Hot?" He sounded shocked.

I don't think he had ever thought about himself that way. For all his confidence, he was totally unaware of the female attention he received. I stopped teasing him. "Yes, I'll be your date for the dance." I sat up and twisted a bit to face him. "I can't imagine going with anyone else."

He chuckled, "Do you know what I've just discovered about you?"

"What?"

"You're a brat. I have heard your mom call you that before and I didn't believe her. But she is right. You, Miss Hilary Foster, are a brat!"

I swatted at him, and he caught my hands easily in his grip. We stared at each other for a few seconds. This was a do or die moment. Was he finally going to kiss me? I could feel my heart pounding so hard I'm sure it shook the entire treehouse. His eyes darkened. His nostrils flared slightly. He reminded me of a caged animal ready to pounce. Drawn into his gaze, I let myself drift forward. My movement seemed to snap him out of his trance. He blinked and pushed me ever so slightly away.

It crushed me. "Why won't you kiss me?"

I didn't mean to say it out loud, but there it was. The question hung in the air between us, pulsating with a life of its own, growing bigger and more un-ignorable with each passing second it remained unanswered.

Finally, I felt brave enough to look up and saw the shocked look on his face. Feeling like I'd made a huge mistake, I backtracked, "Never mind, you don't need to answer."

"You want me to kiss you?" His voice was incredulous.

"Well, yeah. It's what couples do." Then a horrible thought struck me, "Unless all this… stuff." I gestured to the way we cuddled together. "Is just an act - part of your disguise to fit in with the rest of us?" I tried to back away from him, but I was trapped against the wall of my treehouse.

He grabbed me by the arms and held me in place. "Wait, a minute. I'm confused." He paused. "Or maybe I've got it completely wrong."

I wasn't sure I wanted to hear his explanation, but I had to know. "What did you think?"

"Mom and the General spent a lot of time researching how people on Earth interacted while Alex and I learned languages and history." His shoulders slumped. "I should have guessed from how mom was dressing Alex that she'd been selective in what she told us. But with so much of what we learned being right, it was hard to tell sometimes." He gave a half laugh, half groan. "That could also explain why Mom and the General only subscribed to the documentary and retro channels."

"What did she tell you about kissing?"

"No kissing on the lips until the third date and we even though we spend so much time together, we haven't even been a real first date yet." He fidgeted. "I was hoping you wouldn't be too upset if I snuck in a peck on the cheek at the dance."

I looked up at him. In the dim light from my back porch, he looked so hopeful.

I smiled. His mom was definitely trying to mould him into an extreme gentleman, circa the year nineteen-forty.

"Actually, the girls were asking me tonight if you were a good kisser."

"They what?" he seemed genuinely shocked. "So much for mom's rule of don't kiss and tell. What did you tell them?"

"It was easy. I just smiled and blushed like mad. They all assumed you were amazing."

Ben started laughing. "You are something special." He pulled me up onto his lap. He was careful to make sure I didn't bang my head against the ceiling beams of my little hide-away. "I've been so careful not to scare you or make you think I was more of a weirdo than you already did."

"So, do they kiss on your planet?"

"Yes, they do." His laugh rumbled up from his chest. "Shall we compare notes?"

"I think we should. After all, we've compared all the boring stuff like politics and weather patterns."

I looked at him and he looked at me… and I kept looking at him… and he kept looking at me… after an eternity, although I'm sure it was only thirty seconds, we both burst out laughing.

I'm sure he felt the same as me, all this talk and no action. It was completely pathetic and really cute all at once.

I rested my forehead against his. He brought his finger up under my chin and raised my face until our noses were touching. He slid his hand along my skin until his fingers brushed my hair back over my shoulder to fall down my back. Without pressure, he drew me closer. I could feel his breath against my lips an instant before his mouth met mine. All my thoughts scattered, replaced by the sensation of his warm, firm lips against mine.

Our kiss probably lasted only a few seconds, but it felt like hours. When we separated, I was breathing hard, as if I had just run a marathon. So was Ben. He still held me, which was good, because if he hadn't been, I would have melted into a puddle right there on the spot.

Ben's breathing was ragged, and his heart was thumping underneath my hand. He licked his lips before trying to speak and even then, words seemed to fail him.

I didn't have that problem. "Wow!"

He smiled. "Yeah, wow. I may need a week to recover."

"Because it was that good or because it was that bad?"

He looked at me with a mock pitying expression. "I thought you were smart?"

"I am, but it's never polite to assume."

"Well then," He pulled me close again. "I think I need to do some more testing before I give you my complete analysis."

"This kind of testing I can completely appro…" All coherent thoughts flew out the window the second his lips met mine again. Seriously, I've been kissed before, but never like this. He didn't have any unique alien moves or anything. He was just felt-it-to-the-tips-of-my-toes good.

"Hilary, are you still out there?" My mom called from the back door.

I looked down at my watch and gasped. It was after midnight. Ben and I had been making out for almost two hours. "Yeah mom, I'm coming."

"Stay here for a few minutes until I get in the house. My mom is cool about a lot of things, but I'm not sure she'll appreciate me being out here with you this late."

Ben nodded. He didn't need to have any further explanation. He was likely going to face a similar situation when he got home himself. "Careful getting down, I'll see you tomorrow." He leaned over to where my head still peeked out of the trapdoor. He gave me a quick peck on the lips. "Goodnight"

"Night" I leaned up for one more and then two, before I ducked down out of reach and ran to the house. It relieved me to see mom was already in her bedroom getting ready to turn in. I'm sure she would have known something was up. I could not keep the smile off my face.

"Thanks, Mom." I called through her closed door. "I was a million miles away."

I didn't think I would ever get to sleep. Ben kissed me. I hugged my pillow and could not stop grinning. Ben kissed me.

CHAPTER TEN

The next morning, I was nervous before I left my house. I was pretty sure Ben wouldn't regret kissing me, but I had never quite managed Shannon's level of absolute confidence. I waited until I saw him walk out their front door.

Ben looked as nervous as I did as he glanced at my house.

Seeing him look unsure gave me that extra boost I needed. I waved goodbye to mom and dashed out my front door. I walked up to him and put my arms around his waist. "Hi, Boyfriend."

His shoulders relaxed, "Hi, Girlfriend." He leaned down at the same time I stood on my toes. Life was good.

"Enough of that already." Shannon hollered as she crossed the street toward us.

"Eww." Alex added as she walked out their front door. She covered her eyes. "I'm too young for this."

Ben kissed me again quickly on the lips before stepping away. "All right, all right. Get into the car already."

"Maybe I should sit in the front, so you don't get tempted to kiss Hilary while you're driving." Shannon suggested.

I arched my eyebrow and pointed to the back seat.

She tried to look innocent and failed. "I was just thinking of our safety."

"Yeah, yeah, you just want to look cool by sitting in the passenger seat."

"Busted." She raised her hands in mock-surrender.

We burst out laughing. Ben and Alex just shook their heads.

There was a real difference between Ben and me. Now that we got that first kiss out of the way, we were so much closer. It was as if we had stopped pretending that we were dating and became a real couple.

The first school dance of the year was on Saturday. Alex was getting excited. She had made two new friends, Stephanie, and Ashley. The three of them had been plotting and planning ways to get their crushes to ask them to the dance. Shannon and I tried to warn them.

"Usually, we just show up at the first dance with our friends. No one really asks anyone for a date to a dance unless it's Winter Fest or the Grad Dance."

Alex argued. "Ben asked you?"

"Yeah, but we're already a couple. We'd be going together even if he didn't ask me."

Alex and her friends ignored our advice. They were on a mission. After all, we were only seniors. What could we possibly know? I suddenly felt the urge to go apologize to mom for all the times I rolled my eyes at her advice.

By Thursday afternoon, two days before the dance and no dates, the girls grudgingly admitted that we had been right, even if it was only to save face about not having dates.

Finally, it was Saturday morning. The day of the dance and I had to work my regular shift until six. It sucked.

"Ben, you drive Alex to the dance. I'll join you later. I want to come home and change after my shift.

He gave me his you-have-got-to-be-kidding-me look. "Not a chance. Mom is driving Alex in. They're picking up Stephanie and Ashley on the way."

As promised, Ben was waiting for me when I got home. He looked so good standing in my driveway wearing khakis and a collared T-shirt. He opened my car door before I had the engine turned off. I reached up for a kiss and was rewarded with a very good one. All that kissing practice in my treehouse had paid off.

I darted under his arm when he leaned in for a hug. He smelled so good. I knew it would take me forever to un-hug him. He looked disappointed when I looked back over my shoulder just before I ran into my house. "Give me twenty minutes."

"I'm starting the countdown now," he warned.

It felt strange not to be getting ready for the dance with Shannon. This was the first school dance that we hadn't spent the entire afternoon doing our hair and make-up. She made her mom drive her in to the school instead of waiting to catch a ride in with us.

I think her mom was a little miffed at me for getting a job and then a boyfriend.

She'd been reinstated as Shannon's personal taxi driver and Shannon was milking the situation for all it was worth. She figured her mother would eventually get sick of driving her everywhere and finally let her get her driver's licence, which meant I was completely off the hook for deserting her.

Without Shan, getting ready wasn't as fun, but it was a lot faster. I changed in record time. I was back outside with Ben with a few seconds to spare before my twenty-minute time limit was up.

Ben and I walked hand in hand to the entrance by the gym. The dance committee had done an exceptional job with decorations. There were welcome banners, balloons, and streamers everywhere. Ben seemed impressed. He hadn't gone to any social functions at his old school, so he really wasn't sure what to expect. He seemed a little shocked to see police officers standing at the entryway. I explained they were there to help deter teenage drinking and any other mischief.

As soon as we walked into the breezeway, people called out greetings to us. If I was honest, Ben's name was called more than mine. I marvelled at how easily he had fit in here.

When we got into the gym, I saw Alex and pointed her out to Ben. She and her friends had claimed the corner and were dancing in a circle. I was happy to see there were a few brave guys in amidst the girls. There was one guy I recognized from her class who kept staring at Alex as she danced. Ben didn't seem to notice, so I didn't say anything. He was her overprotective big brother. I couldn't wait to tease her about her admirer tomorrow before we over-analyzed every detail until it screamed for mercy. Maybe this time she would appreciate my mature senior's insight.

Shannon must have been watching the door for us. She appeared out of nowhere, grabbed Ben's arm and my hand, and dragged us out to the middle of the floor. Our friends had nabbed the sweet spot in the centre where the blast from the speakers merged at their loudest. Without a word, not that I would have heard her anyway, she pushed Ben toward one side of the circle and me to the other. We automatically started moving to the deafening beat of the music.

To my surprise, Ben hadn't been bragging. He was an excellent dancer. He was grooving along even better than Jason, who was dancing beside Janie, one circle over.

Janie noticed too, judging by the scowl on her face. I'm not sure what promoted me to be her primary rival, but I was sure I didn't like it.

Shannon saw the expression on Janie's face and gave me a thumbs-up.

Yeah, easy for her to say. She wasn't the one who'd become Janie's competition. I sighed. My life was about to go to hell.

The song finished, and the music slowed. Ben had been doing his own research on dating etiquette. He walked across the collapsing circle and spun me around like a ballet dancer before he took me in his arms. He saw the glares he received from the guys dancing around us and grinned. "I got that right, didn't I?" He leaned in closer to my ear so I could hear him. "Mom reminded me when I left to keep at least six inches apart while slow dancing."

She might have reminded him, but he didn't push me away when I pulled him closer until our hips bumped together as we moved in a slow circle. Thoughts of Shannon, Janie, and the evil alien Hurliingen fled from my mind.

We were near the end of the song when I remembered Alex. I peeked around Ben's shoulder. Sure enough, there was Ben's little sister in the arms of a tall, gangly looking ninth grader. Alex was meticulously keeping six inches of space between them. From the look on his face, he seemed so happy she'd agreed to dance with him; he didn't even notice. Kids were so cute.

When the dance finished, Ben and I met the rest of our friends at the all-night restaurant at the Colonial Inn, not that we ever stayed all night. We were long gone before the rowdy after-bar crowd arrived. Mrs. McAllister picked up Alex and her friends so Ben could come out with us.

We greeted Kimmy, the head server, when we walked in. She'd been working at the restaurant for years and loved to tell us funny stories about the drunk people who came in after the bars closed. I could never decide if she exaggerated their stupidity or not. I guessed she was hoping to prevent us from becoming 'those' people when we started clubbing ourselves. I don't think she needed to worry about the kids in my friend group.

She sent us to the back of the restaurant to claim the coveted long table where we could all sit together. I think Kimmy liked it when we got to the table before Janie and her crew. Janie was always demanding or complaining, and she treated the servers like her own personal staff.

Kimmy brought us menus, even though she already knew what most of us would order. The restaurant was a dive with only a few good things on the menu. Since it was the only twenty-four-hour restaurant in the city, it was always busy. We had just finished ordering when Janie and her friends arrived.

There was a new guy in her crowd. I hadn't noticed him at the dance. He seemed to keep himself separate from them, walking several paces behind and sliding in at the end seats at their second table. I was about to ask

Shannon if she knew who he was when I felt Ben stiffen by my side. I glanced over and saw that his knuckles were white where he gripped the table's edge. I put my hand over his and leaned forward so no one else would see his sudden tension. "Ben, what's wrong?"

"One of the guys in Janie's group is a Teglar."

"Teglar?"

"They're from one of the other planets in the Alliance of Eight."

"Do you think he's hiding, too?"

"Depends on which side he's on. They were converting over to our way of governance when the coup happened on my planet. Last we heard, they were having a civil war."

"Come on, you two, not at the table." Shannon joked when she realized Ben and I were having a private tête-à-tête. I glanced over at the other table. The new guy was watching Ben and me with interest, Ben more than me. I felt a shiver run down my spine. He seemed to have recognized Ben, too.

Kimmy and the other waitress were at Janie's table for a few minutes dispensing coffee and taking orders.

The guy watched us.

To be fair, there wasn't much else for him to look at. We were in his direct line of sight, and none of Janie's other friends seemed interested in talking to him. Ben kept a covert eye on him while we laughed and joked with our friends. To any outsider, he looked like one of us. He fit in as if he had been with us since pre-school.

The food arrived at both tables at the same time. It relieved me when the guy from Teglar switched his concentration to his plate and away from Ben.

He seemed an odd match to the rest of Janie's group. They were all laughing loudly, attracting attention while he sat quietly and thanked the server when she took his order. Yeah, he didn't fit in with them. Even though it was September, and we were inside, he hadn't taken off his black wool coat. Underneath, I could see he wore a black turtleneck and black jeans. No wonder I didn't see him at the dance. He would have been invisible.

He didn't join in their conversation any more than they were trying to include him.

When we had finished our meal, we chatted and goofed around while Kimmy handed out our bills. As she handed me mine, Ben swiped it. I raised my eyebrow at him.

"This is a date. This is mine."

Kimmy burst out laughing, "This one," she patted Ben's shoulder, "is a keeper."

I leaned in close to Ben, rested my head on his shoulder, and looked up at Kimmy. "I know. I lucked out."

Kimmy nodded. "Yeah, I never did like that Trent guy."

"Trent?" Ben asked. It was the first time he had ever heard the name.

I don't know if he had even thought about me having another boyfriend before he came along. I wasn't about to explain it to him now either, at least not in the middle of a crowded restaurant with a Teglar sitting less than two metres away.

Shannon said nothing. She just shook her head at Ben. "No stupid guy questions about ex-boyfriends allowed. You will not ruin the best first dance of the year."

The other guys at our table looked sympathetic to Ben's plight but nodded their heads in agreement. There would be time for those questions some other time.

A few minutes later, we all got up and headed to the cashier.

Kimmy laughed as we playfully exaggerated our movements and aligned ourselves to stand obediently in a straight line, waiting for our turn to pay. When it was Ben's turn, I glanced back at Janie's table and noticed the new guy wasn't sitting with them any longer. He'd left and there was money beside his plate to pay his bill. I nudged Ben. His face grew grim, and a wary expression came into his eyes. He leaned over and whispered in my ear, "Grab Shannon so we can leave. I'll get the car."

Shannon was over talking to friends sitting at another table. I said hello before hauling Shannon away. "Ben's already out by the car."

She shrugged and followed me out of the restaurant. "Hey look, there's that odd guy from Janie's table talking to Ben."

"Damn."

I debated. Should I go over to interrupt or let Ben deal with the new guy all by himself? Hah, who was I fooling? As if that was even an option. If Janie's new friend was going to cause Ben trouble, I wasn't going to just stand back and watch. "Hey Ben, what's taking you so long? I thought you were going to bring the car around?"

Shannon kept pace with me as I rushed over closer to where the two boys stood.

The stranger was tall like Ben, but the way he slouched into his jacket made him look less muscular. That was a plus... I hoped. Despite his rounded shoulders, his posture wasn't tense, which made me feel better.

I relaxed even more when I realized Ben was leaning against his car with one foot crossed over the other, his I'm-just-chillin' stance. Whoever this guy was, he didn't seem to be a threat, at least not an immediate one.

I walked up to Ben and slid my arm around his back. It relieved me when he wrapped one of his arms around me. Part of me had been afraid he would push me away to keep me safe.

"Hilary, Shannon, this is Tom."

"Hi Tom," I reached out to shake his hand. I was curious. Here in front of me was another alien. But like with Ben, I couldn't see any difference. I didn't know how he and Ben had recognized each other.

"Kie Catres" Tom spoke to Ben. He sounded confused.

"Jetse Kiet" Ben responded, nodding at me.

Tom looked surprised, and I wasn't sure why. They were talking in a language I didn't recognize.

"What's that?" Shannon burst into the conversation in her usual I'm-here, manner. "Some sort of secret boys-speak? How do you two know each other?"

Tom looked uncertain about how to answer.

Ben answered for both of them. "Our grandfathers did business together."

"But," Shannon countered. "that doesn't mean you know each other."

"Our grandfathers were friends. The families kept in touch, and we've seen pictures of each other, just never met in person."

"Your grandfathers were friends?" I emphasized the word friends, giving Ben a chance to warn me if anything wasn't quite right.

"Yes Hilary, they were exceptionally good friends. They did a lot of collaboration."

My shoulders relaxed a bit more, but I was still wary. Ben had a good poker face. I wouldn't know if something was wrong, especially if they kept talking in their own language.

Tom was watching my reactions with interest, leaving Shannon virtually ignored. This didn't last for long. Shannon was used to being the centre of attention, usually with no effort on her part. This was a new situation for her.

"Where are you from, Tom? I haven't seen you around before."

"I uh." He looked down at his feet. "I just moved to Saint John."

"Cool. How'd you end up in Janie's crowd?"

"My dad knows her parents. I didn't have a choice. Neither did she."

Shannon and I looked at each other. Silly boy. You think Janie wouldn't have dumped you the minute she stepped into the gym for the dance if you didn't have something she wanted.

"Sure, she did." Shannon said sagely, "Janie doesn't do anything she doesn't want to."

Tom pondered this for a few seconds. A smile spread across his face as a thought occurred to him. "Jason's her boyfriend, right?"

Shannon and I both nodded.

"She might have needed to bring him back in line. He seemed a little rebellious earlier this evening, so she told him she would meet him at the dance. When she showed up with me, he backed down and let her tighten the leash again."

I thought for a new kid on the planet, he caught on quickly.

"So, ladies, where should we go from here?" Ben asked.

"Alas, home for me," Shannon said. "Mom and I have to go to my grandparent's place again tomorrow. Grampy is still not feeling well."

"Are you driving?" Ben asked Tom.

"Yeah, mine's the red 4x4 hybrid over there." Tom pointed to a massive H3 that took up two parking spaces near the end of the hotel parking lot.

"That's a hybrid?" Shannon asked.

"We made some modifications."

Ben didn't sound pleased. "What kind of modifications?"

Tom understood what Ben was really asking. "Nothing the DMV… Sensors could pick up."

Ben and I nodded and again Tom looked at me in surprise.

I got the impression Tom didn't expect me to know about the Sensors, either. He took it well. I don't think I would be that relaxed if some strange chick knew so much about my life.

Shannon brought our attention back to her. "Tom, why don't you drive me home? We'll give Hilary and Ben a chance to be alone."

I looked at Shannon in surprise. Didn't she just call Tom odd, like five minutes ago? Now she was looking at him with her head cocked slightly to the side. I groaned inside as I recognized the telltale signs. She was interested. I followed her gaze back to Tom. He was cute enough, but this was a record, even for Shannon.

Tom was still staring back at Shannon. Even though he seemed able to manage Janie without a problem, Shannon seemed to intimidate him.

This was going to get very interesting.

Finally, Tom broke the spell, reached into his pocket, and pulled out his keys. "Sure, come on. Kiet hu Ref?"

Ben hesitated before speaking again. When he did, he pitched his voice low enough for Shannon not to hear. "After you drop Shannon off, meet us back up on the main road. We need to talk."

"Ok, will do."

Tom helped Shannon climb into his truck just as Janie and her gang came out of the restaurant. She barely glanced at Tom until she noticed he wasn't alone, and then when she saw Shannon, she did a double take. Ben and I quickly got into his car before we had to explain why we were laughing.

We followed Tom and Shannon out of the parking lot. "Will she be safe with him?"

Ben laughed, "Yeah, Tom thinks she's hot. That's why he is so tongue-tied around her. I think he was more interested in finding out who she was than learning why I'm here in Saint John."

Tom was interested in Shannon. That gave me another reason to know more about him. "What's his story?"

"What I said was true. His grandfather and mine were friends. My grandfather was helping his adapt our governing system for use on their planet. It was his grandfather's brother who was against the changes and started their rebellion."

"How did you know he was from another planet?"

"It's hard to explain." He paused. "The closest way I can use to describe it is he has an aura. We both do, but they are very faint in your atmosphere. Mine's because of the Tixlar and his is a residue from compounds in his planet's atmosphere."

"An aura?" I looked at him closely. "Why can't I see it?"

"Part of the reason we came here was because your optical functions don't normally see that part of our appearance."

"But Tom could." I thought for a minute, "What about the Sensors and the Hurliingen?"

"No, Tom couldn't see mine. His eyes are more like yours than mine. He recognized me from an image his grandfather had taken of my family during one of his visits just before we had to escape. He wasn't sure it was me, which is why he came out to the parking lot to talk."

"And the Sensors and the Hurliingen?"

"They did not design the sensors to detect it and the Hurliingen come from a different solar system. Even if they knew we had come here, their sight is limited. They'd never be able to see it. Even for me, it is difficult to see different auras on Earth. The pollution in your atmosphere makes them very dim."

Disappointed, I gave up trying to see Ben's aura. "Are you sure you can trust Tom?"

"Yes, his family has been here longer than we have. They have been living in California. They saw the Sensors there too. His dad panicked and went into hiding and moved to Saint John. They had no way of knowing the Sensors had done a planet wide sweep."

"They don't monitor what's going on?"

"They can't. His family barely made it away from their planet alive. Their planet's takeover was purely political. There was no need to keep any of the old regime alive like the Tixlardine on Myonus."

"What happens now?"

"Well, we have a bit of a problem."

I immediately tensed up again. "What?"

"Tom's family didn't have the advantage of having you advise them. As soon as they saw the Sensors, they contacted folks back on their home planet. Tom said they were warned about a spacecraft coming to Earth, apparently crewed by Hurliingen."

"But, if Tom's family's power is just political, why would the Hurliingen be after them?"

"From what Tom said, the rebellion is holding Tom's dad and grandfather as examples. The Hurliingen figure they can quash the rebellion if they can prove Tom's family ran away like cowards."

"Seems like a lot of trouble to track them down."

"The Hurliingen aren't really a military power. They conquer worlds by manipulation. Something like this is right up their alley."

"So, it's anyone's guess who the Hurliingen are really after."

"It doesn't really matter. The Hurliingen thrive on competition. Their entire society seems to be built on outdoing each other. If the group of Hurliingen come here looking for us and find Tom's family or the other way around, it will be an enormous triumph for them."

Ben flicked on his signal light and slowed down to follow Tom and Shannon to the off ramp.

"Can the Hurliingen trace Tom's family here?" It made me nervous. Despite his claims to the contrary, I was still picturing gigantic space warships hovering over Saint John High School ordering Ben and Alex to surrender while another blasted Ben's house, with my mom caught in the crossfire.

"They can trace them to California because of their communication signals, but not to Saint John. The Hurliingen are not as human looking as we are. They can't just walk down the street and ask around."

"Would they care? I mean, wouldn't first contact with a new planet start a new competition or give them bonus points for this one?"

Ben thought for a minute. "Maybe, but from what we've heard, they're stretched thin already. They tried to take over the Alliance of Eight and it didn't work as smoothly as they'd hoped. They need Alex and me back on Myonus to succeed. For them it's all about pride. They're way past the point of giving up and going somewhere else."

"You're sure?"

"As sure as I can be." He tried to lighten the mood. "All I can say is I'm glad you're on my side. If the bad guys had your smarts, we'd be in real trouble."

Even though I was still worried, I smiled. That was a pretty wonderful compliment.

Ahead of us, Tom turned into Shannon's driveway. Ben and I kept out on the main road, just out of sight, so Shannon couldn't see us. I felt guilty for not telling her. She was going to kill me if she and Tom got together… and she found out that I knew from the beginning. Well, we'd cross that bridge when we got there.

CHAPTER ELEVEN

It seemed to take forever for Shannon to get out of Tom's truck. Somewhere during the drive home, Tom must have lost his tongue-tied-ness.

When he finally pulled back out onto the street, Ben waved his hand out of his window signalling Tom to follow us.

We drove a couple of kilometres before Ben pulled into the parking lot of a convenience store.

Tom drove in and parked his truck a few feet away.

The parking lot was well lit, even though the store closed hours ago. We had safety and privacy, exactly what we needed.

Ben and I leaned against the passenger side of his Barracuda and Tom sat on his truck's sidestep.

"Why does Hilary know but not Shannon?" Tom immediately asked Ben.

I answered instead. "They hadn't planned to tell me. I saw the Sensors and told Ben about them. Since I'd already been asking questions, Ben figured he had no choice except to tell me the entire story." I shrugged. "I kind of ended up along for the ride after that."

"And Shannon?" he persisted.

Ben answered this time. "It was a risk telling Hilary, but she'd seen things that our cover couldn't explain. We asked her not to tell anyone else."

"So, you being a couple is just an act?"

"No." Ben answered quickly. "I planned on getting to know Hilary as soon as I saw her." He smiled at me. "The rest has been a bonus."

I smiled back, but I was still worried. It was great Ben was so confident in Tom's loyalty, but I wasn't. His arrival seemed too quick and convenient after Ben's arrival and the Sensor sweep.

"How long have you been on Earth?" I asked.

"We arrived four years ago. My father and his affiliates heard about of the Hurliingen coup on Ben's planet. Even though there were rumours about our planet being targeted as well, dad and the other leaders were sure it was just hysteria, and it would all blow over. The committee was certain there was nothing on our planet that the Hurliingen would want or need. The takeover was fast and caught them by surprise. We were lucky to escape."

"So, why did you come here?" I asked.

"We created a list of planets with an atmosphere we could breathe. Then we narrowed our choices according to how well we would fit in with the inhabitants. We had to look like them and be able to act like them, too. Some, uh… humanoid cultures are more human than others." He smiled at me, hoping I would catch his joke.

I smiled back, even though I was still wary. Tom seemed genuine, and Shannon liked him. Normally, she could spot a pretender at first glance and had no problem calling bullshit. But she was crushing on Tom so I'm not sure I could trust her judgement either.

"The more we could blend in with a planet's occupants, the less likely we'd be noticed. We weren't sure why the Hurliingen were taking over our planet, so we didn't know if they would come after us or not. Dad avoided the planets that we traded with. He hoped that by coming to Earth, we would be too far away if they searched for us. Since it took so long for the Sensors to arrive, I guess we chose well.

Tom raked his hand through his hair. "But then, we screwed up. We panicked when we saw them. They had barely gone away before we contacted friends on Sigvu and Mcoj. Two days later, we received an emergency transmission. A ship was heading to Earth. They said the Hurliingen had hijacked it. We knew we would be easy to catch if we attempted to leave Earth, but this time, Dad prepared ahead. Since we arrived, he had established several business affiliations all over North America under different identities. We flew on commercial airlines with two different sets of passports to eliminate any paper trail. Our… spaceship is still cloaked thirty metres under the surf off the coast in Los Angeles where there is a severe rip tide. No casual divers will find it and if the Hurliingen do, they won't be able to get near it. They can't do water."

Ben nodded, "That's pretty ingenious."

"I thought so. Let's just hope it works." Tom paused. "We left some markers out in the desert area close to where we used to live. We're hoping that it will fool the Sensors and the Hurliingen into thinking our transmission was a lucky shot from an experimental Earther."

"You don't call us Earthlings?" I laughed.

"Never heard the term until I watched a space movie from back in the forties." Tom laughed.

"When will you know if it worked?"

"I guess we'll only know if it doesn't." Tom looked apprehensively at Ben. "We've only just arrived. It is important to protect you and your sister. I'll make sure we move quickly to another location. If they track us here, they'll be likely to find you, too."

"Maybe… maybe not." Ben was silent for a few minutes.

I really wished I could read his mind.

A couple of cars passed before he spoke again. "I think we're safer if we stick together. The Sensors were here before you arrived. Alex and I are probably already on their radar. We can defend ourselves more effectively if we're together."

"You have defences?" Tom seemed surprised.

"We have contacts and access to military expertise."

"Earth weapons against Hurliingen. You're joking, right?"

"Are we really that weak?" Until I'd met Ben, I'd thought we were pretty advanced. It also concerned me how Ben hadn't told Tom about the General. Maybe he didn't trust Tom as much as he pretended.

Ben looked at me with pity. "Yes, Hilary, you are." He quickly amended himself. "Or rather, your military technology and weapons are. You however, are a great asset."

I rolled my eyes and looked over at Tom, who, to my surprise, was nodding in agreement.

"He is right. It surprised me when I realized you knew about us. Just by the questions you're asking, you seem to take it all in stride."

Pleased and a little embarrassed, I could feel the red creeping up into my face. I was glad it was dark. "I guess being a geek and reading all that sci-fi stuff wasn't a bad thing after all, huh?"

Ben chuckled. "It's definitely made you an effective strategist."

"What do we do now?" Tom asked, getting us back to the subject.

"I think we need to compare notes. You said your dad had contacts. Is there anyone who can help?"

"A few Alliance of Eight members." Tom leaned against his truck. "There might be two or three other families nearby." He paused. "It's not a lot. There are probably more of us scattered around the province, but it would be nearly impossible to assemble them all. From what I've heard, most of them are content to stay hidden."

Ben didn't seem as surprised as I was about the number of alien families nearby.

I was shocked. Who knew Saint John, or even New Brunswick, would be a hot alien destination?

"Who is here with you?" I asked.

"My dad, mom and my little brother Danny." He added, "Danny is only eight. I'm not sure how much help he would be. Unfortunately, the same goes for my dad." He lowered his head as if ashamed. "Sometimes I swear I've had more tactical training than him. He was a government man back home, but he looked after the business stuff. Even when he did his required stint in the military, he was in meetings more than on the field. If it came down to a fight, well... I'd rather give a gun to Danny."

"Then it will definitely be better if you folks stay close. You might not be able to help us if the Hurliingen find us, but we can definitely help protect you." Ben paused. "And to answer your other question, we can't defend ourselves against an attack, but the Hurliingen are more about sneaking around. We have enough monitoring equipment to see them coming and can hide our presence and yours too, if they get too close.”

“Are you sure they won’t attack? They can’t exactly stroll down the street and start a rebellion like they usually do, but desperate times…”

“Why can’t they just walk down the street?” I was curious.

“The Hurliingen look like aliens,” Ben said to me. “They’re big, ugly and smelly.” He put a comforting arm across my shoulders and then answered Tom. “The Hurliingen won’t attack this planet’s inhabitants. Alerting Earth’s population to their presence would be counterproductive.” He looked at me. “Your military won’t be effective against them, but they will be annoying to the Hurliingen once they’ve mobilized. We already know the Hurliingen are on alert from seeing the Sensors.”

I tried to hide a yawn. The conversation wasn’t boring, but my body was revolting against yet another late night. It was almost two, and I didn’t even want to think about the homework I had to do before my afternoon shift at the store tomorrow. Ben glanced at his watch. “We need to go.”

Tom and Ben did a weird handshake thing before turning away from each other to head back to their own vehicles.

I was about to open the passenger door when Tom asked one more question. “Do you think, once we get rid of the Hurliingen, Shannon would be interested in going out with me on a date?”

I answered him without giving away Shannon’s interest. “If she’s interested, I doubt you’ll have the chance to wait until after the Hurliingen.”

"Is that ok with you?" He looked as if my approval was important to him.

"Let's get rid of the bad guys first. Once I see how you handle them, I'll let you know if I think you're good enough to date my best friend."

"Ouch." Tom winced. "Remind me never to get on your bad side."

"See that you don't." I looked over at Ben, who stood listening with his driver's door half open. "We all know what's at stake and if you screw Ben over, I'll come after you myself." I climbed into the car and shut my door behind me.

Ben and Tom said something to each other in their own language, which I had no hope of deciphering.

Ben climbed in and started his engine. "That was harsh, don't you think?" He was laughing, but I could tell he was curious. "Do you think he's lying?"

"Do you?" I asked him. "You didn't tell him about the General, so I figured there was something that made you cautious." I shrugged. "Besides, it's not like I could do anything if he is one of the bad guys. I just wanted Tom to know you aren't alone."

Ben leaned over and kissed me. It was just a quick peck on my lips, but the message was clear. We were a team.

Tom started his truck and waved as he pulled out of the parking lot and headed back toward town.

As usual, Ben drove behind their house to park his car out of sight from the road. I was silently regretting Shannon's request for Tom to drive her home. Tom probably already knew where Ben lived.

Sure enough, we had just closed the doors of the Barracuda when Tom drove by in his truck. I saw him first and pulled Ben back into the shadows.

His shoulders slumped as the apparent betrayal.

"Are you going to be, okay?"

Ben shrugged. "Yeah, I just don't know what to think right now." He kicked a stone across the yard, hard enough it almost hit my car. "It could go either way. What Tom said could be true. They came here to hide and found me by accident, or…" he hesitated, as if not wanting to say the words aloud. "He was just the lucky one who found me for the Hurliingen."

"What if I quoted my mom and said don't worry about it tonight, there's nothing you can do, anyway?"

"I'd do exactly the same thing as you would and worry, anyway." A ghost of a smile crept across his face. "Of course, that would be after I rolled my eyes."

I playfully slapped him in the chest for making such an insolent… and truly accurate statement. He captured my hand in his and pulled me close. I slipped my arms around his waist, and he held me tightly. We stood like that for an eternity. It was the first time I have ever actually felt someone's disappointment. Every muscle in Ben's back was tight. His breath was ragged. He wasn't sobbing or anything melodramatic like that, but in a weird sense, I almost wish he had cried. His tense silence was almost too much for me to take. It was amazing how, in less than two hours, meeting a relative stranger could have such an impact on his life.

"You have to go home. You work in a few hours." Ben said reluctantly as he loosened his grip. "I have to wake the General and tell him what happened."

"Do you want me to come in too?" Surely, I figured, I could make it through one night with no sleep.

"No, you need to go to bed. I'll talk to the General and then try to get some sleep myself."

"Some first dance, huh?"

"It had its moments." He gave an unconvincing laugh and then gave me a peck on the lips. "Now scoot or your mom won't ever let you go out with me again."

"I'm going, I'm going."

Ten minutes later, I was in bed, staring at the ceiling. Why did Tom follow us? An hour later, I still didn't know what to think, so I just stopped trying.

CHAPTER TWELVE

Even though I barely slept, I was at Shannon's front door at eight thirty the next morning with two extra-large Tim Hortons coffees and a half dozen of her favourite double-chocolate, caramel gourmet cookies. I needed to do a little investigation of my own. I would pump Shannon for information about Tom, assuming she had stopped talking long enough during their drive home last night to let him say anything.

Shannon's mom looked longingly at the coffee as she waved me up the stairs to her daughter's room.

Shannon was awake, but not out of bed. She looked at me groggily when I opened the door after a brief knock. "It's me."

"Timmie's!" She sat up and reached for the bag in my hand. I passed her a coffee instead and jiggled the bag of still warm cookies slightly out of her reach.

"Ok girl, Spill."

"Spill what?" She feigned innocence.

"The deets on your drive home with the… oh wait, what did you call him?" I paused for a dramatic moment before I snapped my fingers. "Ah yes, the odd guy." I bounced the bed when I plopped down beside her, almost spilling her coffee in the process. It reminded me of when we were seven, and I had done the exact same thing. Back then, it was pink lemonade, not coffee.

"I don't know." She said honestly. "I was listening to him talk to Ben, and I started getting intrigued. I really like the sound of his voice." She thought for a minute,

"He doesn't really have an accent, but… I don't know, I just enjoyed listening to him talk." She took a sip of coffee before setting the cup on her bedside table. "Besides, I figured you and Ben would like to have a bit of extra time alone together." She made a quick grab and snagged the bag of cookies I'd dropped on the bed between us.

"This is true." I said, pretending to ponder. "We enjoyed the extra time we had together, but we were concerned about you taking off with Tom. None of us knows him yet. It seemed really fast, even for a Miss Impulsive like you."

"I know. It was weird. Maybe his voice hypnotized me." She shrugged and took a bite out of a cookie. She had to do a quick double-bite to keep the long gooey strand of caramel from dribbling down her chin. "I mean really, if you had told me I'd be letting him drive me home when we were sitting at the restaurant, I would have said you were full of crap."

I nodded and waited for her to take another bite of her cookie before steering the conversation in a slightly different direction. "So, what did you and Mr. Dreamy-hypno-voice talk about?"

"I don't know. We just talked. I told him about you and I growing up together and he said he wishes he had a close friend like that. He has a brother, but he's still just a kid, so they really don't have a lot in common yet."

"Why is he hanging around Janie and her crowd? He didn't seem to be their type."

"He can't stand them. Janie's dad knows his dad through business. They forced Janie to take him to the dance. Tom said that if she brushed him off, she would get into major trouble with her parents. Janie's dad is trying to suck-up to Tom's." Shannon giggled. "Can you imagine, Janie, finally being forced to behave like a polite human being?"

"Too funny." I laughed as if this was the first time I had heard about the thing with Janie. I had to keep it straight and not get confused between what Shannon knew I knew and what she didn't. Yikes. Maybe I should have bought myself two coffees. All this spy stuff was exhausting. I was going to need a steady supply of caffeine just to get through the rest of the day. Damn, I was barely seventeen and already faced coffee addiction.

"Did he say how Ben and he knew each other?" I gave her an innocent smile. "Ben and I didn't really talk much once we were alone."

"La la la la la." Shannon covered her ears like she used to when we were kids. "I don't want to hear about how you and your hot boyfriend played tonsil hockey."

"Well then, answer my question. How did Ben and Tom meet?"

"Tom said their families knew each other when they were growing up. They didn't really spend time together. That's why Tom waited until Ben went outside to approach him. He wasn't hundred percent sure if it really was Ben and didn't want to make a mistake in front of 'everybody'."

I nodded sagely and took another sip of my almost empty coffee. "That makes sense. Our friends wouldn't have said anything. But if Janie was forced into letting him hang around, she would have a field day at Tom's expense for the mistake."

"Yeah, and since he's starting school with us on Monday, Janie could make something silly like that follow him around all year if she wanted to."

"Tom's going to Saint John High?" This tidbit suddenly seemed more important than my initial plan to find out if Shannon had told Tom where Ben lived. I tried to keep the shock out of my voice and look pleasantly surprised at the news. From the look on Shannon's face, I don't think I pulled it off.

"Yeah, he starts tomorrow. That's why Janie's dad was so insistent about her being nice to him." She started laughing. "She should be more grateful. Can you imagine Janie having to play nice if Tom was a math geek or a science nerd?"

I laughed along with her, but not nearly as much as I should have.

Shannon looked at me oddly. Obviously, I wasn't doing a very good spy job. Lucky for me she must have thought I was still just worried that she was moving too fast with Tom, so she rushed into tell me more about him.

"Luckily for Janie, Tom's pretty cool and he has a wicked sense of humour. He won't be a drag on her social network. But as much fun as it would be to watch Janie struggle against his sarcastic comments, I told him he should hang around with us instead."

An old saying flashed through my mind. "Keep your friends close and your enemies closer." And Tom was still an unknown after last night's drive by.

"Good idea." I said to Shannon. I didn't even have to try to sound convincing because it seemed like the best option for now.

Shannon relaxed and smiled. "I know it's sudden, but I really like this Tom guy."

"Are you sure it's not just his hybrid tank of a truck that has you flashing cartoon hearts out of your eyes?"

She whacked me with her pillow. "Since when did I ever date someone just because he had wheels?"

"Wait, a minute," I raised my hand in mock excitement, "Pick me, pick me, I know this one." I ran to the safety of her bedroom door. "Jeremy Wigginson in fifth grade. He was the first guy in class allowed to ride his skateboard to school."

I darted out of her bedroom just as the pillow Shannon whipped toward my head thumped against the doorframe. Her mom raised an eyebrow and shook her head as I ran down the stairs. I could hear her laughing behind me as I raced out the front door as if a thousand Shannons were after me. I was halfway across the street when Shannon hollered out her bedroom window after me. "Coward!"

Ben must have heard Shannon's shout because he came out from behind his house. He jerked his head in her direction as he wiped the grease off his hands with a rag. "What did you do to Shannon?"

I stood on my toes to give him a good morning kiss. "I was just torturing information out of her."

The way he raised his eyebrows, I don't think he believed me.

"My weapons of choice were heavily sugared coffee and gourmet chocolate-caramel cookies."

"Weapons?"

"Yup," I said. "Give them a few hours and those cookies will land right on her hips."

"You are evil."

"And…."

"And what?"

"You forgot brilliant!" I whacked him on the arm.

"And why," He rubbed his arm, "are you so brilliant this time?"

"I found out that Tom will start classes with us tomorrow and…"

Ben's expression was hard to read, but he didn't seem upset over Tom's transfer to Saint John High School. "And what?"

"Shannon has decided he's 'interesting'"

"That doesn't surprise me."

"It doesn't, how so?"

"When we were talking, she kept looking over at him. She hardly looked away the whole time we were standing there."

"How'd I miss that?"

"You spent all your time looking at me."

"Dang, I'll have to make sure I ignore you from now on when we're out in public."

Ben was still laughing when his dad, or I mean the General, came over to join us. "What's so funny?"

"Hilary thinks she can resist me."

The General rolled his eyes. "I am sure she will have no trouble resisting you if you keep acting smug like that."

I smiled. "Have I mentioned I really like the General?"

The older man sobered a bit before he spoke to me. "Do you have time to come in for a few minutes? We need to talk."

I glanced at his face but couldn't really get a read on him. I wasn't in trouble. He didn't have that sort of look, but he looked concerned. Once inside, we went down to the tactical room in the basement. As soon as I walked in, I saw several additions, since I was there two days before.

Every console was lit up and there were a lot more three-dimensional hologram maps floating midair in the centre of the room. The General pulled out the chair by Alex's terminal and asked me to sit.

I sat but found it difficult to focus. My eyes kept switching back and forth, unable to settle on a single hovering image for long before another caught my attention. Some of the new maps I could figure out. One or two were of Earth. I recognized the shapes of the continents. One looked like it could be our solar system, but it differed from any version I'd ever seen before. I really wanted to take a closer look, but the General paced back and forth through the hologram, making it hard to decipher.

"Ben told me about Tom. If there is a Hurliingen ship already on its way to Earth, we need to know everything we can. It was worth the risk of contacting my colleagues on the Alliance planets not taken over by the Hurliingen. The situation on Myonus is dismal. The coup was successful initially, but things did not go quite the way the Hurliingen planned. Our citizens fought back. There have been riots and revolts. There does not seem to be any end in sight.

"The wars haven't been on just Myonus. Tom's planet and some of our other trading partners were switching over to the model of government advocated by Ben's grandfather. The populations on those planets have also rebelled. The Hurliingen were not prepared for the resistance. Neither were the Tixlardine they had tricked into helping them. Many of them have abandoned the Hurliingen's plan completely and have been fighting to reinstate Ben's grandfather's ideals.

"This makes Ben and Alex even more important not only for their physical attributes, but their capture would demoralize the rebels. The Hurliingen need to have them in their control even more than before, if their plans have any hope of succeeding."

"They won't just give up?"

"No." The General shook his head. "For them, to give up is worse than being defeated."

"How does Tom fit in?" I asked. "He starts classes with us tomorrow."

The General didn't look surprised. "We do not know yet. So far, we've validated his story, but it seems odd that he followed you last night. We'll continue to watch him closely."

"Shannon has already offered to monitor him."

"She knows?" The General tensed and scowled at Ben and me.

"No sir. She thinks he's cute."

The General stopped pacing mid-stride. "She thinks he is cute?"

I smiled. The General was about to learn a whole new strategy. While he was evaluating Tom as a potential threat, Shannon was in the trenches, evaluating him as a potential boyfriend. "Shannon will come in handy. She can keep him close yet distracted at the same time."

Ben had been standing by the door. "For sure, Shannon can be distracting. Gosh knows she rarely lets anyone get a word in when she's talking." Ben winked at me. "And she's always talking."

As much as I wanted to defend my friend, I didn't want to lie to do it.

CHAPTER THIRTEEN

On Monday, Ben dropped Shannon, Alex and I off at the plaza behind the school before driving off to find a place to park. Seconds later, Tom pulled up in his hybrid monster machine. Shannon hopped into the cab and they disappeared in the same direction as Ben.

This was the first chance I had to talk to Alex without Ben or her mother around since the dance. She looked like her feet still hadn't touched the ground.

"So…?"

"Oh Hilary, it's so awesome." She grinned. "Stephanie and I were the only two girls asked to dance. Jenny saw me watching Robbie on the dance floor and when a slow song came on, she asked him to dance. He turned her down and then he came right over and asked me instead. You should have seen her face. We had so much fun afterward talking about it. The moms tried hard to look like they weren't listening in, but we knew they were, so we talked even quieter. It was almost as much fun driving them nuts as it was to be asked to dance."

"Mine did that too." I smiled conspiratorially. "I saw you and Robbie dancing, but I didn't tell Ben. I think you're safe from big brother interference for now. But remember, you are only twelve. Dancing is one thing, but don't rush the other stuff."

I expected her to roll her eyes at my big-sister advice. Instead, her grin got even bigger. Then I realized she'd stopped paying attention to me. I turned around to see the famous Robbie coming toward us. His face broke into a matching grin when he saw Alex.

They were so cute. Alex was practically vibrating as he approached. When he stood beside her, Alex immediately reached for his hand. "Hilary, this is Robbie."

"Hi Robbie." I relaxed a bit. Up close, he looked just as young as Alex and even more awkward than he had across the dance floor. From the way Alex had grabbed his hand, she was definitely going to be the one in charge of their relationship.

"Alex?" Ben, Shannon, and Tom walked up behind her. Ben was glaring daggers at the boy holding his baby sister's hand.

"Hi Ben," Alex said innocently, "This is Robbie."

"Hi Robbie" Ben's voice was low and had a warning in it. He held his hand out to Robbie until the boy took it. By the wince on Robbie's face, I guessed Ben's grip wasn't gentle. This overprotective big brother thing made me glad I didn't have one after all.

I stepped over and poked Ben hard in the ribs. He released Robbie's reddened hand from his grip. Alex glared at her brother.

"Come on folks, the first bell is about to ring, and I'd like to offload some of my books into my locker before homeroom." I pulled Ben along behind me, leaving the rest of the gang to follow.

"I need to find the office and pick up my class information." Tom chimed in.

Alex and Robbie were holding hands again… although I noticed they had switched sides, so Robbie didn't have to use his sore hand.

"I'll take you." Shannon offered and led him into the school.

We barely made it through the door when Janie, followed obediently by Jason, descended on us. "Tom," she said in a saccharine voice, "there you are. Come on, I'll take you to the office to get settled." It took her a second to notice the rest of us and how Shannon had her arm looped possessively through Tom's. When she did, her eyes narrowed.

"I've got it covered," Tom said politely. "But thanks anyway."

The six of us turned and walked away from Janie without a backwards glance.

At noon, Ben brought Tom out to join us at our regular spot. Alex had taken my advice and started spending lunch with her friends. At first Ben seemed pleased with the change, but today, from the way he kept looking back toward the school, I sensed he would have preferred her close by and not necessarily because of the impending Hurliingen invasion.

I felt a wee bit guilty for not warning him about Alex's new beau. I figured it wasn't worth saying anything until he could see Robbie for himself. As I'm sure Ben would have imagined some evil jock-like predator ready to swoop down to claim his sweet, innocent baby sister.

Ben would just have to get used to Alex having boyfriends, especially now that she had permanently ditched the ponytails. If it hadn't been Robbie, it would have been some other guy competing for her attention.

As soon as we gathered, Ben and Tom started talking in low voices, their backs turned slightly toward where Shannon and I were sitting. To distract Shannon I asked, "How was she?" Shannon had first period history class with Janie.

"Mad. She walked into class, glared and me and then strutted over to her desk. She refused to look at me for the rest of the period and didn't even dis my outfit like she usually does."

"Same in English. She was there before me and looked away when I walked in. Tom came in just behind me and sat in front of me. He turned around to talk to me until Mr. Hansen came in. He had his back to her the entire time. She didn't like that at all."

Ben and Tom finished their conversation and joined in ours.

"I was talking to one guy who was in the restaurant with us after the dance. I guess Janie had a fit when she noticed I'd ditched them. I should have told her directly when I left so she could properly dismiss me. Apparently, there are rules to follow when hanging out with her." He shrugged, "She spent the night ignoring me and because of that, no one else dared to include me in conversation." He looked at Shannon. "I spent most of my time watching you guys across the restaurant. You gave me hope there were decent people in Saint John, after all. I was regretting our move when I thought Janie, and her group were the only crew to hang with."

"Glad we could help." I said.

Shannon raised her eyes and placed her index finger dramatically on her chin. "Do ya think we should tell Janie that Tom has downgraded her to 'only if I have to' status?"

Ben almost choked on his soda. "I think we should just keep that to ourselves for now."

"There you are Tom," Janie appeared on the opposite side of the street. She walked slowly over to us as if it was really the last thing she wanted to do. "I've been looking all over for you. I thought we were supposed to have lunch so I can show you around the rest of the school?"

"Sorry Janie," Tom said as he casually put his arm around Shannon's shoulders. "I thought I made it clear this morning that I'd be able to handle getting around on my own." He reached into his pocket and checked his cell for a missed message. "You should have called me and saved yourself the trouble of searching for me."

Her shoulders snapped back, and her chin jutted out just a fraction. "I would have if I'd realized how long it would take me to find you."

The look on Tom's face was unreadable. "Well, you don't have to worry about looking after me any longer."

Janie paused, as if suddenly realizing she had overstepped and wasn't sure what Tom would do in retaliation. "I'm sorry Tom. I didn't mean it quite like that."

Tom shrugged, "Whatever."

Janie paused, as if not sure what to do, since she was the one who'd been dismissed. "Er, Okay."

Shannon raised her eyebrows as Janie walked away and whispered, "Wow. I have never seen Janie that submissive before. What do you have over her?"

Tom replied. "Nothing. I think her dad is putting on the pressure. Probably threatening to take away her car if she doesn't behave. I feel kind of sorry for her. I've met her dad, and he's all about his business. Her mother." He shook his head. "She is some piece of work. All she cares about is making a statement. My mom thinks she's ridiculous…" He paused with a chuckle, "and we're from LA."

We all burst out laughing and from the corner of my eye, I saw Janie look back. She looked resentful. We hadn't heard the last of her.

After Ben drove us home, I had precisely an hour to eat, change, and head back over town for my six o'clock shift. I had only been on the sales floor for thirty minutes when Ben and Tom walked in.

I was with a customer. Ben caught my eye and indicated I should come talk to them when I finished. When I walked up behind them, they were talking in their weird language again. It sounded really cool. I thought I should get Ben or maybe the General to teach me at least a few phrases, so if something happened, I could figure out what was going on.

As I approached, Ben and Tom switched effortlessly over to English. The transition caught me by surprise. It didn't register they were talking to me until Tom repeated his question.

I still missed what he said. "Sorry what?"

"We need to have some sort of portable communication that will let us talk but not give away our location like a cell phone. Ben and I have been thinking that it would be good to have back-up communication in case the Hurliingen found us. All cell phones have built in GPS and since we don't know how knowledgeable the Hurliingen are in Earth technology, we thought it would be a good idea to come up with something less traceable."

"Walkie-Talkies," I said. "They have a range of up to 10 kilometers and some have multiple frequencies."

Ben and Tom looked at each other, with duh… why-didn't-we-think-of-that expression on their faces.

"And you call yourselves geeks. I scoff in your direction." I waved my fingers dismissively at them. "You're nothing more than tech-Neanderthals." With that, I flounced away, laughing as I led them to another section of the store where the walkie-talkie display had them hung in two-packs and four-packs, batteries not included, of course.

I stood back to let them look over the different choices. I knew which one I would choose. But it was best to let them make their own decision just in case there was something in one of the lesser models they could integrate with their own technology to extend the range of an emergency message.

Jocelyn, my shift manager, came over to say hello as I rang up their purchases. "I wish all my staff had boyfriends who bought as much stuff as you do." She looked pointedly at Samantha, who was stocking a nearby shelf. "Half of them come in just to demo the new games."

"We can do that?" Ben asked with a mischievous grin while rubbing his hands together at the prospect.

I looked at him, confused for a second because I had never heard him talk about playing video games before.

Then he winked at me.

I shook my finger at him. "You play it, you buy it."

Jocelyn looked at me and I nodded. "Smart girl." and walked away.

"Can you meet us at Timmies when you get off work?"

"I still have three assignments to do for tomorrow."

Ben looked disappointed, but he didn't push me.

I could feel myself relenting while I searched my memory to see if I'd had a full night's sleep since meeting Ben. Dating an alien who had interplanetary pirates coming to kidnap him at any moment was very time consuming. What the heck, I was young and could sleep later. "I can't stay long. I'll be there about quarter past nine."

The rest of my shift seemed to take forever. It still felt like I was in the middle of a sci-fi movie. It was exciting to know I was one of the very few Earthers who knew aliens existed. Really, you would think they'd be more likely to tell some high-ranking military person instead of me, a regular seventeen-year-old girl. Ok, so I'm a really, really smart seventeen-year-old girl who is good with computers and other electronics too, but still.

Nine o'clock finally rolled around, and I waved goodbye to Jocelyn and the other staff before heading out the door to rendezvous with the boys.

CHAPTER FOURTEEN

Ben and Tom were waiting for me in the parking lot outside the Tim Hortons, on Waterloo Street. As usual at this time of night, the parking lot was deserted and there were no cars in the drive-thru or even passing on the street. This section of the city became a ghost town during the week.

The two of them were standing in the space between their vehicles to prevent anyone from parking there before I arrived. I rolled my eyes at the unnecessary precaution. As soon as I pulled in, Ben motioned for me to unlock my doors. At the sound of the click, Ben hopped into the passenger seat and leaned over to give me a cramped half-hug across my stick shift, while Tom climbed into the seat behind me.

"So?" I looked at Ben and then twisted around in my seat to see both of them while we talked. "What have I missed?"

"We've been testing the range on the walkie- talkies, and you are brilliant. We can hear each other as far out as the highway at the end of Rothesay Avenue from the Lancaster Mall. That's over twelve kilometers." Tom said.

Ben added. "And that's with a clear transmission. We get static-y after that, but don't completely lose each other until we're almost to that big gas station before the turnoff for the airport."

"That's what I figured. Keep in mind, that intersection by the gas station is on a hill near the river. The water probably helped to boost your range."

"That would explain why we didn't get nearly as far when we headed out on the Loch Lomond Road."

"Exactly. That stretch of road is in a valley. You'll find the same thing heading west to Grand Bay. That highway is hilly. The walkie-talkies will lose reception as you go through the parts that dip."

"That makes sense," Tom said. "We didn't even think about how terrain could be an issue."

"Well, you needed something low tech that couldn't be tracked." I paused. "So, what's the plan of action with these new toys?"

Ben answered, "We figure Alex, Tom, you and I should each carry one. Then each of Tom's parents and, of course, Mom and Dad."

I noticed Ben still wasn't referring to the General by his title. It made me curious. He also bought three four-packs. Four walkie-talkies were still unassigned. "Who gets the other walkie- talkies?"

"We have someone else to keep in touch with." Ben said quietly.

I noticed the tone of his voice. Obviously, I wouldn't like who he was about to name, but nothing prepared me for….

"Janie."

"She's one of you?" I asked incredulously, "Why didn't you tell me?"

Ben shook his head as if he was still having trouble believing it himself. "I didn't know, neither did Tom until tonight." He shrugged.

"How does she fit in?" I tried not to sound as horrified as I felt. I mean, not that I didn't like Janie, well, ok, I didn't, but that was mostly because of the crap she shelled out to the rest of us. She was probably a delightful girl on the inside... really, really, really deep inside.

"She's a half-breed. That's why I didn't see her aura."

"I knew her father was from Myonus, but I just assumed she and her sister were his stepchildren." Tom said.

"Does she know?"

"She does now. She had a fright when Ben first showed up at school this year."

"What does Ben have to do with it?" I asked, slightly perturbed at any hint of a link between Janie and Ben.

"She could see my aura and freaked. She thought she was going nuts like one of her mom's great-aunts. Her mother made her talk to her father, and he told her about his side of the family tree."

I tried to feel sympathy for her... really, but I laughed instead.

Both Ben and Tom looked at me oddly.

"I'm sorry, but if you guys knew the crap she pulled on us in grade seven, you'd appreciate the irony. Shannon and I won an award for the best model of the solar system. Janie spent the rest of the year making beeping noises at us and calling us spooky space girls. I wish I could tell Shannon. She'd find this hysterical too."

Tom shook his head and looked at Ben as if to say. "Females."

"If it's any consolation," Ben said, "she's pretty upset that you seem to know more about where she comes from than she does. She doesn't enjoy knowing that she may need to depend on you if the Hurliingen find us.

I can't say I liked it any more than Janie did. "What happens now?"

"Well, you go home and finish your homework, then get some sleep. I still have a brutal math assignment from Mr. Morrison to finish and the… Dad won't let me use my computer."

I grinned, knowing exactly which computer he was referring to and it was not the laptop I sold him.

Tom agreed. "I have an English assignment due at the end of the week. What's up with that? This is my first day and I'm already behind. Not fair!"

Ben gave me a quick peck before opening his door. Tom was already in his truck by the time Ben stepped out.

I took the long way home.

It blew my mind that Janie was an alien. Sure, there were times she was so over-the-top bitchy that I was sure she must be from another planet… but I never in a million years thought it would be true. Right or wrong, I wasn't sure I could suddenly become her best friend. My dislike for her was a well-earned constant in my life. It was part of the foundation that made me well… me.

Meeting Ben turned everything I thought I knew upside down. I just wanted something to stay the same. Maybe I'm just being childish and will look back at this one-day and laugh. But right now, there were too many other things that required my attention, and playing nice with Janie shouldn't have to be one of them.

I face-palmed. "Oh God, how would I ever be able to explain this to Shannon."

CHAPTER FIFTEEN

"Make it stop."

I whacked my screeching alarm clock and buried my head in my pillow. It couldn't possibly be time to get up already. I opened one eye and peered at the display. Ugh, less than four hours of sleep.

Stumbling out to the kitchen, I looked out the window and saw frost. It was almost enough to make me crawl back between my covers again. I knew it had been cold last night, and the frost reminded me how quickly winter was coming. It was annoying to have to bundle up when you didn't get the trade-off of a snowball fight as a reward.

By the time I was ready to leave, Ben was already outside with his ice-scraper. I stopped to watch while he pushed the little plastic ice-remover across his windshield. His back was toward me, and I just paused for a few moments to admire the view. I was grateful that he had already started his car. It would be nice and toasty by the time we got inside.

Then again, maybe the cold air would help me wake up. I stepped outside and took a deep breath of icy air.

"Alex, I love your hat." Shannon hollered as she came across the yard.

I agreed. It was cute, and it made her look way older than her twelve years. I wondered if her mom had noticed.

Shannon had just a smidge more make-up on than usual. Her dark eyes looked smoky. "Nice make-up job Shan."

She turned red.

"Omigod, you're blushing." I could count on one hand the number of times I've seen her face turn scarlet. This was serious. Tom had better not screw her around. Alien, member of the Alliance of Eight or not, he's toast if he hurts my best friend.

Frost still clung to the pavement as we walked across the drop-off plaza behind the school. Shannon, Alex and I decided to wait inside for Ben and Tom to get back from parking their vehicles.

Just as we saw them walking across the street to the plaza, Alex spied someone else. "Bitchface at nine o'clock."

"Alex!" I had never heard her swear before. Then I looked over my shoulder toward nine o'clock, Janie. I leaned in close to Alex's ear so Shannon couldn't hear my next question. "Alex, how do you say shut up in Myonusian?"

"Mimp fur."

"Is that somewhat polite?"

"Of course, I'm not allowed to use any of the good words yet."

I was about to point out that hadn't stopped her from calling Janie a bitchface, but I decided not to.

It was the moment I had been dreading. Was she going to act like a decent human being, even though technically she was only half-human?

Janie stopped, crossed her arms, and waited until she had my attention. "Don't think this means I'm going to let you hang around with me."

I stared at her. It took me only a second to figure it out she needed to keep the status quo as much as I did. "No worries," I said casually. "I wouldn't want to cramp your style. God knows it's barely holding together as it is."

"You are a bitch."

"You taught me well."

"I don't have to put up with this."

"Um Janie, you're the one who came to me. I certainly didn't ask for this conversation."

She started to say something else when I saw Ben and Tom approach.

I held up a hand. "For Pete's sake Janie, mimp fur!"

She looked like I had struck her. I wasn't sure if she knew any of Ben's language, or not, even if she didn't, her thinking I did, would kill her. I probably went too far, but seriously, the General, Ben, Tom and I were busting our butts trying to figure out what to do if the Hurliingen found them. She could at least show a little gratitude instead of being such a twit.

Ben and Tom stopped in their tracks.

Janie looked stunned then spun on her heel and strode away.

"What was that all about?" Ben asked.

Shannon answered. "I honestly don't know. It's like she came out of nowhere and attacked Hilary."

Then she turned around and looked at me, "What did you say to her, anyway?"

"I heard her saying it to one of her friends the other day. I'm pretty sure it means shut up." I looked over at

Ben for confirmation. Ben was looking at Alex, who was innocently looking out the window, waving at Robbie, who was just walking across the plaza.

"Sort of," Ben said, "Although it's pretty harsh."

"Harsh enough that I'll have to apologize?"

Tom clarified, "Not from what I heard her say to you."

"Whew."

"What was going on.? I've obviously missed something." Shannon looked at each of us.

I shrugged. "Janie and I might have to work together on a project, and I don't think she's thrilled about it."

The bell rang, saving me from further explanation.

CHAPTER SIXTEEN

Robbie was waiting when Ben dropped us off at the plaza on Thursday. Alex wasn't with us. She had a dentist appointment, her first cavity.

"You might as well go inside." I told Robbie, "She may not make it here before the bell rings."

"That's okay. I'll wait for her just in case she's early."

Shannon and I bumped shoulders as we walked into the school, trying hard not to let Robbie see us giggling. "Isn't he adorable?"

Shan and I stood just inside the building watching for Ben when Alex and her mother drove up. Robbie practically sprinted to the passenger door.

"Don't do it Robbie." I warned him, even though I knew he had no chance of hearing me.

"Oh, no." Shannon's voice was even louder than mine was.

Robbie opened Alex's door and gave her a kiss on the cheek when she climbed out of the car.

From where we stood, it was hard to tell if Mrs. McAllister saw it. At least she didn't leap out of the car, which was a good sign. We wouldn't know for sure whether Alex escaped a lecture until we got home after school.

After school, Ben and I went downstairs as usual, and Alex went upstairs. We could hear Mrs. McAllister follow her down the hall to her room and then all hell broke loose.

I don't really know who I felt more sorry for, Alex or her mother.

Mom didn't like it at all when I came home all starry-eyed after my first kiss. At least I was fifteen - Alex was twelve, and it obviously hadn't been her first kiss. Robbie didn't know how young Alex really was. No one at school did. Alex, Ben, Shannon, and I had decided it would be better if no one else knew her true age. Secondary School is hard enough without the added burden of being a child genius.

We'd warned Alex to keep things slow, and she was, but seriously, even an innocent kiss on the cheek in front of a parent is dangerous ground when you are in grade nine, no matter how old you are.

Robbie should have known better.

We heard the General try to intervene, but it didn't work. Alex wasn't his child, and he was wary of overstepping his bounds. By necessity, the General had full reign over Ben, as it was crucial for him to be trained properly, not only for their protection here on Earth but in case they ever made it back to their home planet. They would expect Ben to be part of the new government. Alex was under her mother's exclusive care, which explained her little-girl style of clothes when we had first met.

There was nothing we could do, so Ben and I escaped out to my treehouse to contemplate the issue in quiet. "You realize there's nothing they can do... right?" I asked him. "She's just going to sneak around to see Robbie, which could lead to some experiences she's really not ready for. We girls can do some pretty stupid things when we're rebelling against our parents."

"I can't imagine you doing anything stupid."

I thought about my ex-boyfriend Trent, "Trust me, it happens."

Ben's arm tightened around mine. "I just hate knowing Robbie's having… thoughts about my little sister."

"Ben, she will always be your little sister, even when she's fifty. Shannon and I are watching her and Robbie carefully and we have warned Alex that if we think she's going too far, we'll tell him how old she really is and that will ruin everything." I sighed. "There are times it would have been nice to have an older brother or sister to look out for me. You and Alex are lucky. You have each other."

Ben pulled me in a little closer. "And I envy you. You can do what you like whenever you want, and never have to watch over your shoulder to see if there is a bad guy chasing you."

We sat together for a while, each lost in our own thoughts.

Suddenly, the walkie-talkie squawked out from Ben's pocket. Tom's panicked voice filled my treehouse. "The Sensors are here again."

Ben banged his head on the roof of my little hideaway, trying to look out the window. We both searched to see if we could see any nasty little purple lights floating out over the bog.

Nothing. The bog was dark.

Ben was closest to the trapdoor, so he got out first, stopping only long enough to lift me down behind him.

We ran to his house.

Alex and her mother were still arguing.

The General looked up when we barged in. Apparently, the arguing had been so loud he hadn't heard his walkie-talkie. He looked almost relieved when Ben signalled for him to follow us downstairs to the tactical room.

The room glowed. More hologram maps were hovering in the middle of the room since I had been there last. One of them had a swirl of dark purple, like a satellite image of a hurricane hovering over the south-western states, but there were tentacles spreading over the entire continent of North America. The mass pulsated and twisted, changing its shape every few seconds. There were only a few strains of purple over our end of the country, and lucky for us, they seemed to shrink back to gather over Montreal and Toronto.

The General pointed out other blips on the hologram that were bright yellow. "This is your military. They seem focused on investigating the biggest concentration of the Sensors. See, the planes from Camp Gagetown have gone north toward Montreal, instead of coming down this way."

"That's kind of silly," I said. "Wouldn't we be a big target, too? I mean, we're sitting between a nuclear power plant and a huge refinery."

"Yes, you are right, but there are many better targets, especially for a first strike. Heavily populated areas are better targets, plus the prevailing air currents would push most of the nuclear fallout out over the Atlantic, which further minimizes the damage they could cause."

It confused me when Ben stepped out of the room before squeezing the trigger to talk on his walkie-talkie. Then I remembered how as soon as I left the tactical room, all the noises from inside disappeared. Ben obviously didn't want Tom to hear the sounds from their heavy-duty electronics.

"I see them, they seem to be leaving."

I looked at the new maps while listening for Tom's reply. The one of our solar system showed a lot more detail than the one Shannon and I built in middle school. In fact, right beside the space station was a huge object that seemed composed of a bunch of smaller ones. I pointed to it. "General, should we be worried about this?"

"No, to my knowledge, the Kichra have been here since the early eighties." He grinned at my shocked look. "A few Earth Scientists seem to suspect there is something nearby. Despite their size, the Kichra ships are invisible to the human eye."

"Who are the Kichra and do they know you're here?"

"I'm sure they do, but they don't really care. They are here to observe Earth's culture. We hold no interest for them."

"Would they tell the Hurliingen you're here?"

"It's not likely. The beings in those ships are the most advanced culture that we know. They came through our solar system a few centuries ago. Their mission is to seek advanced cultures to learn from them. Apparently, we had nothing new to teach them, so they left."

"Then why are they here? Your technology is way more advanced than ours. What do they find so interesting on Earth?"

"I would imagine they're intrigued by the volatile way your cultures work together on one level and fight with each other on another."

"You're sure they aren't waiting for a good time to attack us?"

"Trust me, Hilary, your planet has nothing they'd want, or need."

"If the Hurliingen attacked, would the Kichra help?"

"Probably not. Their mandate is to observe and not interfere with another civilization's progress."

It freaked me out that there were observers from another planet just watching us. I felt as if someone had broken into my house and read my journal. It was creepy.

Tom's voice came through the walkie-talkie again. "They're gone. We were out at the mall to get my brother some stuff and they just passed by overhead. They hovered here and there, but then they went up really high and took off."

Ben came back into the tactical room. He took another look at the Sensors tracking map and saw the purple mass creeping even farther away from our location.

I had always thought Saint John was too small a city to be exciting. Who knew that would be what would make it appealing to Ben, Tom, Janie, and their families? Luckily, the Sensors couldn't rationalize where alien families might choose to live to avoid detection.

So far, the General figured they were safe, and judging by how the Sensors never stayed long, it seemed they were right.

Tom's voice came across the walkie-talkie again. "It looks like they've really gone. Do you see any?"

Ben stepped out of the room again before replying. "Nothing. We didn't see them at all this time."

Ben keyed in the lever again. "Tom, do you know any more families in Saint John?"

There was hesitation before Tom spoke. "Yes, but I think we should wait until we're in person to continue this conversation."

Holy Crap! Just how many aliens were living on Earth, anyway? Those old 'Men in Black' movies were becoming a little too real for comfort. I was beginning to feel like Will Smith. Every time I turned around, there seemed to be more and more of them popping up.

It seemed to concern the General as well. "You think he's still holding back what he knows?"

Ben replied, "I really don't know. He mentioned there were others before. While I don't think he will do anything to harm us, I can't completely trust him yet. Every time something happens, he conveniently drops a new bombshell."

The General nodded. "Good analysis. I'll do some more digging to see if I can find out more about both Tom and Janie's family backgrounds. Your dad and grandfather amassed quite a library of information. My only concern, of course, is that what we have is severely out of date. Even though we have only been away for a few years, a lot could have changed."

"I know," Ben said. "That worries me, too."

"These other folks," I asked, pointing to the hologram of the solar system and the big ship near our space station. "Is there any chance they have been observing your home planet too? Would they be willing to share information?"

Ben looked surprised.

The General shrugged. "She asked. I told her." Then he looked back at me. "I doubt they'd tell us, as it would fall under their mandate of not interfering."

I thought for a minute. "Do you think it would be worth reminding them that this whole scenario wouldn't be happening if you hadn't chosen to hide here?"

Ben and the General pondered this as a tear-stained Alex and her equally upset mother walked into the room. "What's going on?"

"Sensors." I pointed to the map that showed them still circling over Montreal and Toronto. The mass seemed to move farther west. For a minute, I wondered if they were just randomly crisscrossing the continent.

Alex shuddered. "I hate those things. They give me the creeps."

"Me too." I replied. "I didn't know they existed until you folks showed up." I frowned. "Do you think they've been following you and are just reporting back until someone else arrives?"

"No." The General said. "We've been monitoring your solar system since before we arrived on your planet and didn't see any unusual traffic that could be considered a threat. Otherwise, we would have chosen another planet to hide on." He sat down at his station and started drifting his hands over virtual keyboards, making the hologram of the solar system enlarge. We started with the sun, examining each planet from every angle, leaving no place for a Hurliingen ship to hide.

I asked him a lot of questions. There were so many things showing on the hologram of our solar system that I didn't understand. The General explained that while our technology was no longer primitive, we still could not see much of what was actually out there. We didn't know that just past Uranus was a major trade route between the Neciuts and Bokilvns.

"I'll keep a closer eye on this," the General said. "And set up more alerts for anomalies."

"What about your invisibility devices?" I thought back to the disappearing act Ben and Alex did just after they moved in, not to mention the very room I was standing in right now.

"They only work on the naked eye by reflecting light in the surrounding atmosphere."

"You mean that whatever you have in the backyard can be found with a metal detector or radar, but just not with our eyes?"

"Yes, but we've taken extra precautions. There are other defences in place to ensure it's not detected by the usual means."

"What exactly is 'it'? None of you have told me what is in your backyard."

"You should probably show her." Alex piped up. "Having someone besides us know how to drive it might come in handy."

Mr. McAllister and I looked at each other. My initial thought was drive what, but really, I already knew. I could feel my heart leap up into my throat. It was already beating faster from the left-over adrenaline after Tom saw the Sensors. Now it kicked up into overdrive. Was I actually going to see a spaceship? Like for real? Images flashed through my mind, Star Trek, Star Wars, Battle Star Galactica. The jumper from Stargate seemed the most likely, at least for the size of the space in their backyard. Like mine, trees encompassed it. The biggest open space was only about fifteen metres across and maybe twenty back.

"Let's go." The General and Ben said in unison. They were grinning like two boys eager to show off their favourite toy.

Ben grabbed my hand and pulled me out of the tactical room, followed by Alex, his mother, and the General.

Even though I had seen the cool stuff in their basement and heard Ben talk about growing up on a different planet, I was strangely apprehensive. It was a whole different ballgame to see an actual spaceship.

As I looked out over their 'empty' lawn, I realized, maybe 'seeing' wasn't the best choice of words.

The backyard looked the same as it had before they moved in. Well, except for Ben's sweet Barracuda parked by the back porch. Alex ran ahead and disappeared, followed by the General. Ben must have sensed me holding back. He slowed his pace to match mine. "What's wrong?"

"Nothing, just give me a minute." I stopped completely. "This feels like one of those defining moments, and I'm not sure I'm ready."

Ben put his arm around me as if he understood, although I'm not sure how he could. This stuff, space travel, Sensors, Hurliingen, it was all normal for him.

I thought to myself, what on earth have I gotten myself into? This time, I smiled at my internal joke. None of this had anything to do with Earth at all.

Ben quirked his eyebrow.

I just shook my head and took a deep breath. "Okay, let's go."

CHAPTER SEVENTEEN

I was about to learn how to drive a spaceship. A freakin' spaceship!

Ben tugged on my hand again. This time I followed. Just like in the basement, I watched Ben disappear and then my hand, my arm and suddenly I was inside. I didn't close my eyes. It still felt strange, but I was getting used to watching myself disappear.

I stopped just inside the door. I was in a spaceship. A real… live… spaceship. I looked around and felt my shoulders droop. It didn't seem that much different from the tactical room except for the two RV like seats in front of a huge display screen and a small window looking out over the front of the ship. It would have been nice if I could have seen it from the outside. Although, I could see the nose of the ship, and was surprised to see it was the same metallic blue as Ben's Barracuda.

Behind the seats were two banks of computers running down each side of the ship. They were beeping and displaying enough different coloured lights to make the ship's interior look like a carnival. In front of each of the long panels were two chairs. They were on rails so they could move back and forth. I imagined that would come in handy if there was such a thing as space turbulence… or, I guess, if they were attacked and their artificial gravity failed or something.

I pushed that thought away. No one was going to be attacked.

I stood behind the General who had seated himself in what was clearly the pilot's seat. His hands moved over the console so quickly I couldn't comprehend what he was doing. Mentally, I upgraded the ship's insides to a tech-geek's fantasy RV.

Suddenly, I was standing in the middle of a hologram. Ben pulled me over to the side so I could get a better look.

Suspended in front of me was a three-dimensional image of a spaceship. The exterior of the ship was bright blue. Through the window, I could see myself standing inside the spaceship as if I was looking in from the outside. It was really freaky. It was like standing between two mirrors. You could see your reflection multiplied to infinity, getting smaller and smaller until you eventually got so tiny you disappeared from sight. I couldn't resist. I waved out the window. In real time, the image of me standing inside the hologram did the same thing. Way too cool!

"Why is it blue?" Out of all the questions I could have asked, I am sure that was probably the dumbest.

"That's the way the metals from our planet reflect light to appear here on Earth." Alex said. She was obviously enjoying my awe and I'm sure she felt good about being the expert in our relationship again. This time, I was the awkward alien.

I cocked my head to the side. "I think the ship needs racing stripes, or at least flames flaring down the sides." I made a joke, hoping it would give my brain a chance to absorb everything I saw. Even though I had been prepared, it was still a lot to take in and convince myself I wasn't dreaming. My arm was black and blue from all the pinching I've been doing lately.

I took another look around the inside of the ship and compared it to the hologram image. The cockpit seemed to be a very small section of the ship. I could feel myself frowning as I realized there was no way the entire ship could fit in the backyard.

According to the image, there should be stairs between the two banks of consoles. "If we're here, then where are the stairs… and the rest of the ship?"

Alex answered again. "The rest of the ship is somewhere else. It's hidden away where no one can find it."

"Huh? But it's there." I pointed to the hologram.

The General clarified. "Yes, but see, it is a different colour. It's just not attached right now, although it is still being monitored by the security scans we have in place."

I must have looked as confused as I felt.

"Think of it like an SUV towing a travel trailer. This is the SUV where the driver sits. The rest can be attached or detached as needed. It contains the living quarters, auxiliary fuel and supply holds. We have it hidden in a remote area, carefully cloaked from detection by Sensors and any earth technology."

Ben added, "It's prepped and ready to go in case of an emergency. It appears here so that we can see it and make sure it's still safe."

I nodded. That made sense.

"How did you get the ship here if you didn't leave a trail for the Sensors to find?"

"We transported it on the roof of my car."

"What?" The room I was standing in had to be at least three metres wide by five long and I couldn't touch the ceiling even if I stood on my tippy toes. "There's no way you could have moved this on the top of your car without squishing it."

"Our metal isn't like yours. It is very light. Plus, there were wheels extending down over the car mostly supporting this part of the ship. It was slow going, but we drove overnight to avoid traffic."

"Ok. That explains why I didn't see Ben's car drive in, but I should have at least heard it." I remembered wondering about that when I first saw the Barracuda. It made a satisfying rumbly sound whenever we drove it, so I had wondered why I hadn't heard it arrive that first morning.

"The car has a dual engine. It can run either on the regular engine or electronically. We switched over to electric when we drove to make the car silent."

"Ah," I shook my head. I looked around the spaceship and remembered the hologram of our solar system. "Everything I thought I knew has changed. Pretty soon, you'll be telling me the Earth is really a triangle."

"No," Alex scoffed, "don't be silly, it's still a square."

I looked at Ben, "Please tell me she is joking." I was more relieved than I cared to admit when he and the General started laughing. "Whew, at least something I learned in school is still right."

Ben and the General showed me around the ship. There were sections hidden behind the panels that I would never have noticed on my own.

When I was ready, I changed the subject. "Ok. How do I drive this thing?"

My first attempts on the flight simulator were dismal. Even though the controls weren't any more complicated than a video game, I'd never been into gaming. Now I wish I'd paid a bit more attention when they demo'd them at the store. Finally, on my eighth try, I managed to lift off without hitting their house or crashing into the hill behind the bog.

Two hours later, I had the controls memorized and had passed the basic levels of the training programs. Luckily, I wouldn't have to worry about sub-space hyper-drive navigation. An onboard plotting system controlled it. I could hit the icon marked Myonus and the ship would do the rest. I was confident and ready to take this baby out for a test run. At least I would have been if starting the real engines wouldn't have painted an enormous neon target saying 'we're here' in the middle of the McAllister's backyard.

It would be a shame to waste all this cloak and dagger stuff we had been doing over the past month just so I could play.

I felt a twinge of guilt about Shannon not knowing about any of this. If she ever found out I had been keeping secrets from her, the Hurliingen would be the least of my worries.

Mrs. McAllister came in. "It's getting late. Come on Alex, you still have homework and then it's time for bed." She looked over at her son. "Ben, I'm sure Hilary needs to get home, too."

I glanced at my watch, surprised it was already seven o'clock. I had been so involved with learning about the ship I had completely missed supper.

Alex trudged out the door ahead of her mother. She didn't look at her mother at all, making it plain their argument hadn't finished.

Mrs. McAllister looked helplessly after her daughter.

I left the controls, walked over to her, and gave her a quick hug. At first, she was stiff, as if not really knowing what to do in this situation. I released her, but I left my hand on her shoulder. "It's temporary. I did the same thing to mom when we had a fight. She'll come around." I felt her relax a bit.

Then I had a brilliant idea. "Why don't you come over to our house this weekend? I think you and my mom would get along well and I'm sure she can give you some advice on how to deal with a headstrong teenage daughter."

Mrs. McAllister looked like she was about to refuse.

"I think Mom is a little lonely. She works from home and doesn't get to see people much anymore. You'd be doing her a favour."

I don't know if she saw though my ploy, but she accepted the invitation. "Thank you, Hilary. I'd like that."

I thanked the General for his patience with my training, then left. Ben followed me out. He grabbed my hand and guided me around the side of the garage, where we were out of sight of the adults. "Have I mentioned how amazing I think you are?"

"No, but I'm intrigued. Tell me how amazing you think I am."

"You're so compassionate. I think Mom has been feeling a little left out since we got here. When we first arrived on Earth, we kept to ourselves. We spent a lot of time at home with Mom and the General. You and Shannon have absorbed us into your world, which is fantastic for Alex and me. The General has enough to do in the tactical room to keep himself busy. Mom helps him, of course, but her focus has always been on looking after us. Now, I'm sure she feels left behind. If she and your mom became friends, I think she'd be happier."

"I figured as much. Mom was the same after dad died. He had been sick and while she looked after him, she'd lost touch with many of her friends. When he died, she was afraid she'd smother me, so she started working a lot. She still works too much. I'd like it if she had someone around to talk to."

"Yeah, and Mom could never go out and make friends. It wasn't safe. I'm sure she wanted to, and it's been so long, I am wondering if she even knows how. Having your mom next door is the perfect solution."

I gave him a hug goodbye and walked the rest of the way to my front door. Just before I went inside, I called back to Ben. "Just remember, whatever my mom tells your mom about me, it's all a lie. I was a perfect angel who never did anything wrong or had an embarrassing moment… ever."

CHAPTER EIGHTEEN

At school the next day, Ben, Tom, and I dodged Shannon during the mid-morning break to have a quick conversation.

"I think it's time we gathered everyone we know together to talk about our options." Ben said. "If the Hurliingen come, we'll have a better chance of defending ourselves if everyone living in Saint John from the Alliance of Eight Planets pooled their resources and stood together. We are all in danger. Anyone who had the means to come to Earth is important enough to be used for leverage on their home planet."

Tom agreed. "I think it's time we bring Shannon and a few others in to help." He watched us closely, as if to gauge our reaction. "Janie and I had a talk with our dads after we saw the Sensors last night. Dad's Alliance contacts in California have been apprised and they are spreading the word to everyone else they know. Janie's father didn't bother to cultivate many friendships. He is aggressive and competitive in business. It seems he has more enemies than friends, even among us. After our talk, Janie and I decided we wanted Jason and Shannon to know what's going on." He shrugged a bit defensively, as if expecting an argument. "It makes sense. They'll figure out something is up, eventually. And honestly, I can't think of a good cover story. And who knows? They might come in handy since the Hurliingen aren't after them."

Ben pondered this for a few minutes while I tried to keep my feelings to myself. This was not really my decision to make, even though it would make my life much easier if Shannon knew what was going on. I couldn't count the number of times I would almost let stuff slip or make a comment about how quickly Ben and Alex have adjusted to life on Earth.

We decided to meet the next day during our lunch break. We'd go up to Queen's Square, which was close enough to the school but far away from where the students usually hung out for some privacy. Strategically, it was an excellent location. Out in the open with park benches where we could sit. It would be easy to see if anyone was close enough to hear our conversation and the traffic on the streets around the park would give us a protective layer of white noise for anyone just casually walking by.

The next day was sunny. I walked up to the park alone and was surprised to see Janie and Jason already there, sitting on the bench, deep in conversation. Apparently, they'd cut last class and from the look on Jason's face, he'd just been told the news.

I'll admit, I chickened out and let Tom tell Shannon. I'd help with the fall out afterward... if she was still talking to me.

Alex was the next person to arrive. She was alone. Not being allowed to tell Robbie still upset her. She'd tried to argue that it was only fair since I knew. That was until Ben, not so gently, reminded her I was never supposed to know. It was her spoiled-brat, hissy fit that gave their secret away.

I was a good girlfriend and held back from reminding him I'd seen him and the General disappear first. Besides, I agreed it wasn't a good idea to let Robbie know. Hell, I didn't think it was a good idea for Jason to know either, but if it helped keep Janie out of my hair, it was probably worth the risk. Shannon finally knowing was an enormous relief. At least I hoped so. It all depended on whether she ever forgave me for keeping something this huge secret from her.

Tom and Shannon were the last two to arrive. Shannon's face was hard to read, even for me. I think she was trying to decide whether the fantastically unreal story Tom told her was the truth or whether he was just teasing her. Her eyes narrowed when she saw Janie, Jason, Alex, Ben, and I gathered together. That probably helped to make it more believable, since Janie would never voluntarily hang out with us.

Ben spoke, "Since we're all here…"

Tom interrupted, "Not quite." He pointed to the opposite corner of the park. "Here come some of the others." From the direction of St. Mac's, one of the other downtown schools, another group of people, three teenagers and someone who looked like a teacher, walked toward us. A car alarm beeped and from the curb beside them, another group of six teenagers and another teacher exited two cars and a pickup truck.

I was speechless and a little worried. Why were the teachers here? As they got closer, I recognized many of the kids. Some I had gone to middle school with, others I had met at different sporting events or through my job.

Ben was silent, but I could feel the tension radiating from him.

Janie stood up and left Jason, who still looked a little dumbstruck, on the bench. She motioned to Ben and Tom to follow her as she walked through the crowd and introduced them to a couple of people, who then introduced them to the others in their group. The rest of us greeted each other awkwardly. It took only a few minutes, but by the time Janie finished with the introductions, Ben looked a lot more relaxed and even smiled at something one teacher said.

I was so intent on watching them; I didn't see Shannon come to stand beside me.

"You knew."

It was not a question; it was a statement. Actually, it sounded more like an accusation, which I was expecting. What surprised me was Alex stepping in to defend me.

"She wasn't supposed to know. We were supposed to fit in and be normal. I let Hilary see something she shouldn't have. I hoped that if she found out we'd have to move away, and Ben would have to spend time with me again."

I couldn't believe that happened only a month ago. She seemed so much more grown up now.

Shannon was not ready yet to be mollified. "Hilary could have told me any time."

"Not really." I reminded her, "It wasn't my story to tell. If it wasn't for the Hurliingen threat, you still wouldn't know, and I would still think Alex played a trick on me. I didn't learn the whole truth until after I saw the Sensors."

"How long have you known about Tom?"

"Since Ben recognized him in the restaurant." I shrugged, "Those weren't sweet nothings Ben was whispering in my ear. He was freaking out because he wasn't sure if Tom was a friend or not."

"But you let me go home with Tom that night." The look she shot me was definitely accusatory.

"Like I could have stopped you." I snapped back.

"Yeah, but if I knew he was an alien, I might have listened."

"Really? You would have believed me if I told you that Tom was an alien?"

"Well, probably not." She relaxed a bit.

"Even if I'd said there was something I didn't like about him. You would have told me I was being paranoid."

She knew it was true. Had I created a fuss, she would have been even more determined to make him drive her home. I tell you the girl has entitlement issues.

When Janie, Tom, and Ben returned, everyone started talking at once. I looked at my watch and called out to Ben. I pointed to my wrist.

He nodded, "Ok folks, we have limited time. We have to get back to class soon. Here's the deal. We have Sensors circling around our heads and have heard rumours that the Hurliingen are coming toward Earth, but we know nothing for sure. Until a week ago, I didn't know there was anyone else on this planet from the Alliance. I am amazed that there are so many of us here in Saint John. Did you all know about each other before today?"

The teacher stepped forward. "Most of us have kept our secrets. I knew of only two other families. It seems they knew of two more families." He pointed at one kid who came in the van with him. "I've had Steven in my welding class for three years and didn't know."

Ben nodded. "I wonder how many more of us are nearby?"

"I know someone in Fredericton."

"Me too."

"I know someone in Moncton."

"I know three families up in the Miramichi from Echyhl."

I shook my head in disbelief.

Shannon stood silently between Tom and me. She was holding his hand but was gripping my arm hard enough that I knew there'd be a bruise there tomorrow.

Ben took control of the crowd again. There was something regal about the way he stood, spoke, and took control. I don't know whether it was the way his mother raised him or his natural charisma, but he suddenly seemed to be more like a military leader than a teenager. I found myself a little in awe of him and felt suddenly shy when he caught my eye.

"The Sensors have been here twice in the past few weeks. We have access to some tracking equipment, and we know there are a lot of them swarming over the earth. Right now, they seem to concentrate on the over Central Canada and the U.S. West Coast. I don't think they know we are here in Saint John yet and personally I would like to keep it that way.

There were nods of agreement around the circle.

"We've come up with some ideas to help keep the families we knew about safe, but those are inadequate considering how many of us there are here today. We did not know there were that many of us when we created our strategy, so we will have to make new plans. The most important thing right now is not to contact anyone back on our home planets. Communications are easy to track and will give away our location. Now that we know there are so many of us here, it is more urgent than ever. It is no longer just our own families we are trying to protect.

One guy piped up from the back of the crowd. "Who put you in charge?" I noticed he was not someone Janie or Tom introduced Ben to at the beginning.

Ben straightened. "Apparently, you haven't been paying attention. I am Krohxa."

I didn't know what Krohxa meant, but the guy who challenged Ben stepped back and seemed to shrink as if trying to disappear. I had obviously missed an important nuance somewhere in the McAllister's story. There were many undertones happening here that I didn't understand. From the reaction of the crowd, Ben, this… Krohxa, was even more powerful than his mother and the General implied.

Ben and I needed to have a chat… soon. I might even make him skip afternoon classes to explain.

Ben kept on talking. "Tom, Janie and I have walkie-talkies. I suggest we all get them if you can. Hilary works at Cole Electronics." Ben pointed to me, and I waved to the dozen or so people I hadn't met yet. "She'll make sure you all get the same models as we have, or at least ones that can be tuned to the same frequency to use as an emergency channel. We have already used them once, and they did exactly what we needed them to."

"If we keep to old analogue Earth technology, it will make it harder for the Hurliingen to locate us. But be careful what you say when you're talking on your cell phones since those signals travel a lot farther than the walkie-talkies and they have GPS."

"While the Sensors don't have the power to rationalize a plan of action, they report back to the Hurliingen. The Hurliingen may not be military minded, but they are great at using manipulation and coercion, which makes us all targets. While they hadn't harmed the inhabitants of any uninvolved planets yet, they seem more desperate than we've ever seen them. I can't guarantee their restraint any longer."

I knew I should be grateful for the sales Ben just handed me, but the last thing I wanted to do was work tonight. I had so many new questions to ask Ben and the General.

Tom spoke. "From what I can tell, we have representatives from all eight of the Alliant planets here plus a few Earth dwellers who have willingly or not quite willingly come along for the ride." He glanced over at Shannon and smiled. "The best scenario we can hope for is that the Sensors are just here exploring and will leave soon. Unfortunately, they have been here for a while. Every day they stay lessens our chances of remaining undetected. The Hurliingen are after anyone who can strengthen their positions back on our home planets. While Ben and Alex are important for them take over Myonus, none of us are safe. The Hurliingen have already caused civil wars on most of the Alliance of Eight planets and if they get Ben or Alex, the Hurliingen will be unstoppable.

Tom looked over at Ben as if for permission to continue.

Ben nodded.

"In case you're wondering why Krohxa has taken charge so quickly here on Earth, it is because General Tsad has trained him."

There was a gasp throughout the crowd.

Apparently, the General was pretty big potatoes too. Geez, I'm not half as smart as I thought I was. How did I miss all this? I glanced over at Shannon; she was looking a little stunned.

"I'm sorry for not telling you." I said to Shannon. "There was no way I could explain this to you without their help, and they asked me to keep their secret."

"I probably would have taken you to the psych ward, anyway." She gave a wry laugh and shook her head. "I'm still not entirely sure we shouldn't all head there, just in case this is a group hallucination or mass hysteria or something."

"It's real. Ben and Tom can explain things better than I can. It's easier to believe when you see some of the hologram maps."

"Holograms?"

"Yeah, they're completely cool."

"I think I died and resurrected in the middle of a sci-fi flick, and you know how much I hate science-fiction."

"Well, this isn't exactly fiction and right now I don't like this any better than you." I glanced back over to Ben, where he stood talking. "This whole kidnapping threat is nasty."

"What? Wait! Who is going to kidnap who?"

"The Hurliingen." Alex piped in. "Tom's father has political power. Ben and I have special genetic codes that the Hurliingen want. They'd use Ben until he's exhausted, and they'd breed me, trying to make someone even more powerful than Ben."

Shannon paled.

"That's the same reaction I had."

"Oh my God, what are we going to do?"

"I don't know Shan, I really don't know. But I'm in too far to even consider backing out now."

Janie came over to where Shannon, Alex and I were standing a little apart from the rest of the group. She looked tired and, for the first time ever, a little vulnerable.

"Have you seen Jason?"

"He was just here," I said as I spun around to where Jason had been standing not two minutes before. I looked around and then saw him running out of the park, away from the school.

"Ben." I shouted.

Ben followed the direction of my pointing finger just in time to see Jason disappear up Charlotte Street. His expression turned grim. Jason was a track star. There was no way any of us could catch him.

Ben jogged over to us and said to Janie. "Any idea where he's going?"

"No, I brought him up here last period so I could tell him about me and what's happening. He didn't believe me and was about to leave when you guys showed up. Seeing everyone arrive must have finally convinced him I was telling the truth. But I don't know where he's going now."

A horrible thought occurred to me, "Janie, is there any chance he might know some way to cause trouble for Ben and the others?"

Janie shook her head but stopped. "Oh, God."

"What?" we said in unison. The others, who were still standing around, became riveted on our little group. They strained to hear what we were saying. Even though they couldn't hear the words, they could probably tell from the tone of our hushed voices something was wrong. They started to look worried.

"Jason's dad just got laid off. He told me not to tell anyone. They built that big new house out in

Milledgeville, and they have a lot of debt. He could sell my story to TMZ?"

Leave it to Janie to make it all about her.

Ben, Tom and I looked at each other. There was a market for everything. All you had to do was find the right buyer. Hell, the internet was full of them, and they wouldn't bother asking for any proof. Jason could potentially get his family out of their financial crisis by risking everyone else with a stupid story.

Janie was in tears.

For the moment, I forgot she was Janie, the bane of my existence. I put my arms around her and let her cry on my shoulder. For the first time since I'd met her, she didn't hold herself aloof, pretending she was better than everyone else. Instead, she shuddered and cried harder.

Saint John High's first bell rang. The one at St. Mac's echoed it almost immediately.

I motioned with my head for Ben and the others to take off. I would stay with Janie and calm her down before we went back to class.

Ben moved everyone away from us, shouting instructions to meet outside the Tim Hortons downtown, at nine thirty.

Nine-thirty was great. It would give me plenty of time to get there after work.

Ben and Tom decided they'd better skip afternoon classes and go look for Jason. They headed to their vehicles.

Shannon and Alex walked back to Saint John High together. As they walked away, I heard Shannon peppering Alex with questions. She was taking this a lot better than I had expected and, thank God, a lot better than Jason.

Once everyone was out of sight, I said. "It's ok Janie, they're gone."

Janie lifted her head. Her make-up was a mess. It shocked me a bit. Even in Phys. Ed., I don't think I've ever seen her with a hair out of place.

She looked around in time to see the girls disappear down Harding Street toward our school. The St. Mac's kids were already out of sight. "I really messed up."

"No worse than anyone else did. I wasn't supposed to know, but Ben and his family weren't very careful, and I was more observant than they were expecting."

"I don't know why I told Jason. It's not as if he really cares about me, he is just in it for what being part of 'Janie & Jason' could do for him." She sniffed. "Tom was so insistent that Shannon should know, and he just assumed that I'd want to tell Jason. I didn't want to sound like a loser. Besides, coming here today alone would have really sucked."

"I'm not sure I've behaved any better." I motioned over to the bench so we could sit. "I left it to Tom to tell Shannon because I knew she was going to be furious with me for keeping something this big away from her."

"How long have you known?"

"I've known about Ben and Alex since the beginning of the school year. Shannon just found out."

"At least she didn't run off to sell the secret to the highest bidder." Janie's voice was bitter.

"We don't know he did that." While it was the truth, I wasn't sure what Jason would try to do this new knowledge.

"Face it, Hilary. Jason wasn't running as if he was scared. He looked like he was running toward something. Focused, just like when he races."

"I don't know Jason very well, but I don't think he'd sell you out that fast. Maybe he just freaked out and had to be alone to process it all?"

"Not a chance. Jason hates being alone. He started playing sports because the teams hung around in packs. He and his little brother still share a room, even though his little brother hates it and wants his own space. If he wasn't so gorgeous and easy to manipulate, I would have written him off a long time ago."

Believe it or not, I was glad to see signs of normal Janie coming back. "I'm not sure what we can do, but hopefully Ben can track Jason down soon, so we'll know what's going on with him."

Janie nodded, obviously feeling better but still bearing an enormous weight on her shoulders.

"If he blabs on us, you can just tell everyone he's afraid of the dark and has a Blue's Clues nightlight in his bedroom."

Janie laughed aloud. "And Barney pyjamas."

"See? Not so bad after all."

We got up and started walking back toward the school. Just as we crossed the plaza, Janie stopped me. "Thank you, Hilary. You didn't have to stay with me."

"I couldn't leave you alone. That just wouldn't have been cool at all. There's a lot happening and we're all in this together."

CHAPTER NINETEEN

My shift that night at Cole Electronics was nuts.

People were waiting for me when I arrived. We sold out of the model Ben bought within a few minutes and the next model down was gone shortly after that. Walkie-talkies were a novelty item. We didn't keep a very large stock and obviously no one else did either, because by the time my shift was half finished, every store in the city was sold out. I knew because I'd spent most of my shift calling around to see who else might still have them in stock.

Jocelyn, my supervisor, came over to me between phone calls. "What is going on? Why does everyone suddenly want a walkie-talkie?"

I knew Jocelyn would ask and I couldn't say I didn't know because, thanks to Ben, most people were asking for me by name. I'm not a talented liar, so I spent most of the drive out to Cole Electronics practicing my explanation. "Some kids were talking today about some nostalgia group their parents were forming. They wanted to re-live the seventies and play with their old toys only in their updated versions. Last month was Rock 'em Sock 'em Robots, this month it is walkie-talkies. I told them we had a bunch of them in stock." I could feel my stomach clench. It sounded much better when I said it in the car. There was no way Jocelyn was going to believe me. "If I had known sooner, I would have asked you to order extra units."

Just then, another bunch of people came into the store. I recognized two of them from the noon meeting at the park. They waved at me.

Jocelyn shrugged, "Weird," and walked away.

Ben was waiting for me outside after my shift. Even though it was chilly, he stood leaning up against the hood, waiting for me to come out. I walked over, slid my arms around his waist, and put my head on his chest. We stood like that in silence for a few minutes. He seemed to need it as much as I did. Eventually, I leaned back far enough to see his face. He looked tense, but strangely more relaxed than he'd been since we first saw the Sensors. I know for me, having a plan was always better than feeling like a sitting duck. Looks like Ben feels the same way.

"How was Janie?" he asked.

"I haven't seen her since last class. She was better, but still worried about what Jason could do. He didn't come back to class."

"We couldn't find him." Ben rested his chin on the top of my head. "I don't know where he could have gone. We even checked his house. There were a lot of cars in their yard, but his wasn't one of them."

"Maybe we'll get some answers tonight." I squeezed him slightly before I let go. "We'd better head over to Timmies or else we'll be late."

I stepped away from him, and he pulled me back. His tug on my arm was gentle but firm. "Hilary," he seemed to struggle for a minute, "Thank you. I don't know of anyone, on any planet, who could be as unfreaked-out about all this as you are." He bent down and gave me a kiss.

It was short, but the emotion transferred in that brief contact between his lips and mine had me wanting to forget all about the meeting, the Hurliingen and everything else. But I didn't. I reached up and touched my palm to his cheek. "We've got to go. Time to save a world… or nine."

Ben followed me to Tim Hortons in his Barracuda. Luckily, he didn't tailgate because as soon as I turned onto Waterloo, I slammed on my brakes.

I was shocked at the number of people who were there waiting. There had to be at least fifty people standing around the parking lot. Part of me wondered if we were going to have the police arrive to investigate. There were so many of us in what was usually a ghost town at this time of night.

Then I saw the two police cruisers parked on the side of the road. Three officers were standing, with Tim Horton coffee cups in their hands, talking to the teacher we had met at Queen Square during lunch.

Much to my surprise, I was waved into the parking lot. Tom and a few of the others were guarding two spaces. Ben pulled in beside me.

This time, there were hardly any kids in the group. It was mostly adults. Standing alone, near the corner of the building, was the General. I started to raise my hand in greeting when he shook his head as if to say don't. So, I didn't. Apparently, the General preferred to be incognito. It was weird knowing that Ben, Tom, and I would lead this meeting while the General stood on the sidelines.

Ben leaned against the rear of his car. That seemed to be a universal signal for all the side conversations to halt and for everyone to gather close. Sound would carry farther tonight, echoing off the silent business buildings surrounding us. Even though there was the background hum of traffic from the highway, we needed to be cautious.

I wondered what anyone driving by would think. In hindsight, this probably wasn't a very smart place to hold a secret meeting. Some folks in the front sat down on the pavement to let the people in the back see and hear better.

I glanced behind the crowd. The General had moved in closer, but he remained on the outskirts of the group. I wasn't sure if he was doing surveillance or just waiting until the right time to identify himself. Ben still hadn't told anyone besides me that the General was here with them. Everyone seemed to assume Ben's training took place back on Myonus.

Ben looked around the group. "Thanks everyone for coming. I know how distressing this must be for most of you. Until now, I am sure you were like us and felt it was safer to stay hidden and blend in with the Earthers. Unfortunately, things have changed.

"Now, not knowing each other might become our biggest weakness instead of our strength. We were under the assumption the Hurliingen were looking for my sister, Alex, and me. We didn't know anyone else was here. Then we met Tom." Ben hesitated. "And learned that we weren't alone."

"The truth is, we are all commodities that can be used in negotiations back on our home planets. None of us would have had the means to escape and take refuge here if we didn't have power or influence. If we stand together here, we may be able to reverse the tide and be able to help end the trouble that the Hurliingen have started on our home planets.

"From what we have learned, this clan of Hurliingen have spread themselves too thinly. They need Alex and me to be successful on Myonus. If they get us, they'll not only have access to all the energy they need, but our capture could crush the spirit of those still fighting. If Myonus becomes their stronghold, it could make the rest of the Alliance fall. If we can defeat them here, we should be able to help turn things around on our home planets. Eventually, we can start living again instead of just hiding and trying to survive." He looked over at me, "I've recently learned the difference between surviving and thriving and I have to say I'm not prepared to be forced back into survival mode."

There were nods of agreement throughout the assembled group.

"I wish I could tell you we have a plan, but we don't. Right now, we don't even know if the Sensors have discovered we are here or are simply investigating all possible planets in this sector. We know there is a cloud of Sensors over North America. They're mostly staying high and out of sight. The Earth military knows they're here, but they haven't made the knowledge public. There doesn't seem to be much activity over the other continents, but that could change. It is hard to predict because we don't know why they are here. If we contact our home planets through regular channels, it could lead the Hurliingen right to our doorsteps.

"We've come up with a preliminary avoidance strategy until we know what our options are. Most of what I am going to say is common sense, but in stressful situations like these, it's best to be overcautious and state the obvious. Don't contact other planets using home technologies. The Sensors have little independent flying range, which means they got here somehow. Even though we haven't found them yet, we know there is at least one Hurliingen ship out there looking for us.

Ben held up his walkie-talkie. "In case of emergency, use the walkie-talkies. The Earth's military is on high alert. Cell phones have GPS and thanks to the paranoia created by the Earth's media, it's almost certain your conversations will be recorded somewhere. The Hurliingen are especially good at using information to gain trust from powerful people. We want to make it as difficult as possible for them to know how many of us are here and that we know they're coming.

"For the walkie-talkies, we have a main emergency channel. Thanks to Hilary, most people who purchased them tonight have the same brand or similar frequencies. If you have something else, let us know and we can tweak them to all be on the same emergency channel. Spread the word. I don't care if other folks make themselves known to us or not, but they must have a walkie-talkie to know what's going on."

"Do not use your craft. The one thing we know for sure is that the Sensors are here, and they can track your exhaust from twenty kilometres away, possibly farther. Which I don't need to tell you will put your entire family in jeopardy."

The crowd murmured for a minute. One man near the front asked. "What about the monitoring equipment we have on board?"

Ben answered the question. "That's fine, as long as you don't have to start the main engines to use them."

As Ben spoke to the group in front of him, I couldn't believe this was the same guy who worried about kissing me. He made me feel young and silly for being concerned about stupid things, like whether Alex was wearing pigtails. I was in awe as he kept on talking.

"Please be careful. In many ways, the chain system where each of us knew only a few others was working. I won't lie. Gathering in one place and having conversations like this is dangerous, but it's also the only way we can plan well enough to beat the Hurliingen, instead of allowing them to pick us off one at a time.

"What we need to do is compile a list of all Alliance of Eight technologies we have. Before you leave, please, will you help us by listing what monitoring equipment and weapons you have here on Earth? Include items that aren't working. I suspect we'll have enough spare parts to fix anything that's broken." Ben held up a handful of pens and a package of loose-leaf paper. He laughed. "As you can see, I've chosen to go with really old earth technology for this part."

The crowd laughed with him.

Ben was such a natural at this.

"Once we have a list, we can see where we stand. If anyone knows any Earth substitutes for Alliance parts, please write them down too. We need to collect as much information as we can and keep everyone updated. We're all in this together, so if you know about equipment someone else has, who is not here tonight, please write that on a separate piece of paper, so we know it is from a separate source."

People rushed to Tom, who was handing out the paper and pens. Others milled around Ben, asking questions he really didn't have the answers for yet. I looked around for the General. I couldn't see him anywhere. But there were so many people all standing close together as they talked that he'd be easy to miss. I stayed close to Ben, looking out over the crowd for Janie and Shannon. I assumed they'd both be here, but they weren't. Instead, a rather plain looking, middle-aged man approached me. I didn't pay him much mind at first, figuring he just wanted to talk to Ben.

"Hilary?"

The sound of my name startled me. "Yes."

"I'm Janie's father. I would like to thank you for helping my daughter today. All this is new to her. I am afraid I took the coward's route, and I gave in to her mother's preference to ignore my background. Honestly, I hoped Janie and her sister would never have to know."

I looked at him, trying to see traces of Janie. She obviously looked like her mother. Not that he was ugly, I'm sure he had been more pleasant looking when he was younger. Now he looked extremely stressed. I shrugged. "I couldn't just leave her there alone."

"Yes, you could have." He sighed. "I love my daughters dearly, but we've taught them to be competitive and stay ahead no matter what the cost. If your roles were reversed, both of them would have left you and laughed about you all the way back to class."

I started to protest, but he waved my words away. "Hilary, I know my daughters. You don't need to defend them. I just wanted to say thank you. We're all learning valuable lessons this week." With that, he turned and walked away, leaving me feeling strangely sorry for him.

By the time we finished, Ben had a sheaf of papers almost an inch thick. Some seemed covered with lists of equipment and supplies. It made me feel like we were in the ending scene of "It's a Wonderful Life where the townspeople all gave money to help pay off the big bill at the end. Only in this case, it was electronics, not dollar bills. Either way, it was still a huge vote of confidence for Ben.

I am not sure if Ben realized how big a thing this was. No one seemed to have recognized the General at the gathering. This was all about Ben and the amount of faith these people had in him by reputation alone. They might have come because of his lineage, but they stayed because of him. If he hadn't earned their trust, they would have just gone home and prepared as best they could on their own.

CHAPTER TWENTY

After the crowd dispersed, Ben, Tom, and I stayed by our cars talking. It was almost eleven, but we were too wired to go home just yet. They had accomplished a lot even though there was still a long way to go before we were anywhere near a solid plan of defence, let alone action.

And there was still no word about Jason. No one had seen him since noon.

I got tired around eleven-thirty and said goodnight. I had to get home before I was too sleepy to drive.

Ben walked me to my car and kissed me goodbye.

As I drove home, I tried to stop my mind from spinning. I turned on the radio to listen to my favourite station, trying to relax.

Instead of the golden oldies I was expecting, there was a panic-stricken voice on the air. Within seconds, I was wide-awake and pulling a U-turn. I had to get back to Tom and Ben.

I raced along Union Street, attracting the attention of one of Saint John's finest. Lights flashing, he followed me as I did an illegal left turn onto Waterloo Street. I hoped the cop was one from earlier. If not, he would have to write the ticket without me. I sprinted across the street to where the boys were still standing. The cop was right behind me.

"Guys, quick, turn on the radio!"

The cop skidded to a stop beside me. "What's happened?"

Ben was already in his car, fumbling with his keys to put them in the ignition. "What channel?"

"CKCW."

"The golden oldies?" He probably would have laughed at me if he hadn't heard the urgency in my voice.

I shrugged. It was dad's favourite channel.

"… purple lights swirling out over the bay surrounding a large hovering tanker. I'm not making this up. Dude, look out your window."

Ben hauled out his walkie-talkie just as a couple of other cars came screeching back into the parking lot. "Did you hear?" Panicked voices filled the air.

"Gen… Dad, come in, Dad?" Ben barked into his mouthpiece over the din of even more arriving cars.

The General's voice came over the speaker, but he was hard to hear over the growing chaos as even more people returned.

"Dad, what's going on? The radio is reporting lights over the Bay of Fundy?"

It took a few minutes for the General to respond. My guess was that he had been upstairs filling in Ben's mother on the meeting and on how well her son had done. He had to run down to the tactical room to investigate.

"There is nothing on the screen here."

"Are you sure?"

I could hear exasperation loud and clear in the General's voice. "Yes, I'm sure."

"Give me a few minutes," I said to Ben. I ran back across the street. I drove up Paddock Street and flew over the viaduct to the North End, only to screech to a halt at the back entrance to Fort Howe, the second highest point in Saint John. Damn, they already blocked off the entrance for the winter. I jumped out of my car and ran up the hill.

I ignored how spectacular the city looked at night. It was clear enough that I could see the past the harbour and all the way across the Bay of Fundy to the lights of Digby, Nova Scotia, over fifty kilometers away. From this height, I could also see down past Coleson Cove to the nuclear reactor in Point Lepreau.

"Ben?"

"Yeah, Hilary."

"I'm up at Fort Howe. I don't see any Sensors. According to the radio, I should see a sea of purple. I think the General is right."

"Then what's the point?"

There was dead air space while Ben, I assumed, was talking to the crowd that was re-gathering around him.

Impatiently, I waited, wondering if I should go back or just continue home. I didn't want to interrupt, but I really wanted to know what the hell was happening.

After listening intently for a few minutes, Ben's voice scared the heck out of me when it came back over the line.

"The police officer called found out that the radio station opened its lines for a contest. When the caller got through, the DJ was so shocked, he didn't properly switch over to music like they're supposed to for prank calls. The entire call was aired by accident.

"Jason?"

"I don't know." There was a pause. Ben's walkie-talkie seemed to click on and off a couple of times.

I waited, but Ben didn't say anything more. I stared out over the harbour. Nothing was out there except for the lights of one of the oil tankers waiting to come into berth over at Courtney Bay. I gave up waiting for Ben to say anything more and keyed in the microphone again. "I'm heading home. I'll update the General when I get there."

"Night, Babe."

"Night, Ben."

I smiled at the endearment. I don't think I ever heard him call me babe before.

CHAPTER TWENTY-ONE

"They have Ben." The General said as he strode across the yard toward me. He'd been pacing back and forth when I drove in.

Suddenly, I was wide awake again. "What do you mean they have, Ben? I was just talking to him. He told me the thing with the radio was just a hoax."

Then Ben's last endearment echoed in my brain. Had he been trying to warn me? Voices could sound distorted over walkie-talkies and Ben never called me babe. Was it even him? I frantically tried to remember anything that should have tipped me off that something was wrong. Wait a minute, Jason called Janie 'babe' all the time. Was it Jason on the walkie-talkie instead of Ben? Jason wouldn't have any reason to kidnap Ben. Would he? I collapsed against my car in shock.

The General was already at his front door. "Hilary?" Just for an instant, under the light, he looked like a tired old man instead of his usual intimidating self.

He needed me. Ben needed me. I straightened my shoulders. "Where's Alex?"

"She and her mother are downstairs searching for leads. I needed quiet to think. Try to remember who was there tonight."

I walked toward the General and gave him an awkward half hug. "We'll find him."

As we walked into the tactical room, I asked. "What do we know about Jason?"

The General looked at me curiously. "You think he has something to do with Ben disappearing?"

I shrugged as we walked into their basement. "Something's bothering me about my last conversation with Ben. Jason seems to be a good place to start. If he's just a local jock, it shouldn't be hard to investigate his family and rule him out as a problem beyond the inconvenience of him bragging about dating a half-alien."

"Hang on." Alex, in her pyjamas, worked the keyboard on her console for a minute. "Yeah, he's suspicious. He and his father appeared out of nowhere five years ago. They've only been in Saint John for a year. They seem to move every twelve to fifteen months." She looked at her mother, the General and me. "They were trying to cover their tracks, but naturally I found them. Here's where they've lived." Just like on TV, driver's licence photos and school IDs came up in front of us to see. The names were unfamiliar, but there was no question it was Jason and the man we had to assume was his father.

"Did you find birth records for Jason, or do we assume he's an alien, too?"

"No birth records for Jason, although there is an adoption certificate for a younger brother dated three years ago." She paused. "Something else is odd. Jason has both a Social Insurance Number from Canada and a Social Security Number from the States. According to the dates on the applications, they requested the cards at the same time." She crossed her arms. "Something wonky happened there."

My mind was racing. Alex was right. "Were you able to search financial records? Janie said something about Jason's family having money problems."

"Ben and I were checking them before the meeting tonight." The General moved to a different console and brought up another hologram showing bank accounts and tax information.

It still boggled my mind that they could hack into our highly secure systems with the touch of a few buttons. That first night we'd seen the Sensors, I had mentioned it. Alex said our encryptions were a joke. It had offended me, but right now I was glad it was so easy. Especially since it gave us the answers we needed.

I studied the numbers even though I didn't know what I was looking for.

The General came to my rescue. He pointed to a section on the hologram. "There are a series of cash deposits, but I can't find the source of the money. It just appears. They started as soon as the bank accounts opened." He pointed to the last line on one statement. It was double the amount. "This last one was a week ago. Jason's family is not in any type of financial trouble."

"Why would Jason lie to Janie then? It doesn't make sense. He must have known she'd drop him if she thought he had money troubles." I looked at the General and then at Alex while thinking aloud. "If he's supposed to be tracking members of the Alliance of Eight for the Hurliingen, I doubt he'd cut ties with a valuable lead. Besides, wouldn't he be trained not to give anything away? Aren't they master manipulators or something?" I shrugged. "We didn't think of him as anything more than Janie's jock boyfriend until he ran out of the park."

Alex nodded. "She's right."

"Maybe he's not a bad guy. Maybe he's just hiding, too? Is there any way to trace him back to one of the planets? Anyone reported missing that wouldn't have purposefully hid?" I knew I was grasping for ideas. At least they didn't seem to think I was stupid.

Mrs. McAllister's fingers started flying over the controls at her terminal. "I can't think of anyone, but there was a lot happening before we left. Let me look."

"Jeremy!" Alex called out.

We all turned toward her. Her mom and the General looked as confused as I felt.

"When I was little, I remember Ben came into my room to say goodbye. He was sad because he had been playing in Dad's office and broke something. He thought he would be sent away, just like his friend Jeremy." Alex paused for a minute, as if trying to remember the details. "Ben was convinced that Jeremy broke something while they were playing and the next day, they took Jeremy away. Ben thought the same thing was going to happen to him. I was only four, but I remember Ben made me promise never to play in Daddy's office. Ever."

"Yes, yes, I remember Jeremy." Mrs. McAllister scrolled through the records so fast it made me dizzy.

The General swung back to his own console, which I learned accessed Myonus' military records. I thought Mrs. McAllister was fast, but the General broke records. "I remember the incident. Someone kidnapped Jeremy. We had a full-scale search for the boy. His parents were non-Tixlardine members of the new council. They quit political life shortly after Jeremy was taken. Someone showing the correct papers citing a family emergency took him from class and he was never seen again. The military was involved because he was the son of a council member. We did not know the Hurliingen were a threat back then, but even knowing what we do now, I do not see how he would have any value for the Hurliingen since he was non-Tixlardine."

If Jeremy was Jason, it still made no sense. Why would Jason turn up on Earth and what motive could he have for kidnapping Ben?

While the General kept scrolling through the holographic database, I looked at the map of the world that was tracking the movement of the Sensors. Since there was nothing else for me to do to help, I watched it.

"I wonder if there is a way to track the Sensors back before we saw them." I didn't mean to say it out loud, but I obviously had.

"Of course." Alex moved over to a different console. In seconds, the maps had changed. "Even though we weren't tracking them specifically, the data was all recorded. How far back did you want to go?"

"How about back to when you first came to Saint John?"

She manipulated the controls to give me a time-lapse view of the Sensors' movements. The Sensors were still there. But they seemed to hover high over Eastern Canada, so they couldn't be seen.

"That's weird. They were here, but then they left to go to California just after we saw them."

The General must have heard what we were saying. He stopped what he was doing and came over to look at what Alex and I were doing. "Alex, go back farther."

"How far?"

"We have data from the ship when we arrived," he said. "Start there."

Alex made some more adjustments to the hologram. This time, when the hologram changed, the bulk of the purple cloud was over Florida. As it cycled through the time since they'd arrived, the cloud moved every few months, but the bulk stayed over Canada's Eastern Seaboard, right over our heads.

The General look confused. "When we were investigating Earth, we couldn't see something as small as Sensors. Because we did not see any ships come near the planet, we didn't specifically look for the Sensors when we arrived. They have a very short range and without a ship to carry them, they would never have been able to make the journey from the Alliance Planets to Earth."

"So, they were here before you arrived."

"Apparently so." The General looked frustrated that he had let something as like this evade his notice.

Mrs. McAllister put her hand on his arm, much like I had seen her do to Ben when he was upset with Alex. "Hakunor, there is no reason to be angry. We had no reason to expect them to be here before us."

"Regardless, I should have checked." He frowned, completely ignoring her comforting gesture. "I've put you and your family in danger by my carelessness."

"I don't think so." I muttered, half to myself. "The Sensors were here before you, not only on the planet but here in Saint John, too. If they had seen you arrive, the Hurliingen would have been here and captured Ben and Alex already. My guess is they are still looking, especially since they moved to explore California when Tom's family contacted their home planet. Since you drove here, they'd have no way of monitoring your movements." I had a strange urge to giggle. "You're hiding right under their noses. You probably couldn't be any safer."

"Except that someone has Ben." Alex reminded me.

My grand theory crumbled into dust, clearing the way for another thought. "Where is Tom? Has anyone heard from him? And how do we know Ben was taken? When I left, eight or nine people surrounded them, and one of them was a cop. How could anyone have taken Ben and left everyone else behind?"

The General answered. "One man who recognized me at the meeting we spoke and exchanged contact information. He is the one who called me just after I returned home. He said Ben and Tom had been talking to a few of them, trying to figure out why someone would call in a prank call about lights over the Bay.

Ben was talking to you on the walkie-talkie. Apparently, he said goodbye to you, looked at Tom and said, "We've got trouble." Tom looked over to where Ben was pointing and said something like "What the Hell?" then they both vanished.

"But you folks vanish all the time."

"We can make things vanish, especially if they're made from the metal from Myonus. It's harder to make people disappear."

"But not impossible."

"No, not impossible."

Alex interrupted us. "Who was the disc jockey at the radio station tonight?"

"George Stacey."

Alex ran back to her console. "Hilary, look." She pointed to a half page spread from the National Post. Beside it was another similar article from the Vancouver Sun and several newspapers from south of the border in the United States. The DJ's name is not always the same, but the hoax was. "Look at the locations. They are the same as on the list of places Jason's family had been living." The General and Mrs. McAllister rushed back to their stations, hands flying over virtual keyboards.

I looked around the room and knew I wouldn't be any help here. I needed to be doing something... anything. "I'm heading back into town. Maybe someone who was still hanging around saw something."

"I'm coming too." Alex stood up to follow me.

"No." The General and Mrs. McAllister said at once.

"Yes." She stood with her hands on her hips. The difference in Alex's voice amazed me. This was no longer the carefree twelve-year-old I'd come to know. Something had hardened inside her. Her voice was crisp and authoritative. "If they have Ben, they knew where to find him. That means I'm safer in Hilary's car than I am here." She looked at her mom. "I'm sorry, Mom, but this is important. You can't protect me. Not this time." She turned to the General. "I think we'll need the emergency kits."

CHAPTER TWENTY-TWO

The General handed me what looked like a regular utility belt while Alex raced upstairs to get dressed again. There were so many switches with strange markings on them. Halfway through the General's training, I must have looked overwhelmed. There was just so much going on and I hadn't had a full night's sleep in days. "Don't worry Hilary, Alex knows how to use this if you forget anything."

"I'll be fine." Even to my own ears, I sounded more confident than I felt. Star Trek, eat your heart out. This thing had it all. I could override any type of lock by pressing a few simple buttons. There were also a couple of features that would come in handy if we ran into problems.

It made me think back to that day just after the McAllisters moved in when Ben suddenly appeared beside me from out of nowhere.

"General, does Ben have one of these?"

"No, we keep these here for emergency use only." He opened a second compartment and swore before opening the rest of the storage areas.

"Two of them are missing."

I sighed in relief. "Maybe Ben hasn't been kidnapped. Maybe your friend just misinterpreted what he saw?"

"Then we'd better go find out what my big brother is doing." Alex grabbed my arm.

"Wait" The General handed me another belt. "Take an extra one, just in case."

"Come on Hilary. Let's go!"

I was beside her in an instant and we were out the door in a flash.

Somehow, it didn't surprise me to see Shannon standing by my car. She looked worried. "I was waiting for you to get home, and then I saw Ben's dad pacing, waiting for you, too. What happened?"

"Thank God," I said, "Get in. We'll explain on the way." I thought to myself 'Go, go, Ben and Tom's rescue team' as we climbed into our version of the bat mobile, and we raced back into town.

While I drove, we filled Shannon in on what had happened since this afternoon. It was a wonder she understood anything because Alex and I were both talking at once, and fast. Shannon, used to such communication, took it all in stride and was making her own suggestions before we got to the Harbour Bridge.

First stop, Tim Hortons. We had to find out what really happened. I made Alex lie down on the floor in the backseat, just in case this was a trap to get Alex out of the house and away from the General's protection. It didn't seem likely, but if we made a mistake in bringing her, I would not make it an obvious one.

We drove down Paddock Street, then along Waterloo where we could see the parking lot before we parked. Ben's car was still there, so was Tom's truck. There were a few people standing around talking, but there was still no sign of either of them. Off to the side, I recognized Janie's father. He must have come back after I left.

I pulled a U-turn on Peter Street and parked across from the coffee shop. As I hopped out of my car, I remembered at the last minute to pull my work T-shirt over my new utility belt. I didn't want anyone else to see it. Luckily, it wasn't too bulky and wouldn't be noticeable unless someone was looking for it. Shannon and I approached Janie's dad.

"What's going on? I thought everyone was going home after we figured out the Sensors were just a hoax."

"Hilary, it's insane. Ben and Tom were standing there discussing the prank at the radio station when they disappeared into thin air. Just like that." He snapped his fingers.

"Do you know of any technology that vaporizes people to transport them?" I asked, "You know, like in Star Trek?"

"You mean like beam me up, Scotty? No, we have nothing like that. Totally vaporizing someone to move them from place to place is beyond our capability."

"Does anyone else have that technology?" I asked.

"Not that I've heard of. But Hilary, I have been living on Earth for over twenty years and I put my old life behind me. I'm the last person who would know." He stopped and stroked his chin for a moment. It was hard not to laugh; it was clear where Janie got some of her dramatic flair. "Although, before I left, one lab I did business with had been working on a prototype, but that was for inanimate objects with only moderate success. The object would become opaque but not actually disappear. In fact, they were planning to scrap the project." He paused again. "The only race I know that could be even close to that sophisticated is the Kichra, and they're nowhere near Earth."

"Who are the Kichra?" I asked, even though I knew exactly who they were and wasn't about to tell him they were here orbiting Earth.

"The Kichra are a super advanced race that came from a universe we haven't discovered yet. Their mission is to observe emerging cultures and watch them grow."

"So even if they were here, they wouldn't help us against the Hurliingen?" I asked even though I knew what the General told me, but it couldn't hurt to see if Janie's dad had a different opinion.

"If they were here, they wouldn't interfere, but there have been no traces of them for decades. In the time of Ben's great-great-grandfather, they came to the Alliance of Eight but other than a brief communication at the beginning, they just let us be and we didn't approach them." He watched my reaction. "You don't look very surprised?"

"After this past month, I'm not sure I have any surprise left in me," I said, "but they sound like they have the same mission as the Enterprise on Star Trek. Their mission was to observe too, wasn't it?"

"Yes," he agreed with a laugh. "In fact, I often questioned if Gene Roddenberry was really from Earth. Some of the technology he included was curiously similar to items on the Alliance of Eight planets. If he wasn't one of us, his muse certainly was."

"Really? I thought that stuff was just all made up." I resisted the urge to touch the belt around my waist and hoped Ben's disappearing act was because he was wearing a belt too. Once I knew for sure he was safe, I was going to kill him for putting us through this.

Shannon rolled her eyes at the mention of Star Trek. "Back on topic. Has anyone been over to the radio station to talk to the disc jockey?" She spoke loud enough for the other people standing nearby to hear. Sure enough, a few of them came over to join our conversation.

I was glad she had seen me come home and came over to help. Sometimes you just really need a best friend by your side.

The crowd talked around us. Everyone seemed to have an opinion. My head was spinning.

Shannon stiffened. She and I were standing at an angle to each other with our shoulders touching. It was a communication system we developed back in middle school as an early warning system so we could warn each other if we saw Janie or one of her friends trying to sneak up on us.

"Hilary, I think we forgot something in the car." She was being more subtle than usual, but I understood. We had to get to Alex. She walked away, leaving me to say goodbye.

I turned my attention back to the group. "It's late. I have to get home." Without further explanation, I turned to follow Shannon. I caught up to her just as she stopped in front of my car. She was looking at the empty sidewalk beside my passenger door.

"What did you see?"

"I can't see it now, but when Janie's dad was telling you about the cloaking devices not completely making things invisible, I thought I saw movement over here beside the car. We both looked, searching for anything that would show an invisible person was standing there.

There it was. A slight distortion that was moving towards us. I grabbed for Shannon's arm, but she was already moving toward it.

"Hang on, Hils." She crouched down beside my passenger door. In a split second, she started whispering furiously. Three seconds later, she disappeared.

I stifled a scream and stepped back quickly.

"Careful, people are watching. If you touch me, you'll disappear too," Ben's voice came out of nowhere.

"Ben, what the hell happened?"

"What do you mean, what happened?" He sounded confused.

"Your mother thinks someone kidnapped you. The General was waiting for me when I got home with the news."

"What? Why would they think that?"

"A person the General was talking to tonight called to tell him you'd disappeared. The General didn't know that you'd taken two of the belts until he was giving them to us." I glanced over my shoulder, only slightly disoriented when I didn't see him standing beside me. I looked at where I figured his eyes would be, based on the distortion, and met what I hoped was his gaze. "He's furious at you for taking the belts without letting him know."

"I've been carrying them with me for a few days, just in case we had to get away fast."

"I told you disappearing was a bad idea." Tom spoke from the distorted airspace crouching beside my car.

"You called me babe. It made me think Jason kidnapped you."

"What do you mean me calling you babe made you think Jason kidnapped me? How did you come up with that?"

"You've never called me babe before, and that's what Jason calls Janie all the time. When the General told me you'd been kidnapped, I assumed you were giving me a clue about where to look."

"She is brilliant." Tom said. "She figured out who we were talking to without us saying a thing. On purpose, anyway."

"You were talking to Jason?" Alex's muffled voice came from the backseat.

"Shan, let go of Tom so people can see you and pretend to get something out of the back seat so the boys can get in. We need to talk where people can't see us. I mean, see you and Tom." I stepped away from Ben and walked around to the driver's side while I hit the button on my key chain twice to unlock all four doors.

Once we were out of sight of Tim Hortons, Ben and Tom switched off their cloaking devices and Alex got up from the floor to sit between them.

"Okay, spill." I ordered. "No, wait. First, call the General and your mom. They're worried sick. Tom, call your parents too. I'm sure they've been told you're missing by now, too."

They both hauled out their cells and dutifully dialled.

"No Mom, I wasn't kidnapped." Tom said, "I didn't realize that's what people thought, or I would have called sooner."

"No sir. I understand it was a stupid move. We have one last thing to do in town, then I'll be home and give you a full debrief." Ben sighed. "Yes, sir. I understand the trouble I've caused. Yes, it was not the best choice, but I have important information for you. Yes, sir." Ben hung up, followed an instant later by Tom.

I didn't give them a break. "Now spill."

"As I was saying goodbye to you, I saw Jason waving to me from the side of the Tim Hortons building.

I suppose that is why I called you, babe. I noticed he calls Janie it all the time and most of the girls seem to enjoy being called babe or sweetheart. It just sort of slipped out."

"Jason looked panicked, and since some folks lingering had been at Queen's Square at noon when he ran away, I thought it best not to call attention to him being there. When I thought no one was looking, I grabbed Tom's arm and hit the cloaking button on my belt."

"Jason was confused and needed to talk to me. What I said at the park contradicted everything he'd learned since he was a kid."

"So, does that mean he had nothing to do with the hoax at the radio station, after all?" Alex asked.

"Not him. It was his adoptive father. He and the DJ have been working together over the past decade, flushing out refugees from the Alliance of Eight and monitoring their movements. They are bounty hunters, working for the Hurliingen. Jason was actually born on Myonus."

"Then why is Jason working with them? Oh, wait. He's the little boy who was kidnapped when you were little, isn't he?"

I glanced in my rear-view mirror and the stunned look on Ben's face was hysterical.

Tom started laughing. "How does she know this stuff?"

"I can't take the credit for this one. Alex remembered him being kidnapped when you were kids."

"Really?" Ben looked at Alex. "But you were only little when he disappeared. How could you possibly remember?"

"Alex, you can explain it to him later." I winked at her in the mirror. "Right now, we have more pressing things to discuss, like what happened to Jason after he was kidnapped?"

"The elites, the ones who were trying to oppose my grandfather, took him away from his parents. They originally planned to let him be found in a hovel on one of the old work farms and then blame my grandfather for the kidnapping. They wanted to discredit him.

"But the Hurliingen had been watching and decided these renegade elites were doing it wrong and decided to help them with the takeover. They snatched Jason away from the planet completely. They filled him with stories of how the Alliance of Eight was evil and needed to be destroyed."

Tom interrupted. "When Janie told him this afternoon about her true heritage, Jason couldn't believe it. He was sure he'd recognize one of us from a mile away. We would be so horrible that we would be impossible to miss. Meanwhile, he's in love with one of us."

"Wait what?!" Shannon and I screeched together. "He's in love with Janie?"

"Yeah. The guy has horrible taste in women." Tom shuddered.

"Anyway." Ben took over the explanation. "Later, when I announced who I was, Jason remembered something from when we were in school together. Apparently, one of the older boys had been picking on him and I stepped in to help and the bully refused to touch me because I was Krohxa. The Krohxa being a good guy, confused the hell out of him, and he had to get away to think. That's why he ran."

"So, he wasn't planning to sell out Janie and the rest of you?"

"No. While I was talking at lunch, he started putting the two histories together and saw there were several gaps. He needed to talk to his father, so he skipped afternoon classes. When he arrived home, he saw their yard filled with cars. Jason snuck in through the back window and crept to the top of the stairs to listen through the door."

Tom interrupted again. "They know we're here and a Hurliingen ship is on the way."

Shannon and I gasped and in the rear-view mirror, I could see Alex's face go pale. Ben put his arm around his little sister and said something that sounded comforting before continuing. "There is a massive search to find me, Alex, and any of the other Tixlardine who have escaped Myonus. The Hurliingen have resurrected the genetic research program and ended up learning how to alter the DNA of Myonusians to make them Tixlardine, but they still need us to make it work properly. Their entire takeover of the Alliance of Eight planets is in jeopardy if they can't get us back."

"Where is Jason now?" Shannon asked.

"He went to go get Janie. He needs to explain everything to her."

"Will she be safe with him?"

Tom spoke up, "I think so. Jason is so confused, but he's really into Janie. He won't hurt her."

"Blech." Alex rolled her eyes.

"So now what do we do?" I asked.

"Tom and I were heading back to get our vehicles when we ran into you. We're going to meet them out at the main parking lot out at the UNBSJ Campus. Assuming Jason can get Janie to let him explain himself."

CHAPTER TWENTY-THREE

"Should we take Alex home? She's probably more important than you are right now in the Hurliingen's new plan." I asked.

"It doesn't matter," Ben answered. "From what Jason heard, they know where we live. We are very lucky Janie was the one to tell him we were all from the Alliance of Eight. It gave him a chance to see another side and make some independent judgements. Otherwise, we'd be sitting ducks. It shocked him to see how frightened we all were of the Hurliingen. He thought we were the aggressive race who attacked the Hurliingen. It made him question everything they had taught him."

Since it was almost midnight, there wasn't much traffic. It didn't take us long to get out to the university campus. As I turned onto Tucker Park Road, which led to UNBSJ's main entrance, I was busy planning a strategy. Shannon protested when I missed the entrance to the university. But I held up a finger for her to wait. A few seconds later, I pulled off onto the side of the road.

Shannon's face cleared. She knew exactly where we were.

I turned around to see three very confused faces. "Here's the plan."

I didn't need to make sure I had everyone's attention, but I did anyway. "Shannon and I know these parking lots well. We did a Girl Guide orienting course here when we were kids. Alex and Shannon, make yourselves invisible. Walk up through this access road to make sure

Jason and Janie are alone. If you see anything suspicious, run up to the exit side of the parking lot to let us know. I'll come in that way."

"Don't forget to stay off the road, so we don't hit you with the car." Tom joked.

"Yeah, good point." I stroked my steering wheel. "I don't want anyone denting my precious car."

It seemed weird to me we could joke when we'd just had it confirmed that there was a lot of bad coming our way. But I'd much rather see us cope this way than stress-out and scream at each other.

"Why don't we use the walkie-talkies?" Alex looked puzzled.

"They're noisy and will give your position away. Plus, Janie has one." Ben answered. "But take one with you anyway, just in case."

"I'll give you a five-minute head start. That should be plenty of time to see if we're going to be ambushed. We'll drive around the university loop and then enter the parking lot through the exit. When I get out, I'll leave the door open so Ben and Tom can climb out my door too. Everyone will stay cloaked but me. But I have a belt on, so I can disappear in an instant if necessary."

Alex asked. "What's Jason driving?"

"Either in his dad's pickup or Janie's Toyota. Or both. Janie might not be willing to get in a vehicle with him after his explanation." Tom said.

"How long do we have until we have to meet them?"

"They should be there already."

"Okay, then let's do it."

CHAPTER TWENTY-FOUR

Shannon and Alex got out of my car and disappeared before their doors closed behind them. Even though I had been expecting it, it was still freaky to see my best friend vanish before my eyes.

I drove down the street toward the hospital, which was conveniently located beside the university for all the nursing students. The road widened enough at the parking lot entrance to give me room to do a U-turn. On the way back to the university entrance, I glanced in the rear-view mirror and met Ben's eyes. "We're close. You might want to get into the front seat and cloak yourselves. That way, it will be easier for you to get out once I park. Someone might notice my car rocking back and forth all by itself as you move around."

Ben nodded, then disappeared. I felt my seat shift slightly under his weight as he maneuvered through the space between my bucket seats. Despite his attempt not to disrupt my driving, he was too wide for the small space. His shoulder, and then his hip, brushed against me as he stepped over my car's center console onto the passenger seat. I heard the thump against my windshield a split second before an "Ouch" and an impatient "We need a minivan for stuff like this."

"Don't dis my car." I glanced sideways at him, forgetting for a second that I couldn't see him. "It could be worse. We could be in your Barracuda."

Tom laughed from the back seat. "She's got a point. Though we should have done this when we dropped off the girls."

"Hey. I'm not the only one who's supposed to be thinking strategies."

"Sorry." Both guys apologized.

A couple of grunts later, Ben said, "Tom, I'm as close to the door as I can get. Watch where you put your feet when you climb over."

My seat shifted again as Tom crawled into the front seat. Even though Tom wasn't as wide as Ben, he was just as tall. His "Ugh" echoed close to my ear before he had pulled himself completely forward. He elbowed me while he tried to slide through the seats.

"Hey watch it." Ben's voice was loud. "I need those."

I burst out laughing a second before screaming. Tom kicked my shoulder, trying to pull his foot into the front seat. The shove knocked my hands from the steering wheel, causing us to head for the ditch. I righted my car, then had to duck to give Tom room to slide his foot along the top instead. His shoe must have caught on the overhead switch because suddenly light flooded the inside of my car.

If I wasn't so stressed, I probably would have found it hysterically funny.

By the time the guys settled in the front seat, I was driving along the long circular road surrounding the university. We passed the entrance to the first parking lot. I was glad Shannon and Alex were checking things out. The bushes were thick between the parking lot and road, we couldn't see much.

"I see a car and a truck, and it looks like Jason is talking to the driver of the car." Ben said.

Tom added, "That's Janie's car."

I drove slowly past the Student Union Building and the stadium as the road swung back around to the main gates. "I don't see anything that seems out of place." I said. "Not that I know for sure how many cars should be out here, but there doesn't seem to be anyone lurking around."

"Do you think we've given Shannon and Alex enough time?" Ben asked.

"I think so. The access road I dropped them off at is only two hundred meters long and it's closer to this side of the parking lot, so they didn't have far to go."

I shut off my headlights, put down my window and stopped my car just before the edge of the bushes at the parking lot's exit, to give Shannon and Alex a chance to warn us if they needed to. We waited for a full sixty seconds just in case, and even though I was looking at my watch, it seemed to take a lot longer. As we drove into the parking area, Jason was still standing outside Janie's car.

I couldn't tell if he was angry or pleading with her. He barely seemed to notice our arrival. I kept my eyes out for anything that might suggest we had company, even though I didn't know what I should be looking for. Ben and Tom had been almost completely invisible under the bright streetlights. This parking lot was a lot darker. We wouldn't be able to see any cloaked attackers until it was too late.

I took a deep breath, climbed out of my car, leaving the door open behind me.

Janie was still in her Toyota. She sat staring straight ahead and I could see tears still glistening on her eyelashes. Her hands clenched the wheel. Her knuckles were white.

Jason was begging Janie for forgiveness.

I hated to interrupt, but I suspected Jason had been at this for a while. At least it minimized the chances of Jason noticing the muffled oomph's and ouches of Ben and Tom climbing over my stick shift and out of my car. "Hey, guys."

Jason turned to look at me. I couldn't read whether he was unhappy, or relieved that I was there and might help him make Janie forgive him. "Hilary, I'm glad to see you." He looked around, confused when he didn't see Tom and Ben with me. "Where are the others?"

I shrugged. "They're coming. There is too much going on for all of us to be together right now. At least until we figure out who is who, and what side they're on." I let my voice trail off.

Jason didn't look happy about my hesitation, but he nodded.

"What happened, Jason?" I asked.

He walked away from Janie's car and came over toward me.

That helped. It gave Janie room to decide whether she was going to come out and join us or listen through her partially open window.

Janie must have decided it was safe to get out of her car now that I'd arrived.

Jason started to rush back to her.

"Stay where you are, Jason, or I leave."

Both of us recognized her ice-princess tone. Jason froze.

"Give her time, Jason." I told him quietly as I walked over to stand between them, giving Janie a chance to keep her distance. I could see it was killing Jason, but he stayed where he was. "So, I have an edited version of what's happened from Ben, but I'd like to hear it from you. There seems to be a lot of holes in your story that I don't completely understand." I looked over at Janie. "And I doubt you've done a good job explaining any of this to Janie, since she's barely able to look at you."

Jason's shoulders slumped as he glanced over at Janie, who was staring stonily at her feet. She seemed ready to listen. However, she was not giving away any hints of her thoughts.

"I was eight when they kidnapped me. They sent me to a horrible place to live. It was like a dungeon with only a grumpy old guy there to look after me and he was always screaming at me, so I spent most of my time hiding from him. Everything was always my fault, and he was always punishing me by sending me to bed without eating."

"Apparently, I was only there a year, but it was long enough for me to have forgotten what my life was like before. The old guy looking after me was always complaining about the Alliance of Eight. He said they were a bunch of idiots trying to change the laws of nature. In my mind, the Alliance became the enemy. It was their fault I was there. Then the folks you call the Hurliingen came. They rescued me and took me to live with another man, who was nice. He looked after me and told me to call him Dad. I was happy. I thought that meant that he wanted me and that I belonged someplace."

Janie's head shot up. I could see his explanation surprised her, but her expression didn't change enough to give away her thoughts. Her expression was still unreadable.

I guess she was a better actress than I thought, after all.

Jason looked at her for a long moment before continuing.

"Until we arrived here, they didn't tell me much. I was merely a piece of their strategy. They kept me healthy while they told me stories about the evil Alliance of Eight and reminded me of what the Alliance did to me." He paused for a minute. "When we arrived on Earth, things changed. They must have decided I was old enough to be useful. I thought of my dad as a superhero with two identities, just like Batman, so I was excited to be part of a team that captured the bad guys even though I never seemed to measure up…" He paused again. "At least until I started dating Janie."

This time he stopped, staring off for a moment as if he was thinking hard. His shoulders slumped a bit. "Most of the people we'd found so far have been non-Tixlardine, not worth the trouble to notify the Hurliingen, so we left them alone and watched them. Dad figured that if this planet was a safe-haven for the Alliance of Eight, eventually someone important would arrive.

"We saw a lot of ships come, but the tracking equipment they designed for us was only to find exhaust from their main engines."

"Which are shut down just after they enter the Earth's atmosphere." I said half to myself.

Both Janie and Jason looked at me oddly.

I shrugged. "I watch a lot of sci-fi."

"You're right. Most ships have booster engines to navigate within atmospheres. We can't get a strong enough reading to see where they land."

"Anyway, I was sure I'd recognize someone from the Alliance of Eight as soon as I saw them. Even though I knew they'd look like me, I was sure they'd be so mean I'd be able to spot them. That's why I freaked out this afternoon when Janie told me she was half-Myonusian. I've been in love with her since we came to Saint John." Jason looked at Janie. "She is the most amazing person I've ever met, and she's from the Alliance of Eight."

This time Janie returned his gaze.

"Gag," I heard Shannon whisper and Alex giggle behind me. Thank God they were close. I really didn't want to have to repeat this conversation.

Neither Janie nor Jason seemed to have heard. "Go on." I said after a few seconds, "Enough with the starry-eyed stares."

Jason turned red. "Sorry Hilary." He broke his gaze from Janie as she reached out and took his hand. Holding her hand, his voice got stronger. "I was so stunned at first. And then Ben, Tom, Alex and everyone else showed up and you were all terrified of us. Then Ben started talking about how we had taken over your planets and how you had all barely escaped. I already knew about the Sensors and Hurliingen, but from the opposite perspective.

"Then, as Ben was winding up his speech, it hit me. Just the way he said something made me have this flash of memory… I knew him. I remembered hum from before I'd been taken away from my family. He defended me against some bullies in the playground. How could someone who helped me be evil?" This time, he looked at me. "I didn't know what to think anymore, so I ran. I needed to talk to the man I knew as my father before I faced any of you again."

Jason took a deep breath. "By the time I got home, it was two o'clock. I thought I would have a few hours to think before dad got home. He was supposed to have a job interview this afternoon. But, when I drove down my street, our yard was full of cars, and there were more parked out by the curb. I drove around the block and then snuck through the neighbour's yard and in through our basement window. I heard voices upstairs in the kitchen, so I crept up the stairs to listen.

"Dad and the others were celebrating. They knew about Ben, Alex, and Tom… everybody. Dad even made a joke about how surprised he was that the stupid Alliance brat they had forced him to take care of had been useful after all."

Janie started to hug him, but he stopped her.

"Sorry, Babe, let me finish. This is important." He turned back to me. "They were all laughing about how you were all freaking out over the Sensors when it didn't matter. We already knew where all of you lived. They've been playing with the Sensors to flush out Alliance of Eight members for the past few years. Once they realized they had Krohxa, they decided to have a little fun while they were waiting for the ship to arrive and gather you up like cattle. I heard them making plans for Ben and Alex." He looked at Janie. "What you heard Ben say to the others this afternoon was the light version. They have new ways of extracting Ancfu to purify it to make it more powerful. They've also learned how to create Tixlar carriers from exhausted family lines. These new Tixlardine aren't nearly as effective at extracting the

204

energy from Ancfu as natural Tixlardine. This new method eliminates the risk of mutant defects which plagued our old research. But it shortens the Tixlardine's lifespan because their body is used up faster to support the new super charged Ancfu. They weren't too concerned with fixing that minor glitch because they knew they'd have access to Alex soon who, if bred with their created Tixlardine, the genetic line would remain potent."

I heard Shannon gasp behind me.

"That's why Dad and his friends pulled the hoax at the radio station. They've been doing that in cities where they have found one or two Alliance members and wanted to see if there were more. This time, because there is a ship on the way, they wanted to do a last sweep to see if anyone else panicked and called home so they could pick them up."

"When will the ship arrive?" I asked.

"Soon. There is urgency because of the lack of power back on Myonus and the need for Alex's offspring to provide it. They plan on taking everyone. Some they'll use as hostages to force retaliations on the other planets to stop."

CHAPTER TWENTY-FIVE

"What about me?" Janie asked. "I'm half human."

"They'll take you too. You're a half-breed. I heard them talking about experiments." Jason reached out to hug her, but Janie took a step back and almost screamed.

Alex had appeared out of nowhere behind her. "Don't worry." Alex put a comforting arm around Janie's waist. "We'll protect you and Jenny."

Janie had apparently forgotten all about her little sister. "Oh God, Jenny."

"I'm sorry." Jason looked really upset. "I keep thinking I should have known better and figured out the truth on my own."

I put my hand on his arm. "Jason, you were eight when you were kidnapped and nine when you were rescued by these people. There is no way you could have guessed they were telling you lies."

Ben appeared behind me, followed a few seconds later by Tom. Janie screamed and stepped toward Jason, who was already reaching out to her. This time, she let him hold her.

"What the hell?"

The boys even surprised me, and I knew they were there… well, somewhere close by. We were going to have to work out some kind of early warning system.

"Sorry Janie. Jason can explain it later. We don't have time now." Ben turned to Jason. "Your dad still doesn't know that you know the truth?"

"No. I snuck back out the way I came in and drove around all afternoon trying to separate actual memories from what they told me." He paused again. "I started remembering bits and pieces of conversations I'd overheard that meant nothing then, but now in context they make perfect sense."

"What about your brother?" I asked. No one had mentioned him except for Janie after the meeting at Queen's Square. I wasn't sure if Ben and Tom knew Jason even had a brother.

"He's only seven. They told me they had rescued him the same as me, and they were keeping him safe. He was almost four when he came to live with us. I don't know what planet he came from, but he cried a lot for his mommy when he first arrived." He looked away for a minute, as if he hadn't really thought about how this all affected his adopted brother. He straightened his shoulders and looked back at Ben and seemed to have made a huge decision. "No matter what happens, we have to find his family."

"And yours." I whispered. I thought back to what information the General could find about his family. From what he could find, Jason's family had escaped too and were still alive.

"I was told they were dead." Jason looked down. "Even if they aren't, do you think they would want anything to do with me? I helped them flush you all out. I doubt they'd be proud and want me back."

I started to speak, but Janie interrupted me. "Jason, you were a kid. You couldn't possibly have known. I think what you're doing now would make them very proud."

"Three cheers for Janie." Shannon whispered in my ear. Even though I knew she was nearby, I jumped.

"Why are you still invisible?"

"No one is expecting me to be here, so I'm going to stay like this and keep walking around."

I turned my head away from the group. "You mean you just don't want to talk to Janie."

Shannon laughed. "Yeah, that too. But seriously, I might have to start appreciating science fiction after this. I could pull Janie's hair and she'd never know it was me." Her disembodied giggle was a little creepy. "The possibilities are endless." With that, she flounced away. I couldn't see her flounce of course, but I knew she did. Even under duress, Shannon had a certain flair.

Our exchange hadn't gone unnoticed. While Jason and Janie were busy gazing into each other's eyes, Ben was watching me. He seemed to sense Shannon had left, and then he walked over to put his arm around me. It was nice to lean into his strength and know that he was leaning on me just as much. "Shannon?" he whispered into my ear.

"She's having fun patrolling the area."

"I'm impressed. Who would have thought Shannon would have accepted all of this so easily?"

"I don't think it's sunk in yet. Right now, I think the hardest thing for her is not to pick on Janie while she's invisible."

Ben laughed. "Why doesn't that surprise me?"

"Ahem." Tom interrupted our conversation. "Perhaps we should get back on task?"

"Right," Ben said as he leaned away from me, but kept his arm firmly around my waist. "Jason, are you able to go back and pretend nothing has changed?"

"I think so." Despite his unsure words, Jason's determination came through in his voice. He glanced down at Janie and then back at Ben. "Yes, I can. I need to get my little brother out of there."

Ben and Tom exchanged looks. Ben was the one who spoke. "Good, because what we plan now depends on your ability to stay quiet about everything you've learned today."

"I'll coach you on how to act around your father, so he won't suspect a thing." Janie's fear seemed to have completely disappeared. The diva was back and ready for action. She turned toward Ben. "What do you need me to do?"

Ben answered. "Nothing yet, the goal is to keep ourselves alive and convince the Hurliingen that we're not worth the effort of a full out war here on Earth. I glanced at the lists of equipment from tonight's meeting before I gave them to the General. We're better equipped than I thought we'd be." He glanced around the group. "Many folks had already left their home planets before things got rough. They were more prepared and brought more equipment. Some folks have tweaked Earth technology in some very inventive ways. The General is evaluating our options."

I looked at Ben in surprise. He had mentioned the General in present tense and Tom didn't react as if this was new information. I breathed a sigh of relief. One less secret to worry about keeping.

"Jason, when you go home, it's probably best that you pretend to have had a fight with Janie. It will explain you being gone all evening and coming in so late. It will also help mask your anger towards your father."

Tom burst out laughing, "Brilliant. If he's like my dad, he won't suspect a thing. Dad has already experienced me coming into the house grumbling about Shannon and he couldn't wait to end the conversation." Suddenly, Tom clasped the back of his head. "Ouch Shan, that hurt."

"What's that supposed to mean?" Shannon appeared beside him with her arms crossed and eyes blazing.

"Holy shit," Janie screeched. "Where the hell did you come from?" Shannon appearing out of nowhere was too much for her to handle. Jason tried to hold her back, but she walked right up to Shannon, inches away and ready for a fight. She demanded again. "How the hell did you just appear like that?"

Shannon looked smug. Taking any opportunity to one up Janie was a habit ingrained in us since kindergarten. At least she hadn't given in to her urge to pull Janie's hair, but a catfight wouldn't help anything right now. I stepped forward, but Tom waved me back. He approached on one side and Jason on the other.

"This isn't helping." Tom said as he drew Shannon closer to his side. Jason did the same to Janie. Neither of the girls looked like they were ready to back down.

"Where's Alex?" I asked. I didn't mean it to be a distraction, but I suddenly realized she was gone. "She's disappeared again."

"It's about time someone started wondering about me." Alex said from beside me. "I figured it wasn't smart to hang around in the open, so I just faded away."

Janie looked around, confused. "Does she have one of those disappear-y things too?"

"Yes." I replied. I saw no reason to hide the information, since it was obvious. "Now, can we get back to the plan? Jason is going to go home, pretend to be mad at Janie. Janie is going to go home and give her father a big hug because he's worried and could really use one."

Janie's how-dare-you-tell-me-what-to-do face turned to shame, as if she realized how this all must be affecting her dad.

"Tom, I'm going to drop you and Shannon off at your truck. Please make sure she gets home safely. Ben, I'll drop you off too. You can follow me home. Alex, you'll drive with me. We need to have a talk. I have some tips that might help you deal with your mom, and Ben probably shouldn't be around to hear them."

Ben raised his eyebrow at me. "You're going to talk about boys? Now?"

"Girl-secrets, no boys allowed," I told him with a smile. "And yes now. We have those pesky Hurliingen all figured out. It's time we get to the important stuff."

"Fair enough. I think we're done here." Ben said. "I think we need to meet again in the morning before class tomorrow. I'll have more information from the General about what options we have based on the equipment lists we got tonight. There's no sense brainstorming until we know what exactly we have to work with."

He turned to Jason. "Think about anything you've overheard, bits of conversation, unfamiliar names or words, jokes that might not have made any sense. Write them down if you can. We'll give them to the General to see what he can figure out since he'll have more context to interpret." He paused. "Oh, and try to remember everything about what you heard about your brother when he first came to live with you. Anything you remember will help us figure out who he is and get him reunited with his parents."

Jason nodded. He had aged in the last few minutes. We all had. None of us looked older exactly, but the responsibility of salvaging this situation fell heavily on our shoulders. We weren't playing games any longer. This was real, and the Hurliingen were coming, whether or not we were ready for them.

Ben, Tom, Shannon, Alex and I piled into my car. As we drove out of the parking lot, I looked back to see that Jason and Janie were standing beside her vehicle. They looked like a solid couple again, which made me feel better. Like it or not, we were all part of the core defense. Any crack in our ability to work together could prove disastrous.

CHAPTER TWENTY-SIX

I dropped Ben, Shannon, and Tom off at Tim Hortons and, as promised, I kept Alex with me. Shannon looked a little disappointed that she wouldn't be part of the conversation until Tom put his arm around her again.

"You can teach me how to make my mother behave?" Alex asked me once we had driven away from the others. She sounded like she didn't believe me.

"Not exactly." I turned onto Union Street and headed toward the Viaduct. "But there are things you can do to make her not freak out as much."

"Is that even possible? I mean, you heard her, right?"

"Yeah." I glance over at Alex with a grin on my face. "She sounded exactly like my mom used to." I felt my shoulders relax. It felt good to talk about something other than evil Hurliingen.

"No way." She shook her head. "Your mom is so cool. She lets you do whatever you want."

"Trust me, it wasn't always like that. In fact, three years ago, my mom was much like yours." I glanced at the clock on my dash and frowned. "And after tonight, I'm pretty sure I'll get grounded for being out so late… again."

"How did you get your mom to change?"

"I didn't actually change her." I stopped for a minute to figure out the best way to explain it to Alex. She was a smart kid as far as books went, but handling people, especially parents, required a unique set of skills. "She and I used to fight all the time. One night when I was fourteen, she wouldn't let me go out with my friends. I said some pretty nasty things and stormed off to my room."

"I snuck out anyway. I got dressed and crept down the hall into the kitchen. I was just about to go down the stairs to slip out through the basement door when I heard my mom crying. I turned back to look into the living room. She was holding a picture of my father and talking to him. She said, 'I don't know what I'm going to do. She is growing up so fast. Oh David, I can't bear to lose her too.' My mom looked terrified. That is when I figured it out."

"Figured what out?"

"Mom wasn't trying to be mean; she was scared, so she went overboard trying to protect me. Dad was dead, and I was all she had left."

I looked over at Alex again to see if she was getting it. She looked thoughtful.

I pulled out onto Chesley Drive. "I think mom panicked. Until then, I'm certain she had successfully ignored the fact I stopped wearing ponytails and started wearing a bra. I think it scared her I wouldn't need her anymore, and she was freaking out."

Alex was silent for a few minutes. "I never thought about that. All I could hear was mom saying, 'No.'"

"Your mom has it even worse than mine did. Even if we forget about that whole Hurliingen thing for a minute, you are still only twelve. You probably shouldn't be going out with a fourteen-year-old. The only reason Ben hasn't ratted you out is because Robbie seems to let you call the shots and we're keeping a close eye on you. But your mom doesn't know any of this, so imagine her shock when she sees some strange guy kissing her baby."

"But it was just on the cheek." Alex argued.

"But you're twelve and she's your mom."

"Thirteen in three months." She grumbled.

"Thirteen is still young in a world full of almost fifteen-year-olds. I didn't kiss my first boy until the end of grade ten. Even though I was fifteen, I thought mom was going to have a heart attack when she found out."

By the time we pulled into my yard, Alex seemed hopeful. "It will get better, won't it?"

"It takes time. Mom and I still argue, but at least now, she trusts my judgement enough to listen to my side. Although, I'm running out of excuses for all these late nights with you and Ben. I might end up with a curfew before the Hurliingen get here."

Ben must have taken the highway. He was already waiting on the lawn between our houses when we arrived. Alex hopped out of the car and ran to her house. "Thanks Hilary." She called back over her shoulder.

"What exactly did you tell my little sister? And how much will I need to defend you to my mother?"

"You won't have to defend me at all. I told Alex she needs to remember your mom is worried, and that Alex needs to work with her, not against her."

"Do you think it will work?"

"I'm seventeen. I have a car and I don't have a curfew. I'd say it works very well. Wouldn't you?"

"Come on you two, we've got work to do," the General called from the door to Ben's house.

I glanced at my watch. It was almost one in the morning. Mom would not be happy when I walked in the door. I didn't have a curfew because I didn't normally abuse my freedom. Even though she was most likely in bed, I knew she wouldn't fall asleep until she knew I was home. Despite the threat, life goes on and we still had classes tomorrow.

"Ben I can't. Mom is going to kill me if I don't get in soon."

"Ok, we'll talk on the way to school tomorrow." He kissed me and wrapped his arms around me. "Thank you,"

I hugged him back. "For what?"

"Everything."

CHAPTER TWENTY-SEVEN

I passed out as soon as my head hit the pillow.

It felt like only a few seconds later when my alarm screeched on the nightstand beside my head. It was too soon. I would need at least another week of sleep to feel normal again. I groaned when I sat up. My poor brain had finally had more than it could take. It was pounding against the inside of my skull, just like I imagined a hangover would feel.

As I expected, mom was not impressed with me coming in so late. She didn't say anything. She didn't have to. Her disappointed look was enough.

Ben was waiting for me outside. Alex was in the car and Shannon was just coming across the street. She didn't call out like she usually did, instead she waited until she was beside us before saying in a low voice, "That all really happened yesterday, right? It wasn't some whacked out dream from eating too much junk food, was it?"

"No Shannon, it was real," Alex's disembodied voice said from the back seat. Shannon bent down for a closer look and Alex appeared less than six inches in front of Shannon's face.

"Dammit, Alex." Shannon jumped back. "Don't do that to me again unless you have to."

I looked at Ben and rolled my eyes. "C'mon, let's go. I'm sure Tom, Janie, and Jason are waiting for us."

As soon as we merged onto the highway, Shannon and I asked at the same time. "What did you find out from the General?"

"We're lucky. We have enough detection equipment for two fully equipped command posts and two secondary ones."

"Is that it?" Shannon sounded disappointed. "I was hoping for an arsenal of cool laser guns and stuff."

"Sorry. There's never been a need for weapons on our home planet. Since the Tixlar was in our DNA, violence was useless as a method to gain power. There were a few weapons from other planets, but they need to be modified to work in Earth's atmosphere." He frowned. "The General is working on them to see what he can do just in case. Luckily, it's not in the Hurliingen's best interests to start a gunfight, just in case Alex or I get injured. They need us alive."

"What's the plan for this morning?" I asked.

"We meet the others down on the corner of Princess and Germain Street. It should be fairly private, but close enough that we can still make it to homeroom in time."

"What about Robbie?" I asked Alex.

"I sent him a text this morning to tell him mom was driving me and that this time, he'd better wait for me in homeroom."

Ten minutes later, we were walking toward the meeting place. Tom, Jason and Janie and a few others from Saint John High and Saint Mac's were already there.

Shannon stopped dead in front of me with a shocked look on her face. She had missed the meeting last night and with all the excitement, I hadn't had the chance to update her on the newest version of who's who. I waved Ben and Alex on without us.

"What the hell? I can understand Janie being from another planet, but Kristen? We've known her since Junior K. She's our valedictorian, for Pete's sake."

"I know." I watched Ben and Alex join the group waiting on the corner. "It's insane, isn't it?"

Shannon recovered quickly and grabbed my arm. "Come on, I don't want to miss anything else."

"How'd it go last night?" Ben asked Jason as we approached.

"It upset Dad that I was fighting with Janie. Then, as he walked away, he muttered something like it won't matter soon, anyway. I wanted to ask him what he meant, but didn't. Instead, I waited for a few minutes, then snuck back to the kitchen to see if he'd call anyone." Jason looked a bit disappointed. "He didn't. I waited for a few minutes, and I went back to my room. I was too hyped up to sleep, so I started writing everything I could remember." He handed Ben several pages handwritten on both sides. "I don't know if any of that will help, but once I got going, I realized just how much my dad said to his friends in front of me because he didn't think I'd understand."

Ben spent a minute leafing through the pages. "Holy Crap Jason, this is great." He tucked the papers into his knapsack and repeated what he had said in the car to us about what equipment was available.

I noticed he left out any mention of weapons. He talked about the cloaking devices but didn't say how many. I glanced over to Shannon and Alex to see if they noticed Ben's omission. Alex had her hand on Shannon's arm. I'm guessing she had been about to be helpful and chime in, but Alex held her back. Completely confiding in Jason was still a risk.

Shannon was good at reconnaissance, but it surprised me how bad she was with strategic information manipulation. After all, I'd seen her in action with her parents. She could talk them into almost anything when she set her mind to it.

When the second bell rang, we broke apart and rushed to get to class while the others sprinted toward Saint Mac's.

CHAPTER TWENTY-EIGHT

Ben and I met up during our morning break beside my locker. Just as I clicked my combination lock shut, Ben moaned.

The look on Ben's face frightened me. He seemed to panic. He looked past me, searching the hall for something.

I swear I could see the colour drain from his face. The image of Superman faced with kryptonite flashed through my mind as Ben slumped back against the lockers. I whirled around to see what he was looking for. "Ben, what is it?"

"Drained. I feel like I haven't eaten or slept in days." His breath was coming in short bursts. "Even my bones feel tired."

In the crowded hallway, with students rushing to their next class. I didn't see anything, or anyone unusual. Ben grabbed my hand. It felt like a cold, limp fish in my grip. Something was terribly wrong.

The bell rang, and the hall emptied. All except for Ben, me and some guy I had never seen before lounging against the brick wall at the end of our string of lockers.

He smirked as he straightened up and started walking toward us.

The closer he came, the weaker Ben grew. He started sliding down the lockers as if his legs couldn't hold him up any longer. Ben had been right. The Hurliingen won't need weapons. This guy seemed to drain Ben just by being close to him.

My mind snapped to attention. This must be one of those genetic mutants Ben had told me about. He must work for the Hurliingen.

He was less than ten feet away. I had to do something fast. I clicked the button on my belt, bent my knees, and draped Ben's upper body over my shoulders. Then I wrapped my arms around Ben's waist, did a semi-fireman's carry-drag across the hall.

Once we were safely across the hall, I looked back.

By the look on the other guy's face, I guess he was not expecting us to just disappear.

I was relieved the cloaking device worked since Myonusian technology powered it, and this guy was like a black hole. Using his surprise to my advantage, I moved Ben further up the hall. There was still enough background noise as the last students scrambled to class to help muffle the sound of Ben's shoes dragging on the floor.

Having a tall, muscular boyfriend was not always a convenient thing. I was just thankful I was wearing my runners and not the skirt and dress shoes I'd originally planned for today.

Ben started slipping. I grabbed him by the waist, silently apologizing for the wedgie I was probably giving him, as I rebalanced him against me. The mutant, as I'd hoped, walked on the other side of the hall, making sweeping motions with his legs to see if he could find us. Apparently, he had no faith in my ability to move Ben so quickly.

To tell you the truth, I was more than a little surprised myself.

With every step the mutant took away from us, Ben's strength returned. At the top of the stairs, the guy turned around and looked down the hall toward us. "Well done, Hilary… this time." He gave a mocking salute before turning away and running down the stairs.

As he disappeared from sight, Ben could finally breathe in a big gulp of air.

"Man, that guy gives off bad vibes." His humour was as lame as his legs. But hearing it was the best sound I could have asked for. I laughed and leaned against his chest. I was glad we were still invisible, and Ben couldn't see the look of terror I'm sure was plastered on my face. How could we possibly defend him and Alex against someone who could debilitate them just by walking by?

CHAPTER TWENTY-NINE

Five minutes later, Ben still couldn't walk on his own. My head felt like it was on a swivel, looking up and down the hall in case the mutant reappeared to taunt us some more. It sent a chill up my spine when he called me by name. Jason warned us that his father and his friends had already identified Ben and the others. So having him know my identity was not surprising, but it still freaked me out. "Now what do we do?"

"We need to find that guy." Ben tried to stand on his own and managed it for a few seconds before he slumped back against the lockers.

"No." I said firmly enough for my voice to echo down the empty hall. "You are going to delegate this one." I kept my hand on his chest to keep him back. He tried to stand on his own and push my hand away, but he was still too weak. "You and Alex are out of play on this one. Let Jason or Tom handle this."

"We don't know how they'll be affected."

"True, but we know how you're affected and can assume Alex will be the same way. They can come from anywhere. There is no way to protect you."

He let out a frustrated sigh. "You're right. The high level of Tixlar in my body makes me highly susceptible to the mutant."

"Well, Clark Kent, it looks like this mutant guy is going to be your kryptonite, and I, Lois Lane, will be your hero. How's that for a spin?"

From the tension in his body, I could tell he was not too keen on the idea. "I don't have any choice, do I?"

"Not unless you know of some type of body armour that protects against power sucking black-hole mutants."

Ben was silent for a few moments. "The General said someone had mentioned using things from here since many of your basic elements do not exist on our planet. We'll have to inspect those lists again to see if there is anything useful. I'd better call him." He paused for a second. "I can't see my phone. I think it's safe to turn off the cloaker."

I peered up and down the hallway. "Are you sure?"

"Yeah, even if he had one, I'd feel him before he could get close."

I clicked off the cloaking mechanism and watched Ben while he spoke to the General. He was obviously still weak, but the colour was slowly coming back into his skin.

When he hung up, I said, "He gave up awfully easy. Do you think this was just a test to see how his presence would affect you in our atmosphere?"

"Maybe, but with him roaming the halls, he could find elites we don't even know about yet."

"True, as much as I appreciate them giving away part of their game plan, I'm not so sure I enjoy knowing what's coming. Ignorance being bliss is highly under-rated."

CHAPTER THIRTY

At lunchtime, even though we didn't have an official plan, a bunch of us gathered again at Queen Square. This time there were a lot more vehicles full of students and many people in business suits who apparently worked in the downtown core a few blocks away. I recognized Janie's dad and a few other adults from the night before at Tim Hortons. It seemed hard to believe that had all taken place just last night.

It boggled my mind to think there were this many people from other planets living in Saint John and really, these were only the folks from the Alliance of Eight. How many other aliens made Earth their home?

Ben didn't waste time when we arrived. He walked through the group to the park bench closest to the centre. He hopped up and whistled to get everyone's attention. "We have a fresh development."

As he told everyone about our encounter with the genetic mutant, I could feel the tension in the crowd as they listened. "Has anyone heard of anything that can lessen the Mutant's effect on the Tixlardine? I know not all of us from Myonus have the same amounts of Tixlar and the mutant won't affect you the same way as me. But seriously, if you can avoid feeling even half as ill as I did, trust me, you'll want a defence."

One teenager who came from Simonds High raised her hand. "I'm Shelley, we're from Myonus. When we first arrived here, we discovered another family from home. Their son, Barry, was one of the mutants created in the experiments. Your dad rescued him from the labs and helped his family migrate here since he couldn't live a normal life on at home."

"They had been on Earth for over a decade when we found them. Barry loved it here. He didn't affect anyone else in the neighbourhood except for my dad and my brother. We're Tixlardine. As soon as Barry got too close to us we'd get so weak we couldn't even stand up. I was only six back then, and it was really scary."

As she spoke, the crowd parted, allowing her to move toward the centre to where Ben was still standing on the bench.

"They were a really nice family, and we tried many things to make it better. Barry felt terrible."

"Anyway, we went out to the park to fly my kite. The string snapped and my kite landed in the pond. Barry was walking by, so he waded in to rescue it and tripped. He got soaked. We had one of those silver emergency blankets in our first aid kit. Mom tossed it to Barry to keep warm then we noticed Barry wasn't affecting us anymore. It turns out those little Mylar blankets worked as insulation against the effect he had on the Tixlardine. We experimented, and it worked just as well if we wore the blanket."

The crowd had fallen silent while she was speaking.

"Mom made us T-shirts and leggings from those emergency blankets. The material was thin enough so they could wear them under their regular clothes. I used to laugh because they'd make crinkling sounds when we moved, but it was okay because it let us all spend time together like normal families. We'd still be weak after being around Barry all day, but we weren't debilitated like before."

She turned to go back to her place in the crowd when she stopped and snapped her fingers. "Oh, make sure you get the real Mylar blankets and not the cheap silver plastic look-a-likes. We made that mistake once. It wasn't good."

A murmur ran through the crowd when she finished speaking. Even though not everyone would be affected by the mutant as Ben had, there were enough of them who had Tixlar to make this knowledge valuable. It was such a simple solution.

I still had the sewing machine mom had given me for Christmas in grade eight. I could easily make long-sleeved shirts for Ben, his family, and whoever else needed one. Part of me was glad we didn't sell the little Mylar blankets at work. I'm not sure how I could explain a second one-item rush after the walkie-talkie incident, especially one as bizarre as Mylar emergency blankets.

Ben called for attention again. But instead of recapping what he had told us this morning, he said something different that I hadn't heard yet. Part of me was miffed because I hadn't been included in the strategy session. But I'd had a history test just before lunch. Even though he had promised to go to class because it was likely the safest place for him in case the mutant boy came back, he had apparently skipped his calculus class and called the General instead.

"They know we're here and they know where we live. Therefore, secrecy is no longer a valid defence for us. Based on the equipment lists we received last night, we have many options. What we are proposing is that we gather all the non-working equipment and spare parts together and see if we can't get some of them functional again. I don't know how much time we have before the

Hurliingen arrive, and we still do not know their plan. We have to move fast. Communication and defence must be top priority."

"We're still going to use the walkie-talkies as our primary communication, cell phones and land lines as second. Sub-space communications will be re-established, but we will need to use it as part of a strategy to get updates while feeding out false leads. We'll have to ask everyone to limit what they say. We don't want to tip off the Hurliingen that we are preparing for their arrival. We don't want them stepping up their plans to attack us sooner."

"What if they have their own cloaking devices and are listening to us right now?" one man said from the group.

"That's possible," Ben said honestly. "We don't know for certain that they don't."

"Then what's the point?" a frustrated voice called out from the crowd. People started talking among themselves in agitated whispers.

"The point is simple. A week ago, this was all still happening. The Hurliingen were coming. They knew who we were, and they were making plans to take us back to our home planets to use us for bargaining, slave labour or breeding machines. The only difference is that now we know they are coming, but not how or when. It sucks. But working together is the only chance we have." He paused for a few seconds. "Does anyone have anything else?"

There was a bit of shuffling in the crowd, but no one spoke.

"Ok then, General Tsad has a well-stocked garage full of tools, so I'll offer our backyard as a meeting place. Anyone who has broken or spare communications equipment, please bring them to my house tonight. With everything together in one spot, we can get equipment working faster than trying to track down parts individually through the lists."

"Tomorrow night, we will work with weapons and detaining mechanisms. Most of them won't work in Earth's atmosphere like they do at home unless they're recalibrated."

He gave out his address and hopped down off the bench, only to be swarmed with people asking questions.

Eventually, the crowd broke up as people gradually dispersed. The kids and teachers from Simonds had a ten-minute drive to get back to their school, longer if there was traffic. They had to leave now, or they would be late for class.

I was disappointed. I had to work and couldn't watch all the cool stuff arrive at Ben's. My geek heart broke a little over that.

Shannon must have seen my disappointment. She put her arm across my shoulders and said, "Don't worry. I'll be at Ben's making sure the aliens don't get rowdy."

"Hey now." Tom protested, and we all laughed.

My shift took forever.

Growing up, Shannon had often accused me of being a control freak. For the first time, I acknowledged she could be right. It was killing me not to be part of what was happening in Ben's back yard.

The clock crawled. At ten minutes before nine, it surprised me to see the General come into the store.

"Hilary, when you're done your shift, is there a place where we can go talk?"

I thought for a minute. The coffee shop in the mall closed at the same time our store did. Then I remembered the new twenty-four-hour Starbucks had just opened up the hill. I gave him directions and told him I'd be there just after nine. As he walked away, I noticed he looked exhausted. He might be General Tsad and all, but he had also helped to raise Ben and Alex over the past couple of years. This was personal, and the stress was taking a huge toll on him. I hoped for all our sakes, it would be all over soon, so life could get back to normal. Well, as normal as it could be with a family from another planet living next door.

At least I hoped they would keep living next door. After all this, they wouldn't just leave, would they? I shoved the thought out of my head. I didn't want to even think of the possibility.

I rushed out of the store at five past nine and drove over to meet the General. When I arrived, there was another man sitting beside him with his back toward me. I started toward the counter but stopped when the General called my name and pointed to an extra mug on the table. He had already bought me a drink. I turned and wove my way over to their table. The man with the General looked familiar even though I was sure I had never seen him before. His hair was long and pulled back into a ponytail. A thick beard covered his jaw. Yeah, I'd remember if I had met him before.

The General introduced us. "Hilary, this is Jusep, an old friend of mine."

When our eyes met, it clicked.

I knew those eyes. "You're Ben's father." I said bluntly.

The General slid the mug of hot chocolate across the table toward me. "Hilary, please sit. We have a lot to talk about."

I looked at the General, trying to read his expression. Nothing. He wasn't giving anything away. I turned to look at Ben's dad, who was alive and sitting at the table next to me. Holy Crap. "Why doesn't Ben know?" My drink was already forgotten. "They all think you're dead."

"Hilary." The General warned.

"It's okay." Ben's father put his hand up to ward off the General's interference. "Yes Hilary, I am Ben's father." He paused for a moment, as if not sure where to start the rest of his explanation.

My head was reeling. I had so many questions. Before I could formulate one into words, he started speaking again.

"The General didn't know I was alive until the meeting last night at Tim Hortons. I didn't dare try to contact him directly, so I got in touch with another Myonusian who had been on Earth for several years. You can imagine my surprise when he told me that Krohxa, my son, had called a meeting." Jusep turned to the General. "Old friend, I can't tell you how in awe I was to see my child speaking with such authority, taking such control. I can never thank you enough for the guidance you have given him."

The General nodded.

After a minute, Jusep continued. "I was wearing one of the personal cloaking devices, so while Ben was speaking, I approached General Tsad. I escaped from Myonus just after the takeover and I have been searching for my family since. I was able to hide on one of our transports the Hurliingen had taken over and went to the planet Teglar. Things were no better there. It took me a year to find another ship and assemble a crew I could trust. The coup made resources and finding a crew almost impossible."

"But you managed it."

"Yes, Hilary, I did. We were just about to leave for Earth when we were captured by the Hurliingen. They had heard of our destination and commandeered our ship to take them there, too. They had heard rumours that the Krohxa was here. The urge to kill them on the spot was incredible. However, I decided having the enemy with us would be an advantage I could not refuse, especially since they didn't realize who I was. So, we pretended to let them take over and started our journey to Earth.

It turned out our risk was worth it. They knew there was another Hurliingen ship en route to earth from one of their rival clans. Based on the reports they received, the other ship had a head start. I bargained with the captain to let my crew control the ship and I would make sure they got to Earth before the others. He was doubtful at first, but I was able to appeal to his sense of competition. The Hurliingen don't have any honour, winning seems to be the only thing that matters to them.

"They were certain that kidnapping Ben and Alex would be simple. They did not know General Tsad was with them. When we arrived on Earth, we were shocked to see the Sensors already here, hovering around California. If I had any hope of rescuing my family, I had to investigate without them noticing. You cannot imagine my relief when I discovered the ship, they found was not mine. While I kept the Hurliingen engaged with looking for Krohxa in large cities, I had my crew release some of our own Sensors, tweaked to find residue specific to my ship, and programmed them to investigate locations where I thought it likely General Tsad would settle."

"How could you distinguish your own ship from someone else's?"

The General spoke this time. "Jusep and I mixed a special additive to the fuel so he could find us. Although our original plan wasn't to use Sensors, they were an improvisation."

I nodded. Brilliant.

Ben's dad continued talking while I sipped my hot chocolate. "We were hoping to get rid of the Hurliingen and come find you on our own, but then they used their contacts on Earth and found the bounty hunters who had contacted the other clan to arrange pickup of the Krohxa and several other key Alliance members. We knew the Hurliingen on our ship were our best hope to find you before the other clan arrived."

"So now what?" I asked.

"Hilary, we need your help." The General glanced over to Ben's father, Jusep. "Ben can't know Jusep is here. The Hurliingen think Jusep is dead. It's part of why they didn't recognize him when they took over his ship. If they find out who he really is, they'll capture him, too." He looked at Jusep. "We need to protect Ben and Alex. I cannot be with them all the time, so I have to depend on you to get them to safety in case the Hurliingen act unexpectedly."

"Right now, the Hurliingen want to take Ben and the others as quietly as possible." Jusep said. "They are interested in Earth as a future project and don't want to jeopardize it. However, if the other ship gets here before we are ready… I don't want to even guess at what could happen."

"Then why are you telling me?" I was confused. "If Ben can't know that his dad is alive, why tell me?"

"The General can't be with Ben and Alex all the time. We need to come up with some way to keep them safe while they're at school. While Tom seems trustworthy, he does not have Ben's complete trust. You do."

"Yeah, but whatever you have in mind, surely the General could just tell me and leave you out of it." I sighed. "Wouldn't that have been safer?"

"Maybe," Jusep agreed. "But you and Ben have grown up thinking for yourselves and aren't afraid to second guess the General. You are as capable as Ben to lead, and you have the advantage of understanding this world better than we do." He stopped for a second. "I watched you the other night. People came to you for answers as much as they did Ben. You already have the trust and respect of our people."

"Oh." At first, I was embarrassed, but then I groaned. "Ben will never forgive me for keeping this from him."

Ben's father reached across the table and covered my hand with his.

I looked at it for a moment. It was the same shape as Ben's, only rougher, and it had several scars across its knuckles.

"Hilary, if there was any other way to do this, I would. I cannot tell you what it was like to see this incredible young man standing in front of that crowd, and know it was my son. It has only been a couple of years since I have seen him, and he is already an adult. He is physically close, but I cannot talk to him. I can't even let him know I'm alive without putting his life in more danger than it already is." His hand tightened on mine for an instant as he held my gaze. His eyes were so much like Ben's. "I want my family back, and I need your help to do it."

"How can I help?"

As the General and Ben's father outlined their plan, my cell rang. It was Ben. I felt guilty and slightly panicked. There is no way I could make my voice sound normal. I pressed ignore and forced it to click over to voicemail. Shannon called me fifteen minutes later and then Ben called again just as we were leaving. I couldn't think of a convincing story to tell them, so I let the calls click over to voicemail. It was the first time I had purposefully ignored a call from either of them. The lies had already begun.

According to their plan, it would be up to me to make sure Ben and Alex were safely out of the way when the Hurliingen came so the General and Jusep's crew could attack them without worry.

"Ben's never going to go for this," I said.

"He won't have a choice," Jusep replied.

I looked at Ben's father and smiled. "No disrespect, sir, but you don't know your son."

"Hilary, this is the only way we can be sure of their safety. Surely you understand this?" Ben's father looked disappointed that I hadn't gotten it after all.

"I understand." I looked at Jusep. "But I think you're underestimating Ben. He will not sit back and watch other people fight without knowing the full plan... and probably not even then."

As I climbed in my car, I felt the weight of my responsibility crush onto my shoulders. It would be me kidnapping Ben and Alex, not the Hurliingen.

CHAPTER THIRTY-ONE

"Where have you been?" Shannon yanked my door open before I'd even shut off the ignition.

Ben stood behind her. He seemed tense.

"Jocelyn and I were having trouble setting up a display." The lie I practiced since driving across the Harbour Bridge tumbled from my lips.

Shannon rolled her eyes. "Figures."

My stomach unclenched when Ben's shoulders relaxed. First hurdle over. "How'd it go tonight?"

"Oh My God, Hilary. You should see all the weird stuff. It's all blue. Some of the dented stuff looks like abalone." She started walking me over to Ben's house, leaving him trailing behind. "Alex took me down to their tactical room. Holy Crap! How did you keep this a secret from me? I should be really mad at you."

By Saturday morning, we had fixed a lot of the broken equipment that people had dropped off. Ben's basement suite resembled a junkyard of spare parts.

The General gave Ben some money and told us to go get lunch. After our conversation with Jusep, he insisted we use my car whenever we go out instead of Ben's Barracuda. I knew it was because Ben wasn't allowed to drive my car and the General needed me to be in charge when the Hurliingen came. Plus, there was more room in my trunk for the gear the General insisted I keep handy.

I'm not sure what he told Ben to get him to cooperate.

We were just getting back into my car with the food when the walkie-talkies started squawking. Ben turned his up so we could hear.

The General's voice came over the speaker. "They're here. Hilary, you know what to do."

I put the car in reverse and gripped my steering wheel until my knuckles hurt.

Ben looked at me. "What does he mean by that?"

I said nothing as I drove out of the parking lot. I'd spent hours trying to think of what I could say that would make him cooperate. "We're going to the rendezvous point."

"What rendezvous point?" Ben turned in his seat until he was facing me. In the back, Shannon and Tom leaned forward, so their faces filled the gap between the front seats.

"I'm sorry Ben, the General made me promise to keep you safely away from the Hurliingen. He'll meet us there later."

"Bullshit. We're going to my house. I need to protect Alex and my mom." He tried to jerk the steering wheel out of my hand. "Pull over, I'm driving."

"Scream at me all you want, but we need to protect you, and this is how it has to happen. The General made me promise." I could feel the pressure of tears behind my eyes. "Alex and your mom will be safe. He has a plan for them, too." I gripped the steering wheel. "It will work out, trust me."

"Trust you?" He shouted. "You lied to me. Why didn't you tell me what the General was planning? I could have changed his mind."

"I didn't tell you because I think he's right. And don't yell at me for lying to you. I've had to lie to my mom practically every night since I met you."

Shannon and Tom had been sitting in stunned silence in the back seat. But now they erupted. "What the Hell?! Hilary, why didn't you tell me? We can't just desert them."

Words; angry, excited, accusing. It all rained over my head until I couldn't distinguish one from the other anymore.

I tried to tune them out and drive up the Golden Mile on to Manawagonish Road. I could barely see the yellow line through my tears. A seventeen-year-old girl shouldn't carry this much responsibility. It wasn't fair. Suck it up, Princess, I scolded myself. Ben has been carrying this type of burden since the day he was born. Deal with it. The General and Jusep are counting on you.

Ben didn't grab the steering wheel from me again. Worse, he wouldn't even look at me. Shannon and Tom eventually quieted down, too.

Once I didn't have to shout to be heard, I spoke. "The General has someone on the Hurliingen ship. Someone he trusts." I wanted to tell Ben who it was. I was sure he'd forgive me once he knew, but I'd promised not to.

"They've been working together, planning how to get the Hurliingen to walk into a trap. Our inside guy told them he might not be of any use in Earth's atmosphere, that it would be better to make sure Ben would react. But really it was to let us know the Hurliingen had a mutant working for them so we could prepare." I had their attention, even though Ben still wouldn't look at me. "If you see the Mutant Boy, pretend he still affects you unless the General tells you otherwise. You too, Tom. We know you're immune, but the Hurliingen don't."

"I can't see why you couldn't have told me this before." Ben's voice vibrated. He was so angry.

Shannon met my eyes in the rear-view mirror. "There is a lot you aren't saying, isn't there?"

"All you need to know is the General is expecting them. I think that's why he insisted we leave for lunch. He wanted us out of the way and didn't want you and Alex together. He'll have your mom and sister safely hidden where the Hurliingen can't find them. The General will meet us at the rendezvous point when it's over."

Ben didn't relax when I finished, but the anger pouring off seemed to have eased a bit.

"We're almost home. Where is the rendezvous place?" Shannon asked.

"We're here." I pulled into the dirt road behind the old ice cream place. It closed down a few years ago. I pulled in to where the road widened and shut off the engine. We were close enough to get to Ben's house if needed, but far enough away to be safe. We all got out of my car. I half expected Ben to run toward home. It would take him less than five minutes to sprint home. Instead, he paced back and forth like a caged animal.

Shannon came over to stand beside me. Tom had deserted her to stand off by himself. From his posture, he was just as mad as Ben. Shannon put a comforting arm around me, but her voice still held a lot of frustration. "Hils, why didn't you say something? Why didn't you trust us?"

"Shan, trust isn't the issue. The General knew Ben would fight this plan and there wasn't time to come up with a better one."

Just then, a light whirring sound seemed to come from the tops of the trees. "Get over by the car." Ben ordered. Despite being ticked off, he stood in front of me, shielding me from whatever made that odd sound. "That's not one of our ships." he told Tom.

The noise grew louder, and I saw some of the smaller shrubs along the road flatten against the ground as if something was pressing them down. There was a slight ripple in the air as whatever it was, settled on the ground. Then a metallic click sounded just before a bright crack appeared. It widened until I realized it was a drawbridge-like door opening. Ben was right, it was not their ship.

I could see Jusep standing in the doorway. I relaxed. It was going to be all right.

"Dad?" Ben's voice was barely a whisper.

As I started to walk toward Jusep, three hulking soldiers, like something out of a bad sci-fi movie, appeared in front of me. Hurliingens? They sure didn't look… or smell like Jusep's men. I looked over toward Tom and saw three more surrounding him. I looked at Jusep.

He shrugged.

My thoughts raced. Even if we turned on our cloaking devices, the soldiers had us blocked in. There was no escape. I thought of the mini-arsenal I had in my trunk, but it might as well have been a thousand miles away.

Another Hurliingen came to stand beside Jusep. "Cark arak." He motioned to us.

The soldiers nudged all of us forward.

Jusep turned to the Hurliingen beside him and said something.

"Ba arak." The Hurliingen spoke again. They pushed Shannon and I away.

"Jusep, what the hell is going on?"

Ben stopped and looked back at me. "You knew?"

I couldn't meet his eyes. I kept focused on Jusep instead. "Jusep?"

"Things change, Hilary." He stepped aside for a second.

I could see the General lying unconscious at Jusep's feet, blood dripping from his face. I couldn't tell if he was dead or alive.

"Where girl?" the Hurliingen beside Jusep shouted at me.

"What girl?" I hollered back.

The Hurliingen soldier backhanded me across the face. I staggered against my car. Shannon screamed and grabbed me before I fell. "It's not supposed to happen like this?"

Jusep said something to the Hurliingen, then looked back at me. "I think I know where he's hidden the girl. Let's go."

Ben and Tom were forced up the ramp into the ship, followed by the Hurliingen, which blocked me from seeing anything else inside. The doors slid shut and the whirring sound came back.

"We've got to get to the house and get Alex before they do."

Shannon was in the car before I was. My face throbbed, but I didn't have time to feel the pain. I had to save Alex and get Ben back. I shoved my car into reverse and gunned it. Gravel flew as I sped backwards out of the little dirt road and skidded sideways when I slammed on the brakes. My tires spun out, squealing when they hit the pavement until they got traction.

CHAPTER THIRTY TWO

A minute later, we were in Ben's driveway.

Shannon was out of the car and cloaked by the time I fumbled with my own device. It popped out of the belt, dropped to the floor, and rolled under the driver's seat.

"Come on." Shannon pulled me from the vehicle. "We don't have time. Just don't let go of me and we'll be fine."

I couldn't hear the whirring sound, but that could mean they'd already landed.

We raced into the house and down the stairs. "Alex?" Shannon and I both called out at once.

She rushed out of the tactical room. "Hilary, they've got General Tsad. We had all these traps set up outside, but they got him anyway."

"I know Alex." I let go of Shannon for a second to let Alex see me. "We have to get you out of here. Where's your mom?"

"I'm here," Mrs. McAllister spoke from the doorway. "Take Alex. I'll stay here in case they come back." She had a wicked-looking device in her hand that I'd never seen before.

I grabbed Alex with one hand and Shannon with the other. We ran toward the stairs.

I caught my foot against something and lost my balance.

I let go of Shannon to break my fall. In that instant, Alex and I were visible.

"There you are Hilary." I knew the voice even before he turned off his cloaking device. "Hello Alex."

Jusep stood on the bottom stair leading into the basement. "Thanks for getting Alex for me. They couldn't find her earlier."

"Jusep?" Mrs. McAllister whispered from her stance at the doorway to the tactical room. "Is that really you?" She lowered her weapon and started across the room to greet her husband.

I watched his face, hoping for any sign of emotion to let me know I could still trust him and that this was all just a terrible mistake.

Nothing.

"I'm sorry Mihika." He said as he picked up Alex as if she was a toddler. "It has to be this way." He clicked on his device and disappeared.

I grabbed the gun, or whatever it was, from Mrs. McAllister's hand and raced out of the house after Jusep. I didn't know how it worked, but I couldn't just stand there and let them leave. The door to the ship was open. I still couldn't see Jusep or Alex. But I saw Ben and Tom slumped on the floor, still surrounded by Hurliingen and the mutant. Ben raised his head enough to look out the opening at me through the door. The look in his eyes hurt me so much I felt physical pain. I heard someone scream, "No!" It took me a few seconds to realize it had been me.

Mrs. McAllister was behind me, screaming out her husband's name.

Shannon caught up and grabbed my other hand. Instantly, we were invisible. We leapt onto the ramp as it rose from the ground and tumbled into the spaceship, somehow managing to keep hold of each other to keep me invisible.

We landed inches away from the mutant's feet.

Shannon gripped my arm so tightly it hurt. I was going to have one helluva bruise there tomorrow… at least I hoped so. Right now, tomorrow was looking pretty iffy.

The mutant boy laughed and kicked Ben. "Not so powerful now are you, Mr. Big Shot."

The ship shuddered slightly. He walked away from Ben and sat down across from them, then took off the gun he was wearing and put it across his lap before slumping down in the seat. He leaned his head back and closed his eyes. Apparently, he was so certain of his effect on Ben that he didn't think he needed to pay attention. Luckily, inside the ship was noisier than outside. There were strange whirrs and clicks, plus a lot of laughter from further inside. "We need to talk to Ben and Tom." I said to Shannon. "While I don't really want to be in the way if our friendly neighbourhood mutant decided to practice more soccer moves on them, we also didn't have much room to creep up between them without touching them. If they accidentally disappeared, it was game over."

"What's a little extra challenge?" I could tell Shannon was trying to be perky. She failed.

The ship tilted slightly, making Shannon and I struggle for a few seconds to keep our balance and still hold on to each other.

"Okay, a three-handed crawl it is." I groped my hand down around her arm until we could link our elbows. Then we bent our knees until we could get down on all fours. I wedged the weapon I had taken from Mrs. McAllister between our upper arms. "Let's do this."

I leaned over Ben, getting as close as I could without touching him. "Ben."

His eyes opened wide for a split second before closing them again. "No."

The mutant must have heard him. He started laughing. "Geez, you're a wimp. I didn't even kick you that hard."

Tom looked even more worried and rolled over toward Ben. "What's wrong?"

Shannon answered her boyfriend, "Apparently, he's not happy to 'not' see us." She said just loud enough for us to hear.

Tom frowned.

"Surely, you didn't think we'd let you two have all the fun, did you?" Shannon said. Her voice was as tense as the boy's posture. We were all terrified.

"My dad…"

"Was supposed to be coming to rescue you." I looked over at the General and could feel the tears well up behind my eyes. I couldn't believe Jusep had let him die. Everything had gone wrong.

Just then, the General's chest rose. He was breathing.

"The General is still alive?"

Tom immediately started coughing.

The mutant looked over at us. "God, you two sound like a couple of girls. Shut the hell up, will you?"

We were all silent for a few minutes. "For now, Dad beat him up pretty bad." Ben looked worried. "We need to get him help."

"We'll add that to the list." Shannon's said beside me. "He gets top priority right after we figure out how to get the hell out of this."

"First off, we need to get me a cloaking device. I lost mine in my car when we tried to rescue Alex."

"They took ours." Tom said. "Barry, over there has them. He put them in his hoodie pocket."

"The same Barry that girl was talking about?" Shannon asked.

"Yeah." Tom and Ben said at the same time.

I'm sure Shannon was looking at Barry just the same as I was. The good news is that he'd put the weapon down on the floor beside him. The bad news was that he had his hands in his pockets and the way his fingers were moving under the fabric, it looked like he was rolling the cloaking device canisters between his fingers, playing with them. "Okay, that's going to be difficult. What else do we know? How many bad guys?"

"Dunno." Tom said. "There were six Hurliingen outside and three inside when they captured us."

"Plus, Dad and at least three others from the Alliance of Eight." His fists clenched. "I don't understand how he could turn against us?"

"He told the General he was coming to be with you when his ship was stolen by the Hurliingen. He is supposed to be on our side." I paused. "At least that's what he told the General."

"We need to find out what's going on." Shannon's voice was firmer this time, almost back to normal, even though she was still whispering. "We can't afford to wait until we get a second cloaker for you. We need to find out what's really happening now."

Ben and Tom both stiffened again.

"You can't." Tom began at the same time Ben said. "Hils…?"

"We have no choice, Ben."

"I know." His head dropped. "I hate this."

"Me too." I whispered in his ear. "How's the mylar underwear holding up?"

He lifted his hand an inch or two. "So far, so good. I can move and can probably walk without too much trouble, even if that Barry guy is right beside me."

"Good. Hang tight, we'll be back as soon as we can."

"Ready Shan?"

"As ready as I'll ever be."

"Okay, let me hold the gun again and then I'll stand up first."

We stood up without falling, Mrs. McAllister's gun safely in my free hand.

CHAPTER THIRTY-THREE

The ship had levelled out and was steady. Aside from a faint vibration, you could hardly tell we were moving. Carefully, we stepped over the General then walked past Barry into the corridor which extended about four meters each way.

"Left, or right?" Shannon whispered. "I'd say flip a coin, but that would give us away."

I almost giggled. I reached up my hand to cover my mouth and almost bashed myself with the gun. With no visual cue to remind me it was there; I had almost poked my eye out and given us away before we'd even left the entry area.

"Listen." I told her. "I hear voices."

"Daddy, what the hell are you doing?" echoed down the hall.

"Alex." Shannon and I said at once and started down the corridor toward her voice. Ten seconds later, we had entered a large room, obviously the bridge of the ship.

Alex was standing toe to toe with her father with several amused Hurliingen looking on.

Apparently, they didn't understand English because Daddy was a dead giveaway to Jusep's identity.

"Alex."

I heard the warning tone in his voice. But Alex ignored him.

"Alex, calm down. You don't understand."

"Then explain it to me." She crossed her arms across her chest and glared at her father.

Shannon gripped my arm. I could feel her shaking beside me. I was very glad I couldn't see her face, or we'd both burst out laughing.

Even surrounded by bad guys much bigger than her, Alex didn't back down. The Hurliingen were nothing compared to Jennie and Janie. You tell him, Alex.

"It's complicated."

"Daddy, I know you haven't been around for the past couple of years, but trust me, I'm a freaking genius. I'll be able to keep up."

Jusep looked at his daughter with a helpless expression on his face. No matter what made him kidnap his kids, he didn't want to hurt them. Otherwise, he would have had one of the Hurliingen take her to some sort of prison cell for the ride back to Myonus and not bothered attempting to reason with her. That gave me hope.

Then again, maybe not. Jusep bent and picked up his daughter and slung her over his shoulder. "Enough." He turned around and walked out with Alex pounding her fists against his back. She knew her biology. She was aiming at his kidneys.

From the way, his steps wobbled, I'd say her aim was pretty good.

"Damn it, Alex. Stop or you're going to blow everything."

Alex wasn't the only one who stopped. Shannon and I stood stock-still as Jusep adjusted his daughter to hold her on his hip.

"The General and I had a plan, but the other Hurliingen ship arrived faster than we expected. I couldn't leave you alone, not when I needed Ben and the General with me." Jusep looked over his shoulder to where Shannon and I were standing. "Hilary, you know it wasn't supposed to be this way."

"How—?"

I elbowed to shut her up. I hadn't decided whether to confirm we were there, forget letting him know there were two of us.

"I was watching for you. The air ripples around you, just like on Earth. Don't worry, they can't see you." He started moving again. "We need to talk." He led us past a few more doors and then into a room with two sets of bunk beds attached to the walls. He put Alex down before looking back out the door to see if anyone else was coming down the corridor. "We have two minutes tops."

"Okay, talk." I said.

"Hilary?"

I put my hand on Alex's arm to let her know I really was there. When I touched her, she vanished. Scared the crap out of me. I let go immediately. "Go on Jusep."

"We need to destroy the other ship before it reaches Earth. We couldn't get rid of the Hurliingen on this ship like we'd originally planned. Which means the plans I made with the General have to change too."

"So, you beat him up?" Shannon asked.

Jusep was too distracted to realize it wasn't my voice. "Not really. I gave him one of our old training signals. He knew I was going to attack, and he acted like I bested him. He and the boys are waiting until we have a plan, then they'll overtake Barry and then come to help my crew with the Hurliingen."

"I don't think Ben and Tom know that part. Ben thinks the General is almost dead and that you are a traitor."

"Damn it. I hoped the General would have been able to tell him it was a fake fight. The Hurliingen gave me no choice. By the time we landed, I was supposed to have taken back control of my ship. The General approached, and I had to do something, or they would have killed him for real." Jusep looked back out the door again. "Damn."

I had another question. "How are you not affected by the mutant?"

"The Hurliingen have been using them to flush out the Tixlardine. We learned how to minimize their impact on us before we left. The General said you'd found a way too."

"Yes. Once we saw how that guy affected Ben, we found a solution."

"Good. Hilary, go talk to the General and Ben, make sure they're ready." He waved us out of the room, leaving Alex behind. "Stay." he ordered.

"Make sure they're ready for what?" I asked as he pulled the door shut between Alex and us.

"I honestly have no idea."

CHAPTER THIRTY-FOUR

Shannon and I had to press ourselves back into the door Ben's father had just closed as one of the Hurliingen and, I assume, one of Jusep's crew members came down the hall toward us. In a small area, the Hurliingen smelled even worse than they had outside. Like dog poop after a couple of hours in the sun.

"What took you so long?" the human asked.

"Damn kid wouldn't shut up." He shrugged. "Thinks I look like her long-lost daddy or something."

"Hah, that kid's father was killed in the first month of the Myonus civil war."

Jusep shrugged. "Doesn't matter. She's out of the way now. Let's get back to work. We need to get that other ship before it realizes we're here."

"Prize ours." The Hurliingen said.

I felt Shannon reach for her nose. I was a split second too late. The Hurliingen's breath was worse than his body odour. It burned in my nostrils. Yuck, how could Jusep stand it?

Shannon and I followed them down the hall and turned off into the antechamber by the door where Barry was still standing guard, well, sitting guard over the General, Ben, and Tom.

Shannon pulled my arm to get me to stop. Barry slouched in his seat even more than when we'd left. He was napping.

Did we dare? Since she was the closest, and let's face it, the bravest in this type of situation, I didn't stop Shannon as she leaned forward.

I moved with her, so she didn't feel like the rope in a tug-of-war. The cloaking devices bulged in his pocket, and one was sticking out enough that we could probably grab it. I hated this. I couldn't see Shannon's hand, so there was no way for me to tell how close she was. It was agony.

"Barry." An approaching voice called.

All three of us jumped.

Shannon and I backed over each other to get away from Barry and the entrance from the corridor.

Barry sat up, pulled his weapon back onto his lap, and pretended to look like he hadn't been sleeping.

This time, I'm sure it was me leaving a bruise on Shannon's arm. I didn't recognize the voice at all.

"Barry, you lazy slug. Just because you weaken them, do not think they aren't over there, plotting how to beat you." The man who entered was the same guy who met us in the corridor with the Hurliingen. He slapped Barry on the side of the head. "Smarten up. If you can't handle a job as simple as this, we will have to re-evaluate your usefulness." He looked over toward Ben and Tom. "What weapons did they have on them, anyway?"

"Nothing, just a couple of those stupid cloaking things."

"Where are they now?"

"Here." Barry reached into his pocket and handed the man both cloaking devices.

Shannon and I slumped together as we watched the man take them. Now, what were we going to do? We couldn't rescue anyone if we had to keep our arms linked to stay invisible. Hell, I couldn't even fire the gun I was still holding. I needed need two hands just to aim it… assuming I could figure out how to fire the damn thing without seeing what I was doing.

The man walked further into the room.

Shannon and I backstepped as fast as we could until we were standing between Ben and the General until there was no more room without tripping over Ben or Tom.

"So, this is the great General Tsad." he mocked. "He doesn't look so great now, does he?"

"He went down a lot quicker than I thought he would." Barry said from his place on his chair. "But I doubt he was expecting to be sucker-punched, either. I bet he saw another Myonusian and thought he was safe."

"Yeah." The man stood over the General. "You'd think he would have known better. The captain is on a few wanted lists back home. But I guess the cushy life on Earth made the General sloppy."

Wait. What?! The man was holding out the two cloaking devices toward Shannon and me. He'd turned so that Barry couldn't see what he was doing.

Did I dare trust him? I looked down at the General and I saw him watching the man through half-closed eyes. It looked like he was smiling. I pulled Shannon closer and tapped the floor beside the General's head with my foot.

He looked up and nodded his head. Like Jusep, he knew we were there.

That was all I needed. I reached forward and took both devices from the man's fingers being really careful not to touch him.

Just then, Shannon nudged me, and the man instantly disappeared.

Barry jumped up from his chair and held his gun in front of him as if he wasn't sure if he should shoot or not.

The man grabbed my hand and took the devices back.

Oh shit, the General was wrong. I'd played right into the man's hands… literally.

Then he burst out laughing. "I love these things." He released the grip on my hand and reappeared holding the two gadgets. "I'd better get these back to the captain. Are you sure they had nothing else on them?"

He turned around again to look at Ben and Tom. This time when he held out the cloaking devices, I took them without hesitation or mishap. As soon as I had them, he walked out past Barry. "Remember, we're watching you."

As soon as he was out of sight, Barry started mocking him. "Remember, we're watching you. Just who does he think he is, anyway? I don't take my orders from him." Barry slumped back down in his chair even further than before.

I tugged Shannon toward the hallway.

Together, we walked out past Barry, carefully sidestepping his outstretched legs. He was staring straight ahead, looking angry. We had to get him away from Ben and the others before he took his frustration out on them again.

The man was just turning the corner into the place where we'd first found Alex.

"Hold the gun." I said to Shannon as soon as we got out of earshot of Barry. The corridor was short. We'd be sitting ducks if anyone came. Even though there were doors, I didn't know how to open them.

"Okay, I think I have this thing on." I unwound my arm from Shannon's and held my breath.

"Hilary!" She grabbed my arm. I had appeared just as a Hurliingen came up from the other end of the corridor. We didn't have enough time to get back into the room beside Barry. We both crouched low and hoped he would stay on the other side of the corridor, which seemed to get narrower the closer he came.

There was no way he could miss us. He was too close.

I felt Shannon move beside me. Suddenly, the gun she'd been holding was visible on the floor just before the Hurliingen kicked it.

His arm stopped mid swing less than two smelly inches from my face.

"Icrej." He bent over to pick up the gun and Shannon whisper-screamed, "Push!"

CHAPTER THIRTY-FIVE

We knocked the Hurliingen off balance and slammed his head into the wall and ran toward the bridge with him screaming behind us. We wedged ourselves in the corner just as several of Jusep's men and Hurliingen ran past us into the hallway to see what was going on.

"Great, now they know we're here and we don't have a gun."

I felt Shannon shrug. "It's not like either of us knew how to fire it, anyway."

We ducked into the almost empty room. The only occupants were a Hurliingen standing behind one of the Myonusian crew members, looking at a hologram. The crewmember was pointing out something, but I couldn't understand what they were saying.

"We have to try this again." I glanced over at the men to make sure they weren't looking our way and flicked the button on what I hoped was the other cloaking device and took my arm from around Shannon's, ready to grab a hold of her again if I needed to.

She let out a sigh.

I looked at my hands and couldn't see them. Relief washed through me. One hurdle over. Unfortunately, there were still umpteen million left in front of us.

The commotion in the hall was coming back our way.

"Against the wall," I whispered. "Once they're all here, we'll go back to the guys."

Instead, they came to us.

Jusep's men half carried, half-dragged Ben and Tom into the room.

Barry followed them then stood off to the side. Close enough to think he was keeping our boyfriends weak, but far enough to keep out of the Hurliingen's way.

Ben and Tom were pushed forward and then they collapsed on the floor, still pretending to be affected by Barry's presence.

The Hurliingen who had been looking at the hologram, turned away from the display and walked over to stand above them. He was the same one who stood next to Jusep when Ben and Tom were kidnapped. "Who here?"

Ben rolled onto his side. "I don't know what you mean."

The Hurliingen stepped closer. "Who here?"

Jusep stepped forward. "You might as well answer. We know someone else is on board. They just attacked a member of the Hurliingen delegation."

Ben and Tom looked at each other for a minute before Tom spoke. "What do you mean someone attacked a Hurliingen?"

"A Myonusian gun appeared in the middle of the corridor. When the Hurliingen bent over to retrieve the weapon, they shoved him into the wall."

"Well then, it's obvious." Tom said. "If the weapon just appeared, then it was the Magic of Disney. Mickey Mouse is on board."

Shannon and I slipped through the doorway back out into the corridor. Even though we could move independently now, we still couldn't see each other. The air rippling around us wasn't as obvious as Jusep made it sound. So, we still held on to each other. Ben and Tom

261

seemed to have a plan. Now was a good time to go see the General.

When we got back to the room where they had kept Ben and Tom, it relieved me to see the General sitting up and talking to the man left to guard him. It was the same man who gave us the cloaking devices.

"No, nothing's broken. I'm glad Jusep held back."

"General." I ran toward him, dragging Shannon behind me. Relieved to see he was all right.

"Uh, Hilary?" Shannon said behind me. "You might want to let the poor guy reappear."

I released the General and sat back on my heels. I reached into my pocket and clicked off the cloaking device. Shannon did the same.

The other man looked surprised to see her. "There are two of you? Jusep said to get the cloaking devices to Ben's girlfriend."

"Jusep doesn't know I'm here." Shannon held out her hand. "I'm Shannon, Tom's girlfriend."

"I'm very pleased to meet you Shannon, and you Hilary." He shook my hand after Shannon's. "I am Nokis."

I turned back to the General. "Do you have any idea what they're planning to do with Ben and Tom?"

"Tom is being a smart-ass in there and is likely to get them both pounded," Shannon added.

Nokis answered. "Jusep had planned to have them disappear once they got on board. But Barry knew they had cloaking devices. The Hurliingen made us take them away." He frowned. "For now, they still think they're in charge. It's better for us to keep the illusion intact so they don't start looking too closely at our actions."

"Where's Alex?" the General asked.

"Jusep has her in a room just down the hall." I told him.

"Yeah, when we found her, she was ripping into her father like you wouldn't believe." Shannon added. "He probably didn't know what else to do with her to keep her out of trouble."

"Yeah, unlike us, who just let the entire Hurliingen delegation know we're here and then gave them our only weapon," I said.

"Stuff happens." She shrugged as if she'd merely put a bottle into the newspaper recycling bin instead of the one for plastic.

"Do we have any sort of plan?" I asked Nokis.

"Jusep thinks we need to wait until after we destroy the other ship before we try to take control of this one. He is arguing with the Hurliingen leader, who does not seem to want to destroy that ship. Apparently, it's more of an insult to the other crew if they're left to confirm their defeat."

"Does it matter?" Shannon asked.

"Yes. The Hurliingen need to get Ben and Alex to Myonus. The other ship will use the return trip to steal them from us if they know they're here. It's a contest and whichever Hurliingen ship has them when they reach Myonus will get the glory. Jusep had no intention of taking Ben and Alex home. He just needed them to be safe before the other ship arrived on Earth. If we get near Myonus, the Hurliingen clans will send out reinforcements. If that happens, we're in real trouble."

"Well, what are we going to do?"

"That's what we're trying to figure out. General Tsad is the best tactician we know."

I glanced over at the General. He looked deep in thought.

"Why don't we destroy the other ship and take back control of ours at the same time?" I asked.

Nokis shook his head. "They're watching every move we make. There is no way to position the ship to fire without them stopping us."

"What if they don't know you're doing it?" I asked. "Is there any way to control the ship from anywhere besides the bridge?"

Nokis nodded. "Down in the engine room."

"What are you thinking, Hilary?" The General asked.

"Well, I'm guessing the bridge has a training program similar to the one I used when you were teaching me to drive your ship."

"They taught you to drive their spaceship?" Shannon's voice was so shrill in my ear it felt like my left eardrum was over visiting my right. "Shh and yeah."

"Anyway, what if we switched the bridge over to the training program and made it look like we were keeping on course, but really, the guys in the engine room would take us toward the other Hurliingen ship?"

Shannon punched me in the arm. "Everyone knows that old trick. It'll never work."

I rubbed my arm. "Everyone except the Hurliingen."

Nokis just shook his head. "Jusep was right about Hilary."

"Is that a good thing or a bad thing?" I was curious.

Nokis smiled. "It is a wonderful thing. Jusep was very impressed with you."

Shannon chuckled as she elbowed me in the ribs. She knew how much I hated receiving compliments. "Way to go. Make your boyfriend's real and pretend fathers both think you are terrific. Outstanding."

I just wanted to flick the switch on my cloaker to disappear and hide for a minute. I could feel my face getting redder by the second.

Nokis sat up straight for a second. "Someone's coming. Hide."

CHAPTER THIRTY-SIX

Shannon disappeared, and I pulled her over to stand against the wall, then we both edged toward the door just in case we needed to make a quick exit. I looked back over to where the General and Nokis were. The General was back on the floor playing dead and Nokis was standing over him, kicking him absentmindedly. The General was good. If I hadn't been talking to him a few seconds ago, I'd have thought he was badly hurt.

Jusep came into the room followed by two Hurliingen, one holding Ben prisoner and the other holding Tom. "Nokis, grab the General and bring him to the storage room. I want these idiots out of my sight. They're annoying me." He turned and pushed past his captives, leading the way back out into the corridor.

Once the last Hurliingen left, Nokis held out his hand for the General who quickly stood up. Then Nokis lifted him with a fireman's carry. As soon as the General was in place, he made his body go limp again. Nokis carried him after the rest of the group.

Shannon and I followed close behind, to use them as a shield just in case we ran into anyone else along the way.

Jusep opened a door to a room filled with what I assumed were supplies. It was hard to tell because everything was in boxes strapped securely to shelves, in case they lost gravity, I guessed.

The Hurliingen pushed Ben and Tom into the room. Nokis followed and stepped around the corner, just out of sight. There was a sickening thump as the General hit the floor.

"Why move? Dead." One of the Hurliingen asked Jusep.

"Not quite."

"Then kill."

"No need. He'll be dead soon enough." Nokis pushed them aside. "Out of the way. I need to lock the door." He looked where he knew Shannon and I were standing. He nodded and pushed the door open slightly wider to give us room to enter.

As the Hurliingen moved, there was just enough space between them and Jusep for us to squeeze through to join Ben and the others before he closed the door.

The door slammed shut behind us and a loud click echoed back through the room. Jusep said, "You two, guard the doors." Another thump slammed against the walls as our guard's heavy armour banged against the wall.

"Now what do we do?" Ben said to Tom.

"Hilary had a great idea, and we're going to use it." The General whispered as he stood up from his place on the floor. "And keep your voice down."

Ben whipped around to face the General. "You're okay?" He closed the space between them in a long stride and hugged the General. "I thought my father hurt you?" Even from where I stood, I could see Ben's shoulders shaking.

The General was actually blushing at the show of affection. "Of course I'm alive. You don't actually think your father would harm me, do you?"

I released Shannon's arm and clicked off my cloaking device. She appeared a split-second later. "Do you really think it will work?"

Ben whirled around. "How did you get in here? Why did you come in here? Why didn't you stay outside to escape?"

"Nokis told me to come in with you."

"Who's Nokis?" This time, it was Tom.

"The guy who made sure he was the one who carried me in here so the Hurliingen wouldn't figure out that I was not injured."

"But he threw you down." Ben said.

"Did he? Or did he just pretend to?"

"Anyway, Nokis told us to come in here for a reason. There has to be another way out."

"The engine room," The General said. "My guess is that there is a way to get into the engine room from here."

"Why the engine room?" Ben asked. I'm pretty sure now that he recovered from the shock of the learning the General was all right, he was eager to get back in the loop of information.

Ben pulled me close as I brought him up to date. "It's a great idea." He looked over my head toward the General. "That means Dad isn't really a traitor?"

"No Ben. Your father and I had a plan to get rid of the Hurliingen who had taken over his ship and then destroy the other Hurliingen ship that was on its way to Earth. We had planned to do it without involving any of you. We told Hilary in case something went wrong. Unfortunately, it went more wrong than we thought possible. We needed you and Tom. Jusep wasn't certain we could get back in time to keep Alex safe from the other ship, so we grabbed her, too."

"Where is she?"

"Down the hall in Jusep's quarters." the General said. "Nokis said that Jusep wanted to keep her out of the way."

"Hah. He thinks a bedroom door is going to stop Alex? He's forgotten what his daughter is like."

The General smiled. "I think he's hoping it will slow her down enough for us to come up with a plan."

"What are we going to do?" Shannon asked. "I get the impression we don't have a lot of time."

"We have to wait for Nokis to tell Jusep what we're planning."

"Yeah, but then they'll have to come back and move us again, which will look strange. The Hurliingen will know something is up." I looked at the General. "This isn't by chance a storage area for the engine room too, is it?"

"No, not in this model. The engine room is on the other side of the far wall. There shouldn't be any access to it from here."

"Should we look just in case Jusep made some extra adjustments after the Hurliingen came aboard?"

"We can try." The General shrugged. "But don't get your hopes up. I would not expect there are many scenarios where he'd want to have extra entrances to the engine room."

Ben and I walked around one set of shelves while Tom and Shannon walked around the other. Tom hadn't let go of Shannon since we had appeared. Then again, maybe it was Shannon who hadn't let go of Tom. Either way, it was cute.

Then I realized Ben, and I hadn't let go of each other either.

After a fruitless search for a secret door, we started opening boxes to see if we could find a stash of weapons or maybe some tools to help get through the wall into the engine room. Some of the boxes were labelled, but since Shannon and I couldn't read Myonusian, it didn't help. Even Ben and Tom had trouble reading some of them because they were not all written in the official language of the Alliance of Eight. Jusep had warned the General and me that stuff had been hard to get since the wars had started and many items had come from planets outside the Alliance.

The General stood behind us looking into each box that we opened, identifying the contents. After about half an hour, although truthfully, I had no idea how much time had passed, Shannon opened up a box of tiny packages of what looked like bright green concrete.

Tom immediately pounced on it and pulled out two of the small containers. "Ben catch."

Ben looked up just in time to grab the package before it hit him in the face. He grinned. "You can't be serious. Way to go, Dad."

Shannon and I looked at each other in confusion while Tom pulled out another small package and handed it to the General. His smile was just as huge.

I looked over to Ben and he had already torn the wrapping off and had taken a big bite. He looked like a little kid the way he held the green thing close to his chest, as if he didn't want anyone to take it.

"Ok I'll ask. What the hell?" Shannon looked at the identical giddy looks on all three male faces.

"Here, taste." Tom said through a mouth full of Kermit coloured… stuff. He held his green thing out to her.

"What is it?"

"Just take a bite, Shannon," Ben said with a slightly emptier mouth. "You'll like it." He held his own square out to me. "Try it."

I looked over at the General, and he had leaned back against the shelf behind him. His eyes were closed, and he chewed slowly as if savouring every crumb. For the moment, our predicament seemed forgotten.

Shannon and I looked at each other again. In unison, we both leaned over our respective boyfriend's hands and took a tentative bite. We didn't break eye contact waiting for the slightest hint from the other that this was not a good idea.

"Oh, my God!" Shannon blinked and then her eyes rolled back as she explored the green fragment on her tongue. "What is this?"

It looked like concrete, but the texture was like dense bread. As soon as it hit my tongue, it melted into a caramel consistency and filled my mouth with a fruity, nutty flavour better than anything I have ever tasted before. I reached out to take another bite, but Ben had already moved it back to his chest where he had crossed his other hand over it as if to protect it from me.

Shannon and I dived into the box and grabbed a green brick of our own, the search for weapons momentarily forgotten as we each savoured this treat. "What is this?" I asked again.

"It's the primary export from Kifcia, one of the other Alliance of Eight planets. It is bread made from the Adjner tree bark. It was my favourite thing when I was a kid. Dad always bought some for Alex and me as a reward when we'd done well at school or after a tournament."

"Apparently, he had a lot of faith that you and Alex would have kept up the good work while you were away from him. There have to be at least twenty more packages in here." Shannon said between mouthfuls.

"Speaking of Alex, we'd better save her some or she'll kill us instead of the Hurliingen."

We closed the lid on the box and shoved it back on the shelf. We hauled out a few more boxes one-handed while we held the green bricks of bread in the other. It was so flavourful that you couldn't eat it fast. I knew I should fold the packing over and shove it in my pocket, but I just couldn't make myself do it. I looked at everyone else and they all seemed to have the same problem.

The next box I pulled forward seemed heavier than the rest. When I undid the latch, I punched the air with my free hand. "Jackpot."

CHAPTER THIRTY-SEVEN

I'd seen them before, small handgun-like weapons that had been brought over to Ben's place. I actually knew how to operate these. So did Shannon. They weren't as big as the gun I'd grabbed from Mrs. McAllister, so they'd be easier to carry.

The General reached in and took out one of the weapons. He looked at the underside, frowned, and tossed it back into the box.

I was a little offended. "These are exactly what we need."

"They would be if they were loaded. They need to be charged and I doubt Jusep has charging faculties set up in here ready for us to use."

Shannon started to help me put the lid on.

"Wait." I reached in, grabbed a gun, and tucked it in the back waistband of my pants.

"Hilary, the General said they can't be charged."

"You know that, and I know that, but the Hurliingen don't."

Shannon laughed as she grabbed a gun and tucked it into her own waistband. Then she handed one to each of the guys.

The General held his hand out as well. "If you get your hands on a gun like this that is charged, be careful. They don't shoot bullets like your guns do on Earth. They are lasers with an adjustable range."

"Well, since these won't shoot, it's one less thing to worry about, isn't it?" Shannon said matter-of-factly. She looked over at Tom. "What else do we have?"

"Just a bunch of maintenance tools." He started to put the lid back on the box.

"Wait." Ben squeezed past Shannon and me. He turned to the General. "Is there a way to undo panels to get us into the engine room?"

The General thought for a minute. "It's been a while since I've studied the diagrams for this style of ship. I am not sure I remember anything more than the basic floor plan." He turned to look at the wall behind the shelving.

"Let's see what else we can use." Shannon said as she pulled out another box. "Maybe we'll get lucky and find a blowtorch."

"That would be helpful." Tom said. He crouched down and gave Shannon a hug. She leaned in, and they clung to each other for a few seconds before she pulled away and continued to look.

I hated not knowing what was happening outside. I had no idea how far away from Earth we had already travelled and to be truthful, just picturing the little blue ball that was my home shrinking into the distance was not half as exciting now as it had been when I was training on the flight simulator. It was a game back then. The longer we stayed trapped in this room, the farther away we went.

The General kept pulling out boxes and inspecting the wall behind the shelves. Occasionally he knocked as if listening for a hollow spot. Several minutes later, he said. "Here."

Ben and Tom moved over beside the General while Shannon and I stood behind them. "I think this will be the best spot. We can dismantle this shelf and detach the panel in behind." He knocked on the wall again. "If I'm right, this will take us into the engine room between the wall and the main computer."

We worked in silence. The boys started unloading boxes from the shelves and handed them to Shannon and me. There were a few near the bottom they had to slide across the floor because the weight was too much for even the two of them together to lift. With the tools from the other box, it took them only a few minutes to dismantle the shelving unit.

We tried to be quiet. Each time we accidentally clanked a piece of metal, we stopped, waiting to see if the Hurliingen standing outside the door heard us.

The wall was built in panels riveted together. It didn't look any different from something you would see on Earth. Which I suppose wasn't surprising when you considered the long history of aliens living on our planet.

The General used some sort of clamp device that looked like a staple remover while Ben used a wedge to pull apart the other side of the panel to pop the rivets holding it to the rest of the wall.

With every sound, we held our breath.

It seemed to take forever before we had removed the panel and were staring at a few wires and the inside of the other wall. On the inside of the wall, the rivets were flat. There was no way to pull them out. We were going to have to break through. The General looked at Ben and Tom as if to say let's do this.

They formed a line with their bodies, and each put one foot against the wall near the top of the section.

The General said. "Hilary and Shannon, get behind us to help make sure we don't fall backward into the shelving. We have to do this as quietly as possible."

Shannon and I got into position.

As soon as we were ready, the General said, "On the count of three, push."

"One. Two. Three."

At first, nothing happened. The wall creaked a bit, but that was it. Disappointed, we all relaxed our positions.

"If we try to ram through it, the Hurliingen will hear for sure." Tom said.

"What if we rocked it?" Shannon said.

"What do you mean?" the General asked.

I was pretty sure she didn't want us to sing to the wall. It took me a minute to figure it out. "You mean like when your car gets stuck in the snow?"

"Yeah." she said. "You rock back and forth. Each time you move forward, you gain a little momentum."

This time, it was Tom who looked very proud of his girlfriend. I had to admit; I was proud of her, too. For someone who didn't drive and hated sci-fi, Shannon was doing all right.

After a few minutes and several loud creaks and pops, but happily, no nosey Hurliingen, we were through.

The General guessed well. Had we chosen the panel to the left or the right, we wouldn't have been successful.

"Oh, it's you." Alex's voice came out from a ripple. An instant later, she appeared.

"How did I get here?" I asked.

"Nokis brought me here. He told me your idea and hoped I could figure out how to take control of the computers from here in case you couldn't get through the wall." Her shoulders slumped. "I can't do it."

The General sat in the chair and looked at what Alex had done so far.

Shannon and I put our arms around the younger girl's shoulders. She seemed so small to take on reprogramming a spaceship's navigation system on the fly, all by herself.

"Alex," Ben started to comfort her.

"Alex, come here." The General interrupted. "Here was your problem." He smiled at her. "You would have had it in a few minutes if we hadn't barged in and ruined your concentration."

Before Alex had a chance to see the issue.

The door to the engine room opened. We all froze.

"Well, that solves that problem." Jusep walked further into the room. "Nokis didn't tell me until after we'd put you into the storeroom about Hilary's suggestion. I left the Hurliingen to guard the door so we would know where they were and that would make two less to monitor. I hoped Alex had learned enough about the navigation system to make it work.

"The Hurliingen Captain will not stop watching my navigator. If Alex couldn't do it, I was going to come up with a diversion to get you folks out of the storeroom and in here." He shook his head as he looked at the hole in the wall. "As usual, the General is way ahead of me."

"Alex did well," The General told him. "She had the patch almost ready to go by the time we got here."

Alex stood a little straighter when her dad smiled at her. "I've missed so much." The pride in his eyes was unmistakable.

"Hang on." I darted back through the hole we'd just come through. When I came back, I handed Alex one of the green rectangles. "Daddy, you remembered." She jumped into her father's arms and was engulfed in a huge embrace.

After he released her, Jusep stood in front of Ben. "I am so proud of you. I do not have the words."

Ben stepped into his father's arms and his shoulders shook ever so slightly. I was ready to cry, and I could hear Shannon sniffling beside me.

The moment passed all too quickly.

"What do we need to do now?" Jusep asked the General.

"For this to work, we're going to need the navigator to know what's going on. Have you had a chance to tell him?"

"No, I haven't been able to inform Kerose yet. The Hurliingen leader won't leave Kerose's side at the navigation console. I think he mistrusts us after the attack on his man in the corridor and wants to ensure we do not try any more tricks." Jusep frowned.

"Sorry." Shannon looked contrite.

Jusep smiled. "It was a good move. You would have been caught otherwise."

"Does Kerose speak English too?" I asked.

"All of my crew leaned English for this trip. Most speak Mandarin and Punjabi too. We weren't sure where we'd find you. Hell, even the Hurliingen have been practicing Earth languages."

"Would it work if Shannon and I followed you back to the bridge and talked to him? The Hurliingen leader wouldn't expect us to stand right beside him. We could tell Kerose what's going to happen and if there was a problem, Shannon or I could run back and forth to deliver messages."

"Yes, that could work. However, we have to do it quickly. The further we get from Earth, the more the circulation system will have purged the ship's atmosphere of pollutants. Without them, the cloaking devices do not work well. Eventually even the Hurliingen will see you."

"Ah, it's already happening. I could see the outline of Alex when we burst in from the storeroom. She wasn't completely invisible anymore," Ben said.

"It's an automatic system. It would take me longer to reprogram it than we have available, so we have to move fast. Luckily, the Hurliingen leader has already boasted to the other ship about having both Ben and Alex onboard. They've changed their flight plan and are following us instead of continuing to Earth to collect the others." He turned to Shannon and me. "Let's go."

Shannon and I clicked our cloaking devices, and it surprised me to see how visible we really were. "Are you sure they won't see us?"

"Yes, the Hurliingen's eyes work differently than ours. They depend on contrast much like a human newborn. They cannot see you until your features become distinguishable. But once they know what to look for, they can track your movements."

For the first time since we had jumped onto the ship, I was scared.

Still without hesitation, Shannon and I followed Jusep out of the engine room to the bridge. Once we were there, we stepped away from him and moved behind the Hurliingen leader. Shannon stood back against the wall, and I crouched down beside Kerose. Jusep came over too. He started talking to the Hurliingen.

I leaned close to the navigator, trying to get in front of him, hoping he could see I was there before I spoke, so I didn't startle him. "Kerose, I'm Hilary. Jusep needs me to tell you what's happening."

Kerose didn't react.

I wasn't sure he heard me. I didn't want to talk any louder.

Apparently, he'd been waiting for me to continue. He looked to where I was kneeling and gave an impatient nod.

Quickly, I explained while Jusep kept the Hurliingen leader distracted.

Kerose nodded again, only this time with a smile. He seemed to like this plan.

I stayed low and made my way back over to where Shannon was standing. "Tell the others Kerose is ready. I'll stay here in case something goes wrong."

"Okay, I'll come right back to let you know when it's going to happen."

I watched her walk away. I couldn't make out the shape of her body yet, but the ripple effect seemed more obvious than before.

It felt like forever before she returned. I was considering going to find her when she finally arrived. "They're ready."

I walked over to Kerose again. Keeping low, out of the Hurliingen leader's sightline, and leaned forward for Kerose to see I was back. "Any minute."

He nodded and immediately scanned the panel in front of him more intently. I stood back a little to give him room and to get behind the Hurliingen. No sense tempting fate.

Suddenly, the entire set of navigation holograms went blank. This couldn't possibly be good. A second later, they came back on, and it looked like the ship was shifting direction.

I looked over to Shannon and saw her ripple already moving across the room toward the corridor. I swung back around to the screens and the Hurliingen had leaned over the back of Kerose's chair and was gesturing angrily at the hologram.

Jusep started shouting at the Hurliingen to stand back and let Kerose fix the problem.

The Hurliingen backhanded Jusep, sending him staggering across the room.

The navigation center went blank again and then reappeared. This time Kerose's shoulders relaxed a fraction. He waved angrily at the Hurliingen, said something I'm sure neither Ben nor Alex would ever be allowed to repeat, and then went back to checking the controls.

The Hurliingen calmed down, but seemed even more suspicious. He leaned over Kerose and refused to move back, even when Kerose tried to shove him away.

Jusep limped back toward the two men and the three of them argued. The Hurliingen spoke much better Myonusian it seemed than English. Even after several minutes of argument and no further problems with the navigation system, the Hurliingen still seemed to be angry and distrustful.

I risked moving closer to Kerose when he sat back down at his controls. "Is it working?"

He carefully pointed to a section of the hologram.

The General had shown this out to me when he trained me to drive the ship. It was an indicator that we were in training mode. I remembered because Ben had laughed and made a crack about how we would be dead if I had really been flying since I had just crashed the ship again while trying to land.

I moved back against the wall where I had last seen Shannon. She had not returned. I debated for a moment before deciding to head back to the engine room to see what was happening there. It was probably the safer place to be anyway, since we didn't know how soon it would be before the Hurliingen could see us.

CHAPTER THIRTY EIGHT

When I walked into the engine room, everyone was watching the hologram controls.

The General was barking out orders to Ben and Alex. Shannon and Tom stood together slightly behind them. Tom looked worried, and Shannon looked fascinated.

I looked and could see we'd come round to face the other ship. We seemed to be too close. "What's happening?"

"The big lasers don't work from here." Alex answered. "The General is going to try the smaller guns."

"Why haven't the other Hurliingens shot at us?"

"We have Ben and Alex and since the big guns didn't work, they think we're just defending our bounty. They have no idea we're about to destroy them."

Just then, the General shouted at the console and threw his hands in the air. "Of course, it's a safety feature. We can't fire the shots from here." He looked at me. "Tell Kerose, we have to switch back to his control. He has to take the shot from the bridge."

I switched my cloaking device back on and sprinted toward the bridge. I was halfway to the entrance when another Hurliingen came out of one of the doors. He looked up and down the hall. Damn, I thought to myself, he must have heard the General yell.

I skidded to a stop and had no choice but to wait. My heart double beat the precious seconds ticking by while he peered back and forth as if deciding which direction to investigate. I breathed a sigh of relief when he turned away and strode to the bridge. I quickly caught up and followed as close as I could behind him. My eyes watered. His stench stung my nostrils as if I'd just breathed in black pepper. I wanted to sneeze. I had to pinch my nose to stop the urge. He halted just inside the doorframe with not nearly enough room for me to squeeze past. I was going to be too late.

The navigation holograms in front of Kerose shut down again. This time when they came back up, the Hurliingen leader roared and grabbed Kerose by the collar and tossed him out of the chair.

Everyone started screaming.

Jusep ran to Kerose just in time to stop the Hurliingen leader from stomping on him.

The Hurliingen in front of me just stood there. I shoved him aside and ran to the control panel. He bellowed behind me, but I was already out of reach.

I stared hard at the panel, trying to figure out the controls. They weren't the same as on Ben's ship. Ben and I had played some space attack games in the tactical room, but none of the keyboards we used looked like the ones in front of me either. I closed my eyes and tried to picture what the symbols looked like. Surely, they would be similar. This was still a Myonusian ship.

The Hurliingen leader whirled around and headed toward where I was standing.

I had two seconds to do something before he took over.

There, I recognized one. I couldn't remember what it was for, but right now, it didn't really matter. I triple tapped it like Ben showed me. Nothing.

The Hurliingen ripped the chair out from behind me.

I triple tapped the icon again. Somewhere between the fourth and fifth tap, I saw what looked like a hologram sparkler shoot out from what I hoped represented us, and head toward the other ship.

I dove sideways just as the Hurliingen started flailing at the controls.

The ship rocked sideways as he spun us around, away from the other ship.

It was too late. The other blip on the hologram shattered, then disappeared.

The Hurliingen leader swung around, enraged. He searched the room to figure out who fired the weapon. I tried to fold myself up as small as I could against the wall. When I was at the console, I noticed I could see the shape of my hand. It looked transparent, but I could still see it.

So did the Hurliingen leader. He bellowed again and started toward me.

"Leave her alone." Ben said from the doorway. He had his gun trained on my would-be attacker, while Tom and the General had the other Hurliingen cornered.

The Hurliingen leader turned and took a step toward Ben.

"Don't even think about it."

When he turned back to me, Shannon, Alex and I all had our guns aimed at him.

It looked like a stalemate until Barry and the two Hurliingen, who had been guarding the storeroom door, ran in from the other corridor.

"I'll handle this." Barry strode across the room and headed straight for Ben.

Ben feinted a weak stagger as Barry got closer. Just as Barry reached out to push him to his knees, Ben nailed him with an upswing.

The crack of his jaw echoed through the room.

Ben grabbed Barry's gun from his hand as he was falling and shot the legs out from under the newly arrived Hurliingen.

As they fell, the one closest to me tried to grab my legs and take me down with him. I dodged his grasp and stomped on his wrist when he tried again. I heard something crack. He howled and brought his hand to his chest. I grabbed the gun he'd left on the ground and swung it around to the Hurliingen leader.

We stood aiming at each other while the pandemonium continued around us.

Out of the corner of my eye, I saw the Hurliingen I'd stolen the gun from grabbing the one I'd dropped. He hollered when he fired and realized it was useless.

The Hurliingen leader didn't waver. He waited for me to make the first move, or was simply buying time for his people to take control again.

I wasn't even sure I was holding the gun right. I didn't dare break our gaze-lock to see how he was holding his. Everything seemed to slow down. I didn't know what was happening in the rest of the room; it was just him and me.

Out of the fog, I heard Ben shout, "Hilary."

The Hurliingen leader smiled and swung his body toward Ben, his gun already aimed.

I didn't think. I pressed the button under my finger and felt myself thrown back against the wall behind me.

Everything went black.

CHAPTER THIRTY-NINE

I opened my eyes in a panic and couldn't see anything but the front of Ben's shirt. His chest heaved against my cheek.

He was alive.

I let myself sag against him again.

"Hilary?" Alex's voice sounded worried as she rubbed my shoulder, as if trying to comfort and rouse me at the same time.

"Is it over?"

"Yes, it's over." Ben pushed me back a bit from him and turned so could see the rest of the room.

The two Hurliingen that Ben shot were tied up and shoved against the wall. Barry was still out cold and tied up beside them.

Tom and Shannon stood over the trio with guns aimed, just in case. Jusep was in the middle of securing the other Hurliingen. The General and Nokis were standing over him with guns ready. The other Myonusian crew members seemed to be okay. Although one didn't seem to be terribly pleased as he wiped thick black goo from his face. Where did that come fro… oh?

The Hurliingen leader, who had turned shoot Ben, lay on the floor with his body partially severed from his legs. There was a large puddle under him that matched the gunk the crewmember was wiping from his chin.

"Where's Kerose? Is he alright?"

"He's fine." Ben pulled me close again. "He had to go to the engine room since we kind of ruined his workstation."

I pulled away from Ben and sat up a little straighter. I winced. My shoulder and the whole right side of my chest hurt. I put my hand on his shoulder and tried to stand. Pain shot through my whole torso. God, it hurt.

"Hilary?"

"Give me a minute." I tried again. This time, I rolled up onto my knees. It still hurt, but I made it.

Ben, already up on his feet, put out his hands to steady me as I stood.

Once I had my balance, I looked at Kerose's navigation station. The chair was in pieces, and the hologram controls winked on and off like dying fluorescent lights.

I tried to walk and would have fallen if Ben hadn't been beside me to catch me. I let out a yelp of pain. Seeing the terrified look on Ben's face, I cracked a joke. "I guess they didn't design Hurliingen guns for someone my size, huh?" I tried to laugh and would have if it didn't hurt so much. "That baby had quite the kick."

Jusep, now done with the Hurliingen, came toward me and drew my head in toward his chest. "Hilary, I don't have words…"

I braced my hand against his chest and looked up at Ben's father. He looked like he had aged over a decade since I met him.

"We did it."

CHAPTER-FORTY

The trip home was much less eventful than the ride into outer space had been. Kerose had repaired the main navigation panel, so we could watch as we travelled home.

Unlike in my imagination, we had not lost sight of the Earth. It was still quite large on the viewscreen, and it grew bigger with every passing moment.

Ben stood behind me, his hands resting lightly on my hips. It hurt too much when he'd wrapped them around my shoulders. The General thought I had cracked a few ribs when the Hurliingen gun recoiled and threw me into the wall. Apparently, according to Shannon, there were already bruises forming on my back. Despite them, I leaned against Ben's chest.

Shannon and Tom stood beside us watching the Earth approach, with Alex wrapped securely in her father's arms on their other side.

"We should be there just before dawn," Kerose said as he looked up from his console.

"Mom is going to kill me." I groaned.

Shannon winced. "Me too. I am so dead."

"We just have to keep Mom from killing Dad until we can explain." Alex giggled.

The sky was just getting light when we landed on the lawn between my house and Ben's.

"Uh oh." Alex said from her position near Kerose. "We are not alone."

She dashed out of the bridge and raced toward the doors. The rest of us followed a bit more slowly. I still could barely walk. We made it to the exit just as Jusep lowered the ramp.

"Mom, it's ok. We're ba..." The rest of Alex's words were swallowed up by her mother's hug.

"Hilary!"

"Mom?" I shuffled forward out of Ben's protective hold. "What are you doing here?"

She started to hug me and stopped when she looked at the expression of pain on my face. "What happened? Oh Hilly-bean, are you all right?"

"She might have a couple of cracked ribs," Jusep said behind me.

"Jusep!" Mrs. McAllister pushed Alex away from her and walked up to her husband and slapped him hard across his face.

"Mom, stop." Ben stepped in and held his mother as she broke down and started sobbing. "He had to take us in case something went wrong. He had no choice."

"He could have warned me. I was so worried." She glared at Jusep over her son's shoulder.

I looked back at my mother, afraid to see her reaction. Mom was staring at the inside of the spaceship behind us. The only part she could see was beyond the open doorway. It seemed to hang in midair because the rest of the ship was invisible. "I thought she was nuts." Mom said. "I stayed outside with her because I thought she'd completely lost her mind, and I didn't want to leave her alone. But it's true, isn't it? It's all true."

"Yeah." I touched my forehead to hers. "It is."

EPILOGUE

"Do you think Janie is ever going to forgive us for taking off and having all the fun?" Shannon asked me as she helped me get dressed for school on Monday morning. She'd spent the night at my place, with her parent's blessing.

I don't think they cared much what her excuse was for staying out all night once they saw I was injured. We claimed there was a car accident, and she rushed to my aid. I called her a hero, and that was all they needed to know. Hopefully, by the time they got around to asking for a better explanation, we would have one.

It took all of Sunday to fill mom in all that had happened. Mrs. McAllister did most of the talking. Filling in the blanks she'd left during their overnight vigil while we battled the Hurliingen in outer space. By bedtime, my mom was still a little shell-shocked.

"The pain I'm in isn't fun." I said to Shannon. "I'm sure Janie will be upset that we dared upstage her." Without thinking, I took a breath to laugh and stopped. "Wow, that hurt,"

"Are you sure you want to go to school today?"

I looked in the mirror and grimaced. I had a large ugly welt on the side of my face from when the Hurliingen hit me when they first took Ben and Tom. Part of me wanted to stay home and sleep until the bruise went away, but mid-terms were coming, and I couldn't afford any more distractions. "I can't let you guys tell the story wrong and leave out all the good parts."

Just then, a truck pulled into Ben's yard.

"Why is Tom here?" Shannon asked.

"I guess there is only one way to find out." I reached forward and groaned. "Help me with my coat, will you?"

By the time we made it outside, Ben and Alex were already talking to Tom.

"What's up?" I asked, as Shannon went over to her boyfriend.

"Tom is going to drive Shannon and Alex to school." Ben looked uncomfortable.

"Oh." My mind started racing. Ben was going back to Myonus. That's what he had to tell me. That's why he wanted to talk to me alone. I could feel the tears well in my eyes.

"Hilary, are you okay? Are you sure you should go to school today?"

"I'm fine. Just a little pain." I didn't tell him that my breaking heart hurt worse than my bruises.

He opened his passenger door for me and helped me get in and fasten my seatbelt before walking around to the driver's side. He gave me a long look before he started the car and I thought I heard him whisper. "This is killing me."

We drove in silence until we were almost to the Harbour Bridge.

"Ben, what's killing you?" There, I started the conversation. I'd never make it through the day if I didn't know for sure what was going to happen next.

"What do you mean, what's killing me?"

"You said it when you got in the car."

He clicked on his blinker and took the exit just before the bridge. He drove down past the baseball field and then turned right and up the hill until we got to

Martello Tower. The parking lot was empty. He pulled in and stopped the car. "You're in pain, and it is all my fault. You're hurt because you were fighting to save me." He slammed his hand against the steering wheel. "I can't even hold you to comfort you right now, and it's killing me."

I clicked open my seatbelt and leaned toward him. "Screw my bruises. Just hold me."

We stayed like that for what seemed like hours. It hurt, but not nearly as bad as him not holding me. "When do you leave?" I finally asked.

"Leave?" He pulled back just enough to see my face. "Who said anything about me leaving?"

"Isn't that why you wanted to drive in alone with me, to tell me you had to go back to Myonus?"

"No. No! I just needed to be alone with you." He kissed the top of my head. "The General and Dad's crew are going back first. They're taking Jason's adoptive father and his cohorts back with them, so we don't have to worry about them anymore. Once they get things under control, they'll send for us. For now, Mom, Dad, Alex, and I are staying right here."

"Really?" I really tried not to cry, but it didn't work. "You don't have to leave?"

"Of course not. I pulled rank and told them I couldn't leave until after I took you to our Grad Dance."

Thank you for reading my book. If you enjoyed it, won't you please take a moment to leave me a review at your favorite retailer?

Other books by Sue Nelson Buckley

The Trouble With Jake

What do you do when you discover the imaginary protector from your childhood is real?

After catching her boyfriend cheating, Kathryn drives all night. She ends up on the wharf at White's Bluff, where she always felt safe.

Jake watches Kathryn arrive, wanting to help her but can't. He's been a ghost for over a century and observing is all he can do… until this time, it's not.

Together, they test the limits of Jake's existence and wonder if it's possible to create a future.

ABOUT THE AUTHOR

Writing is as important to me as breathing… ok well at least as important as chocolate (trust me - that means it's vitally important). I've been telling stories since I was a kid. Often it was to get myself out of trouble (sometimes it even worked) but most of the time it was to keep my brothers and I entertained.

When I'm not writing, I'm knitting, gardening or taking walks outside with my camera ever ready for the perfect shot. I'm also learning to paint and play the guitar with varying degrees of success. The key is to never stop trying.

Follow me:
Instagram: @suenelsonbuckleywrites